Song For A Shadow

Song For A Shadow

▼　▼　▼

Bernie MacKinnon

Houghton Mifflin Company
Boston   1991

Fic
MAC

Printed in the United States of America

AGM 10 9 8 7 6 5 4 3 2 1

Library of Congress Cataloging-in-Publication Data

MacKinnon, Bernie.
  Song For a Shadow : a novel / by Bernie MacKinnon.
    p. cm.
  Summary: Being the son of a famous rock star creates a troubled
family life for Aaron, who has to live in the shadow of his father's
fame and his mother's mental illness.
  ISBN 0-395-55419-5
  [1. Family problems — Fiction.] I. Title.
PZ7.M1997Lo   1991   90-39647
[Fic] — dc20   CIP
                            AC

For the memory of my grandparents,
Dougald and Rose MacDonald
and Mary MacDonald MacKinnon,
and for my grandfather,
Bernard MacKinnon.

Contents

▾

PART ONE

▾ ▾ ▾

With No Direction Home

1

▼

On the night that his father's nationwide tour opened at Madison Square Garden, Aaron crashed the blowout after-concert party. He didn't stay long.

A few days later, he visited his mother at the psychiatric hospital in Hartford. By then he had made up his mind to cut free of everything. To cut free — it was his one consuming thought as he made the long drive back from the hospital, back to the empty house.

Next morning, nothing felt unusual as he locked the front door. Nothing felt final as he rolled his white Mazda RX-7 out of the driveway. He watched the large blue house shrink away in the rear view. Driving with the sun in his face and an oldies station on the radio, he left Stamford. He was past New Haven before any sensation took hold. Bob Dylan howled from the radio: "How does it feel / How does it feel / To be on your own / With no direction home . . ."

Aaron's hands tightened on the steering wheel. Though he had heard the song a hundred times before, it had never hit him like this. It was as if Dylan's howl was for him alone.

Then he let his hands go limp and stopped listening. It was an old habit — to clutch a song as his own anthem, as a theme for this exact moment. Like a pill, all it ever did was take him high and drop him. Life was no movie. Life had no soundtrack. Maybe it did have heroes, but he was not one of them.

As the song peaked, he tingled in spite of himself. "You're invisible now / You got no secrets / To conceeeaaalll!"

Impatient, Aaron took an exit at random and headed toward the ocean. Another whim steered him left at a fork, down a winding dirt road past boarded cottages. Minutes later he thought he saw what he wanted and stopped. A pair of ruts veered to the right between knolls and gnarled sumacs, ending at a clearing of grass and sand that dropped off suddenly, with the sea beyond.

He got out. He followed the ruts to the cliff and peered over the edge. The slope cut steeply down past rocky outcroppings to a strip of rocky beach. No sign of people. With the breeze snatching at his hair, Aaron gazed across the ocean's glitter. He watched the wheeling seagulls and listened to their cries. When he turned around, the sight of the sumac trees held him there a moment longer; their curling, crimson-budded branches swayed in tribal dance, and his mind swayed with them. It was hard to believe how easily he had discovered this spellbound place. This was the spot.

And this was the day. May 2, 1987 — Day of Escape.

Aaron walked back toward the car, a present from his father. As he neared it, the hate gripped him once more. There would be no more presents. He opened the passenger door, grabbed his black jacket and his knapsack with the sleeping bag attached, and threw them on the ground.

The next thing he knew he was behind the wheel, bumping toward the cliff and the line of ocean. Clear of the trees, the bumping came harder and he held tight, teeth set as the quaking landscape filled his vision. Closer, closer — he had only seconds left, and amid the bucking he heard his mother's voice: "Please, please look after yourself. You're a man almost, but you're still my lone boychild." The horizon shook.

4

He yanked the door handle and tumbled out, rolling clear in time to see the Mazda's rear tip skyward and plunge out of sight.

He scrambled on his knees to the edge and saw the sleek white frame strike an outcropping and disintegrate in a burst of fire. Debris flew. The blast sounded across sea and sky as the crushed, flaming skeleton bounced heavily and then dropped, hitting the water with a big splash.

He lay there, staring down long after the water's surface had smoothed. Then he got up, brushed sand from his knees, and started back shakily toward the road. He didn't know where he was going. But what he was escaping — that he knew in every rotten detail.

He was escaping all the sluggish hours at home, hours spent staring at the walls and fighting an urge to smash every piece of furniture. He was leaving his mother's illness, a weight that made him feel useless at best. He was shedding the kid he had been, the kid who was quiet when others were loud, guarded when others were open, awkward and disconnected when others were plugged in. He was running from the smirks and gossip of people his age, and from all the well-intentioned adults who predicted that he would follow in great footsteps. More than anything, he was running from the great footsteps. It was these, the steps of his father, that made Aaron's life look small and blurred and shallow by comparison.

Wherever he would end up, he hoped it would be a place with no reminders of his father — Danny "Spider" Webb, rock 'n' roll icon. Danny Webb, the legendary Spider — whom he rarely saw in person but whose presence always hovered, ready to descend like a permanent night. Kids at school spoke of coming to see their parents human-sized; this sender of gifts had grown only taller in Aaron's imagination.

When the Mazda had materialized in the driveway just after Aaron graduated, it might as well have been placed there by a giant's hand. While dozing in the back yard, Aaron had seen his father as a colossus towering above the neighborhood, his huge guitar sending down power chords that quashed the sound of traffic. In his last year at school, Aaron had avoided making any reference to the Spider, but someone always brought it up and new acquaintances always found out. On occasion he wondered how much the knowledge kept people at a distance; at the same time he suspected those few who wanted to get closer. It seemed he was born mainly for the curiosity of strangers, and this made him feel more obscure than any broker's or foreman's son. He in fact had daydreams of being such a man's son, ordinary enough to be seen plainly and not through the strobe-lit fog of the Spider's celebrity. With an average, small-scale father he might have stood out for what he was, both good and bad.

Halfway back to the road, he halted. He was seeing them again: his mother beneath the tree on the hospital grounds, his father crouched on stage with his guitar. Fleetingly their faces merged, smiling the way that other couples smiled in air-brushed wedding portraits. He had long felt ridiculous imagining this and would have been embarrassed to tell anyone, but the mirage always returned. Then he felt the tears ready to surge and started walking again. He couldn't afford to get careless. Feeling sorry for yourself wasn't just dumb but sometimes was dangerous, in ways that were hard to see.

He pulled his jacket on and shouldered the knapsack. He kept walking until he found the highway and stood by the on-ramp, thumb extended as cars whipped past. As each car shot by he concentrated on the drivers' faces, dim spots behind the windshield, and they would look away. He tried to picture what they saw in their glimpses: a lanky, pale young man who didn't smile; dark-eyed, with messy black hair. But soon the repetition — car coming, dim face, car gone — lulled him until he was less aware of the traffic than of his usual cycle of thoughts.

It was funny that despite everything, he had chosen to learn guitar. While practicing a song or writing one, he often had to chuckle. "Following in the footsteps," he thought. Like John Dillinger's son raiding a piggy bank or Lawrence Olivier's boy auditioning for a toothpaste ad. Yet he knew that by most estimates he was pretty good for his age. And besides, music was the only thing that could make him forget. A few times while performing with the Gimmix, the band he had joined last summer, he thought he felt the pulse of something pure inside, untouched by his father's fame or anything else. A small, superheated nucleus of his own. But then, at the thought or mention of the Spider, he would again sense himself being measured against the colossus. Gravity returned, pulling him down, and once more he couldn't tell where the legend left off and he himself began. Take away the legend, and how much of him would remain in people's sight? Would he just vanish?

The Gimmix, in any case, were gone from his life. He had sold his guitar. Meanwhile the Spider, enjoying a new level of mystique, had released a record and launched his first tour in six years; backing him were three of the four original members of his celebrated Red Sky Band, with a new young bass player. From Boston to San Diego the Spider's likeness would adorn uncounted T-shirts and posters, his voice and videos would erupt from station to station, and news items would follow his march as though it were a presidential campaign.

Aaron's efforts to recall visits with his father proved strangely frustrating. After each meeting, no matter how flesh-and-blood the man had seemed — however obvious the fact that he slept, ate and drank like anyone — his image would haze over and recede into the far distance, falling away like the booster stage of a rocket in space. His warmly rhythmic speaking voice became garbled in Aaron's recollection, lost in the otherworldly noise surrounding the Spider's career. It was noise that had nothing to do with Aaron or with his mother, and that would now turn louder than ever. Thinking of this set loose an anger that made Aaron curse his father. Anger, as much as anything, had brought him to this highway's edge.

He held his thumb higher but vehicles kept passing.

Finally a hatchback slowed to the side of the road. The driver was a crew-cut middle-aged man who said he was going to Norwich. They talked easily until the man asked, "Where are you trying to get to?"

"I'm going, um . . ." Aaron stammered, amazed at the vagueness of his plan. "To, um . . . Canada."

"Got friends up there?"

"Yeah," he said. "I'll be staying with some friends."

Aaron stared at the swiftly passing scenery. For an instant he could have sworn that the car wasn't traveling of its own power but was being pulled along, drawn by a distant magnet. In the next moment, he wished that the part about friends awaiting him weren't a lie. Where was he really going? Though there was no going back, he wondered if the shadows ahead held worse things than he had dreamed of. Maybe he would vanish after all. The highway's broken midline raced by, a stream of white torpedoes.

The man described a summer he'd spent hitching cross-country, and his stories took them the rest of the way. On a hill near Norwich he let Aaron out and wished him luck.

Aaron watched the car disappear over the crest. It was early afternoon. Traffic whooshed along but he didn't raise his thumb; he just gaped at the road and trees. Incandescent yellow clouds mounted in the west, and a strange buoyancy filled him. It was as if the sky had cracked and crumbled, leaving him beneath a different sky — pure and wild, impervious to questions and reaching forever.

2

▼

Aaron blinked his eyes open. From nearby trees, a flock of starlings announced itself in a riot of cackles. He sat up in time to see a rabbit dart into the brush. In the dawn's dim blue light, a mist hung over the road. It was his fourth day of travel and he was somewhere in New Hampshire.

Having rolled up his bag, he was wiping the moist earth from it when something made him pause. He felt stiff. He felt grubby. But inside him a warm current flowed — not physical, but somehow stronger than his pulse, deeper than his bones. All his fears were gone. Never before had he felt so calmly ready.

"Morning, guys!" he called, startling some birds to the upper branches.

Pulling on his sack, he inhaled the earthsmell and gazed down the road. Its cracked, lumpy pavement faded into the mist, but it was his again. He started walking, then halted as a buck crossed not far ahead, trotting regal and tall and then bounding into the growth with a snap of twigs. Everywhere birds called and trees and ferns dripped as the first rays cut through, chasing the mist away. Aaron's hunger bit, and he remembered the bag of apples in his sack. He got them out and devoured three. Where would he get food next? And who would it be this time, winging out of the country to take him farther? Out here it was just him and his thumb — a game of chance with shifting odds.

Smiling, he spoke to the road. "Come on, who's it going to be?"

During his long waits between rides, a sort of plan had taken form. Canada actually sounded okay as a goal. Maybe that had been his idea from the start, at the back of his mind, for he had instinctively headed north. He had never been to Canada but often pictured it: a cool and roomy fortress, high above America's clamor. Half a continent to get lost in. He could tuck himself away up there, get a job of some kind, and let the past fade.

Bands and song writing were on indefinite hold; ideas such as going to college were laughably distant. What he wanted was to live among people who liked him, who shared his jumbled interests and would let him lower his shield, not caring what he came from. He wanted a girl he could talk to without fear and be with in comfortable silence — someone generous to whom he could be generous, who had drives and challenges inside her but no hopeless complications. As for his own complications, he only hoped that time would undo them and free him from his hate.

When he tried to think more precisely of his desires, fantasy took over. His mind wove vague scenes of triumph with future friends and lovers, until he caught himself and realized that their faces were merely those of people he'd noticed in school, in music clubs, on the street, or even on TV — people he'd thought he might like to know. The scenes themselves felt stolen from movies or novels, growing pale as he tried to bring them in focus, until they just dissolved and left him momentarily stunned at the roadside. Then he would recall his first guitar lesson, when he was twelve, and his toothless instructor Albert leaning toward him:

"Aaron, you know my friend Jack?"

"Jack who?"

"Jack Shit."

"No."

"No what?"

"No, I don't know Jack Shit."

"Good. Admitting you don't know jack shit — that's always the best place to start."

This was another kind of start, Aaron thought. A bigger kind. And it was best to admit that he knew little, and nothing at all of what lay beyond the next ride. That's where the mystery was, and mystery felt better than hard plans and specifics.

Soon he caught a ride from a disheveled young couple in a camper bearing Colorado plates and a bumper sticker that said Oz or Bust. The woman was the more talkative, relating parts of their odyssey as the road curved and climbed and mountains rose in the distance. After this, she said, it was down to North Carolina to visit friends — no big rush.

Seated among the camping gear in the back, Aaron looked

at the bright-colored Indian blanket spread under him, its nature symbols stitched in red. Atop a pile of books behind the driver's seat lay a well-worn paperback on herbal medicine. Aaron listened to the woman's sprightly monologue, thought of the bumper sticker, and tried to wish away the scorn he felt. Then he realized that his mother would have liked this Oz-bound pair, in a melancholy way. For her sake, he could like them. He peered out at the mountains, thrusting up from tree-cloaked bases to bare, jagged peaks. He imagined the lunar bluffs and canyons of Utah, the rainy wilderness of Oregon, the cool fog of Puget Sound, and the flowing gold of the prairies. One day he too would see these places.

Nearing the town of Conway, the camper developed a rattle and they pulled into a service station. Aaron thanked the couple and went down the street to a McDonald's, after which he got a ride from a balding, muscular man in a station wagon. It wasn't until he saw a sign for the Maine boundary that he realized he'd gotten mixed up in Conway, taking an eastern route instead of a northern one. He cursed himself for not having bought a road map.

The driver was telling him about his two small daughters, and Aaron decided to relax about the change in direction. He wasn't on any timetable, and this way he would see Maine — a state he had seldom even thought of, and then only as a place where the parents of some Chase Academy classmates spent their summers. And he would end up in Maritime Canada, a region of which he knew even less. No big rush, as the camper woman had said.

The man let him out on the outskirts of Fryeburg, Maine. The clouds had a silvery luster, hanging just above the hills, and soon they began to sprinkle. Aaron squinted as he held his thumb out, trying to look forlorn for the cars rushing past. Night would probably find him outdoors again and he hoped it wouldn't be too wet. Worries sprouted as he trudged along: find a laundromat, find some place to take a shower — and how much of a hassle would they give him at the Canadian border? The drizzle had ended when he remembered he was different now and kicked his worries aside. Then he heard the sizzle-sound and turned, thumb out for a dented maroon sedan coming at high speed. It slowed and swerved to the side, plowing the gravel.

The door opened as Aaron ran up to it. There were four guys inside, about his age, and a blaster blaring heavy metal. The two in the back shoved over — a blond, acne-chewed kid and a short, beefy one, both in cutoff Iron Maiden T-shirts.

"Howya doin'?" boomed the blond one, lifting a half-empty six-pack onto his lap.

"Kind of wet," Aaron said, climbing in. He sat with his arms around his sack as they graveled off.

The driver was a swarthy, frizzy-haired guy in a camouflage jacket. Riding shotgun, a dark, husky guy with leather wristbands held the blaster in his lap.

"Where you going?" the driver asked above the blaster.

"Canada," Aaron said. "You keeping north or east?"

"East. Goin' to Auburn."

"Good. Thanks." Aaron wiped his hair back, edgy but glad to be moving.

The blond, pimpled guy beside him was in high spirits. "Have a beer!"

Thanking him, Aaron took the bottle and unscrewed it. He could humor them, but wondered when the blond one would ask if he had any reefer.

It was the short, beefy one who asked. "Got 'ny reefah?"

13

"Naw, I don't."

The blond one scowled. "No? Aw, man, then what good are you?"

"Been seeing a lot of cops on this road."

"Aw, man!" moaned the blond one, shaking his head.

"Cops," said the driver. "I'm sick of seein' cops."

The driver talked about the five-band concert they had seen yesterday at a fairground in New Hampshire. Aaron sipped his beer, eyeing the roadside for police as the speedometer passed seventy. "Jeez, must've been good," he said.

The driver slowed as they went through a fair-sized town, then floored it past a mountain scarred with ski trails. He laughed about a girl he had hustled at the concert, and the short one droned about the stuff he had smoked. The blaster shrieked and pounded. Aaron swigged his beer and hoped that Auburn wasn't far.

"Mitch!" called the blond guy. "Let's have some Doors!"

Wordlessly, the dark, husky one shut the blaster off, ejected the tape, and picked a new one from the box at his feet.

The blond one rapped Aaron on the arm. "Like the Doors?"

"Great band," Aaron said, hoping the kid wouldn't start up about Jim Morrison.

"Morrison's a fuckin' classic," the kid said. "He could party!" He gulped his beer and leered at Aaron. "We're gettin' him on for you, man. Reefah or no reefah."

Aaron didn't look at him. "All right."

From the blaster came the pulsing bass, snaking organ, and drum snap of "L.A. Woman." Morrison's off-key snarl broke in and the song raced, turning the driver's foot to stone on the pedal. Aaron finished his beer, gripped the empty, and watched trees whip by. . . . Morrison the Lizard King, he

14

thought — Morrison the growling screwhead stud cadaver in leather pants.

The kid thumped him on the arm and he dropped the bottle.

"Fuckin' great, huh?"

Aaron nodded, tight with an urge to hit the kid and bail out.

"Hey," called the short one, lighting a cigarette. "Sure you don't got 'ny reefah?"

"Sure," Aaron said.

"Well, let's check it out," said the blond one, and grabbed Aaron's knapsack.

Aaron yanked it away. "C'mon, all right?"

Arms braced, the kid stared with small eyes and Aaron saw that nothing could stop it. That sneer and those small, drunk eyes didn't care what was in the sack. "Give you a fuckin' beer and you fuckin' hold out on us, man. Come on, what's in the fuckin' — "

"Lay off!" Aaron yelled, but the guy was on him, clutching at the sack. One hand grabbed his hair and Aaron jabbed an elbow, cracking the kid's jaw, and they were locked in a jerking, cursing struggle while Morrison wailed. The car swerved. Fumbling for the door handle, Aaron heard gravel as a fist hit his lips. The door flew open as he wrenched the sack away. He fell out on his back, tumbling just free of the car's tail, and pebbles sprayed his face.

"Get him!" came the short kid's voice. "Beat the shit out of him!"

The world teetered amid spots as Aaron lurched to his feet and saw the blond kid spring from the car. In an instant Aaron was being throttled and punched. Stumbling sideways he shoved the guy off, then whirled and swung. His fist smashed squarely into bared teeth and the kid tripped backward, holding his mouth. Aaron sprang for his sack but from nowhere came a terrific blow to his ribs, sinking him in a reeling blur. A foot kicked his shoulder and he rolled, glimpsing the dark one above him.

Against the blond one's foaming curses, he heard the short one: "Waste him, Mitch! Waste the bastard!" And he heard the driver: "Naw, leave him, okay? Christ, man. Come on, let's go."

Through a half-shut eye, Aaron looked up at the leather wristbands of his attacker, who turned to say something. Aaron rolled, leaped up, and dove for his sack just as the short one got there and seized it. Aaron's fist caught the kid in the eye. With a corrosive cry, the kid let go and Aaron was running across the highway, holding the sack by one strap, running toward the dark woods and away from the fists and curses and the feet beating after him. Head bowed, he jumped a ditch and plunged into the wet whipping branches, thrashing along with the sack to his chest — thrashing, tripping, plunging, and not looking back.

He didn't know how long it was before he staggered into a marsh, halted, and listened to his ears ring. Gulping air, he thought for a moment that he would throw up. His heart hammered. Sky and wood tilted, tilted, as spots burst and tumbled like smoke puffs before his eyes. The pain was all over him, distant for now but growing, beginning to penetrate. A bird crossed the sky; he wondered whether it was real. Slowly he raised a hand to the side of his head, lowered it and saw the blood, so red. He had to find the road again.

He went left into the woods and groped along, hauling the sack by its broken strap, then cut toward the road, figuring to emerge behind where the four guys had been. His head

16

throbbed and his skin stung in places, and he wasn't sure whether it was rainwater or blood running down his cheek. Then, tripping over a stump, he heard his mother: "I know you have to go, if that's how you feel. But please, please look after yourself."

Branches sliced across his vision, and his mind became a kaleidoscope of scenes, with warped faces and babbled echoes. He saw his mother beneath the tree at the hospital, his father playing a solo in the stage lights. He saw himself on stage with the Gimmix, playing some club; kids he had known in Connecticut and back in Los Angeles; his stepfather frowning; the headmaster lecturing him that Chase was not a reform school.

As he blundered from the trees and crossed the road, he was muttering things in an alien tongue. A horn sounded but he didn't look or run, and the car swept by just inches from his back.

A string of cars passed his thumb. Unmoving, clutching the strap, he stared at the moist charcoal sky as all the shardlike scenes and faces spilled across it like a movie gone wild. And the pain was with him, on top of him, and deep inside. And after everything, he was still the same kid — still the same. And it was dusk and he was alone where no one knew him, and he never should have left.

He didn't look up or raise his hand for the next vehicle. It was only when he heard it crunch along the shoulder that he turned and saw it backing toward him — a red jeep with a white top. Its backup lights blinded him and he wondered if it would run him over. It stopped. With the engine still running, a big shape emerged, shut the door, and moved toward him. Then a deep voice came: "You don't look so good there."

Aaron stood still as the man stepped into the red taillight

glare, and in a twirl of dizziness he found himself staring at a plaid flannel wall, the widest chest he had ever seen. He looked up into a pair of deep-set eyes, like twin hollows in a cliff. A baseball cap was jammed onto the big head and the collar of the open blue jacket was turned up. The man held his hands to his hips. The stance and face might well have meant challenge if not for the eyes, crinkling in shock. "Jeez — you're a mess, pal."

Aaron spoke through swollen lips. "Some guys . . . they picked me up and they . . . they . . ."

"Let's get you into the jeep."

The man took Aaron's arm and they walked to the jeep, where he opened the door for him. Swinging behind the wheel, the man lit a cigarette and shifted gear. Aaron put the knapsack on the floor. As they pulled out he looked at the craggy-faced stranger, whose bulk made the jeep seem too small.

"Thanks for stopping," Aaron said.

"Well, somebody had to, I guess." The man blew smoke. "Now, what happened?"

Aaron told him.

Rolling his window down, the man shook his head. "Some people just oughta be fed down a disposal, face first."

Aching but unmindful, Aaron watched the road winding into the headlights, and soon they passed a sign that said Fox Hill. Then there were lights ahead.

"My wife knows first aid," the man was saying. "If there's anything serious, we'll see about a doctor."

"Thanks," Aaron repeated. "I have money if it comes to that."

The man grunted and tossed his butt out, slowing the jeep as the route became a main street and the town quietly un-folded — darkened shops close to the road, lighted houses

18

farther back. A few streetlights glowed and traffic was almost nil. A hotel, a bar, a service station, a firehouse, a log beano hall, an open restaurant, a closed diner, a Seven-Eleven store with high school kids around the lot — with each sight, Aaron grew more peaceful. Only the pain kept him from doubting his senses.

"The wife's working our store," the man said. "I'm thinking we should go there first thing."

"If you don't mind, right now I just want to lie down."

"Sure. All right."

They bumped over a railway crossing and passed a square with a post office, a library, and a domed town hall. A white church and a bank came up on the right, a hardware store and a barbershop on the left.

Finally they turned left onto a side street marked Lark Lane, then right into the driveway of the first house. The man got out, but Aaron took a moment to gaze at the small frame house. Bathed by the light of an old-fashioned lawn lamp, it was brown with white trim, steep-roofed, with sculpted wood around the door and windows. There was soft amber light within, and a dog's barking. Aaron tingled strangely. His only thought was that a short while ago he had been wandering along the road.

The man came around to help him but Aaron said it was okay and got out, leaving his sack. He followed the man across the lawn, up the steps, and through the door.

Across the varnished hall floor a black Labrador came wagging to the man's hand, then cut toward Aaron and sniffed his muddy sneakers.

"He's all right, Slim," the man said.

Aaron patted the dog's head and got a wag, then bent to untie his laces. He smelled cooking.

"Dad?" came a girl's voice. "How'd it go in Bridgton?"

19

Placing his sneakers by the mat, Aaron turned to see a teenage girl enter the hall and stiffen with a gasp. She was pale, slight, and of average height, with taffy-colored hair past her shoulders and a yellow apron covering her overalls. In stocking feet she stood gaping, fingertips to her mouth. Aaron felt a stab of embarrassment.

"Gail, this guy ran into some trouble," the man said, hanging his cap and jacket on a hook.

"Ho-ly!" she exclaimed, nibbling a knuckle. "That's awful!"

Aaron's brain wobbled and he looked at the floor.

"Take his jacket and show him to the bathroom," her father said. "I'm calling Mom to look at him. He can lie down till she gets here." He lumbered toward the kitchen.

Nearly tripping over the dog, the girl bounced to Aaron's side. Her hands fluttered like moths about his shoulders. "Here, let me . . . Were you in an accident? Is that what happened?"

"Sort of," he said, giving her his jacket. "Thanks."

"The uh, . . . bathroom's upstairs. Oh, I'll . . . Outa the way, Slim. . . . I'll show you where it is." Her voice, though quivery, had an unexpected huskiness.

Following her up the carpeted stairs, he heard her father in the kitchen. "Any customers? . . . Okay, go ahead and close up. I think he'll be okay but you should have a look. . . . Okay, bye."

The girl paused at the head of the stairs and called down. "Dad, take the chicken out of the oven please?"

When she handed Aaron a towel he thanked her again and tried to smile, but it felt like a grimace. She was still staring as he stepped into the bathroom and shut the door.

The face that met him in the mirror was gaunt, with

20

dried blood on one side and along his lips. His eyes were bloodshot and his hair tangled. He took his shirt off, examined the skinned patch of redness on his ribs, and carefully pressed the hurt spot on his shoulder. Gazing at the work of his assailants, he imagined them being fed down a disposal, face first. He found a roll of paper towels, wetted several, and gingerly wiped blood away before washing more thoroughly.

When he came downstairs, the girl had her apron off and anxiously showed him to a sofa with a pillow. There he lay and dozed off to the smell of chicken, the clinking of silverware, and the lowered voices of father and daughter.

3

▼

Aaron awoke with a blanket over him and a woman's face looking down, roundish and pleasant in the light.

"Hi," she said. Smiling, she put a hand to his chin. "I'm just going to have a look at that cut." Gently she tilted his head to the side. Her brow wrinkled. "Wicked," she murmured, and knelt for a closer look. She was attractive in a soft, middle-aged way, with fine long lips and dark hair fringed gray. She removed her windbreaker. From a first-aid kit at her feet she took a pen-light and checked his eyes. "No concussion. And it doesn't look like you'll need stitches."

Aaron looked past her shoulder and saw the girl standing, hands fiddling at her waist as she observed.

"You know, I'm not always a babbling idiot," she said. "I mean, I'm sorry I freaked."

"I sort of freaked when I looked in the mirror," he spoke.

"Gail, quit being such a spectator," said the mother. "You still have homework these days, don't you?"

Sighing, Gail let her hands slip to her sides. "Sure do, Mom. Thanks for reminding me. I mean, the future of civilization's hanging on it, right?"

"No it isn't," the mother said, putting the pen-light away. "It's just a matter of whether you want a crabby old witch on your hands. And you know what that's like."

Gail left with a mutter.

"My shoulder's bruised," Aaron said, "but I think it's okay. The only other thing is my ribs."

The woman pulled the blanket down and told him to unbutton his shirt. Examining his skinned flesh, she squinted painfully. "Oh . . . What kind of crazy morons . . ."

"The kind you line up in front of a wall," came the man's voice. "The kind you offer bounties for. A thousand dollars per scalp, plus a week in the Florida Keys."

"My husband's a frustrated chief justice," the woman said, recovering her clinical air. "Now I'm going to feel gently but it'll hurt some."

Aaron managed not to flinch. Across the room he saw the man slouched in a comfortable chair, smoking as he watched TV with the sound off. His hair was steel-gray, close-cropped. The dog lay beside the chair.

The woman got out adhesive, mercurochrome, and a roll of bandage. "This and some aspirin for now," she said. "Your ribs seem to be intact — just be glad it wasn't down lower.

22

For now we can put you up. There's a room above our store. I'm just wondering if I should drive you to the clinic in Bridgton, to be on the safe side."

"No, no. I'm pretty sure I don't need to."

She went to work on his head.

"Thank you," Aaron said, gazing up at her. He had to stop himself from saying it again. "I'm not talking too well . . ."

"You don't have to," she said, and smiled. It was a unique smile, tucked in at the edges. "And you're entirely welcome. I needed to brush up on this anyway. So tell us your name."

"Aaron . . . uh, Cunningham."

She dabbed the mercurochrome on with a cotton ball. "I'm Peg and that's Jerry, alias Fergie. So where are you from and where are you going and all that?"

"From Connecticut, going to . . . to Canada." Canada nicked his memory like a cold blade.

"Hmm . . ." Peg mused. "Well, so much for your means of travel."

The head wound stung.

"Wanna rest some more?" Peg asked. "Or do you feel like food? My daughter saved us some chicken and salad."

Aaron realized he was famished.

Minutes later he was eating with Peg at the kitchen table, trying not to bolt his food or guzzle his milk. Jerry leaned in the hall threshold. Aaron noted a plaque on the wall by Jerry's shoulder — a coat of arms with "Clan Fergus" lettered royally at the top.

"Do I dare ask?" Peg said, looking at her husband.

Jerry twisted his mouth. "It was sixty bucks."

"Ugh!" Peg stalled over her salad.

"Sixty," Jerry repeated. "All because one uniformed bozo likes to write his name on tickets." Folding his arms, he

23

looked at Aaron. "Local constabulary nabbed me for speeding last month. I had my date in district court today."

Peg wiped her fingers with a napkin. "My money says you *were* speeding, hon. And anyway, you probably got ugly to the judge."

"Not the judge — the law school punk from Portland. My lawyer was worthless, and here's this punk prosecutor up there making like he's running for governor. If any more wind came outa him they would've had to issue a small-craft warning."

Peg smiled at Aaron. "Colorful, ain't he?"

"He's all right," Aaron said.

"Want anything else? Don't be bashful."

"Thanks, no." He was still hungry.

Peg got up and took their dishes to the sink, where others awaited washing. "Well, Jer. I must say you're taking this better than I thought."

Jerry huffed. "Only because I took a long walk to cool off."

"Well, doing the dishes'll calm you down even better. It's past your turn, I believe."

Jerry moved to the sink and started filling it. He gave Aaron a glance. "You can tell who's boss, huh?"

Aaron smiled, but his stomach wasn't settling. "Hey, I'm sorry you had to close early because of me."

Peg waved a hand, retaking her seat. "It's Dead Tuesday, Aaron. No biggie."

Gail strode moodily into the kitchen and Peg asked about her homework. Pouring a glass of Kool-Aid, Gail griped about an essay assignment and how hard motivation came, a month and a half from graduation. The dog came wagging in and sat while Aaron stroked his smooth black head. Aaron looked from the dog to the three faces around him and had to swal-

24

low an urgency that he couldn't understand, afraid that he might cackle or cry.

"What's the assignment?" he asked.

Gail screwed her face up and answered in a stilted whine. "A study of the imagery and other poetic devices in Robert Frost's 'Acquainted with the Night.' "

With sudden gladness, he recognized the title from his Lit class at Chase. "If you bring it down I think I could help you."

Gail arched her thin eyebrows. "Okay." She gulped her drink, then went back upstairs.

Lacing her fingers together, Peg regarded Aaron curiously. "Sure you want to strain your poor head tonight?"

"I can give it a try."

Gail returned with her notebook and anthology and took a seat beside Aaron. He looked at the poem and pointed to a line. "Yeah, you see? It's about this fear which the guy can't explain to himself, and nighttime's the overall symbol for whatever it is that's scaring him. The fear just keeps haunting him. He walks out in the rain and comes back in the rain — and see how it begins and ends with the same line? The idea is that nothing changes. The fear won't let up and he can't sleep, so he just keeps walking."

With Peg looking on, Gail stared at the page. "Poor guy."

"And the 'luminary clock,' " Aaron said, "he's talking about the moon. That usually stands for anything that's not rational."

"Oh!" Gail sparked up, then slouched into a pose of bored sophistication. "I mean . . . I knew *that*. What do you take me for? *Vous avez l'impression que je sois stupide?*"

Peg groaned. "We know you're good in French, dear. Just concentrate on that for a moment."

25

Scrubbing a grill, Jerry gave Aaron a look of amused approval. "A scholar in our midst!"

Aaron continued happily. "Anyway, there's also this line about — "

The phone rang.

"Pardonnez-moi," Gail said, and hurried to pick it up. "Hello? Hi, Dori."

Peg sighed. "There she goes."

Jerry stood drying his hands with a towel. They were small hands for a man his size. "Another exciting fourteen-hour day tomorrow," he grumbled.

The back door opened and a stocky young guy with tousled black hair loped in, his Bruce Springsteen T-shirt blotched with sweat. He looked about Aaron's age.

"Hey, Doug," said Jerry.

"Greetings." Going to the refrigerator, the guy patted the dog and noted Aaron's presence with puzzlement.

"Doug, this is Aaron," Peg said.

"Hi," Aaron said.

"Evenin'." Taking out the Kool-Aid pitcher, he eyed Aaron's bandage. "How . . . How're you?"

Aaron brought a smile up. "Getting better."

Gail plugged her free ear and stretched the phone cord into the hall.

Hanging up the towel, Jerry looked at his watch. "Better take you to the luxury suite, Aaron. You'll be pretty sore and the more shuteye you get, the better."

Jerry went upstairs as Aaron went to get his jacket and sneakers. Putting them on, he heard Peg and Doug in the kitchen.

"How was it tonight?" she asked.

"Wicked slow," Doug mumbled. "About seventy dinners. Hey, why's that guy here? What happened to him?"

26

Huddled with the receiver, Gail let out a laugh.

Jerry came back down with some blankets, a sheet and a pillow, and got his jacket and cap. Aaron called good night to Peg, who wished him a restful night.

Outside, Jerry said the store was just around the corner on Main, and Aaron got his knapsack from the jeep. They didn't speak as they walked. Jerry seemed tired, his stare inward. Aaron was tired again too and his head-to-ribs ache had returned, but so had that odd clutching in his throat.

The store was a two-story white building with gas pumps out front and a grassy lot in back, across which the Fergusons' house was visible with its fenced back yard and soft amber light. A block-lettered sign above the store's door read Ferguson's Corner Grocery. Aaron followed Jerry around the back and up a narrow flight of steps, to a door that Jerry unlocked. Inside, Jerry pulled a light-bulb string and revealed a bare room with flaking wallpaper, one cracked window, and a bathroom in disrepair. A mattress stood upright against the wall; Jerry lowered it with one arm and dropped the bedclothes and pillow onto it.

"Nothing special here at the Hotel Ferguson," he said.

Aaron stood in the doorway, staring at Jerry's wide back.

Jerry rambled on. "Used to rent this out for a song, many moons ago. Then it had plumbing problems. Finally fixed that last summer, but the room still needs a lot of work. Anyway, you should be warm . . ."

"Jerry?"

He turned to Aaron, his face questioning.

Aaron's cheek twitched as he spoke. "I hate to be trouble for anybody."

"And you've really been a millstone around our necks too, kid. You can repay me by strangling a certain cop."

Aaron couldn't laugh. This was a stab in the dark, but it

was all he had. "Is there any way I could . . . Like, do you need help here at the store?"

Jerry put his hands in his pockets, walked slowly to the cracked window, and peered out. "Be straight with me. Are you running from something?"

Aaron opened his mouth, then sucked his sore lip. "No."

Jerry turned his eyes to him, and his tone was as firm as his stare. "Not hiding from the law or — "

"No, no." Aaron shook his hurting head. "Nothing like that."

"How old are you?"

"Eighteen."

Jerry leaned on the sill and lit a cigarette. "Not to pry into your personal business . . ."

"I know — you don't know me."

"Right," Jerry said, exhaling. "I don't know you, even though you seem like a good Joe. My wife and I talked, and we . . . Well, it would have been more comfortable for you at the house, and I'm sorry about that. But you just hear about things that happen to people. I guess I don't need to tell you."

"No, you don't have to explain," Aaron said. "This place is fine. I was just asking . . . if maybe I could stay here and help you, if you needed somebody. Do you need somebody?"

Jerry tapped ashes onto the sill, and Aaron waited.

"Well, it so happens, yes," Jerry said. "I just got rid of a kid who was showing up stoned. My son didn't work out either, but that's another story." His voice took a contemplative turn. "And my daughter's got something else lined up. As it is, my wife and I are having to put in a lot of hours, and she has her part-time job at the library."

Aaron's heart lifted.

28

"Still," Jerry went on, "I decided to be real choosy about who I hired next. Plenty of kids around here need summer jobs, kids from families I know. A few of 'em might even be the reliable sort I'm looking for."

"I'm reliable," Aaron said quickly. "And you wouldn't have to pay me much. Staying here could be most of it."

Jerry frowned at the mattress. "That's a nice angle. I pay fair, though." Again he fixed his eye on Aaron. "Then again, how do I know you won't be booking out in a few weeks? This isn't the thrillingest neck of the woods, y'realize."

"I think . . ." Aaron faltered. "I mean, I want to stay here. Not just for a few weeks. It looks nice to me."

Nodding, Jerry drew on his cigarette. "Interesting proposal." He crushed the butt on the sill. "Well, I'll see what my wife thinks and get back to you. How's that sound?"

Aaron suppressed a sigh. "Thanks, Jerry. I'll understand if it's no, but if it's yes . . ."

"Feel free to sleep late. When you're ready, I'll be down here at the store. We'll rustle up some lunch and see how you're doing." He tugged on his cap. "G'night."

On his way out, Jerry clapped Aaron on his sore shoulder but Aaron hid the wince. He tossed the sack onto the mattress and sat.

Neither soreness nor exhaustion could still his hopeful tremor or keep images of the Fergusons from dancing behind his eyes. Again and again he recalled their voices, their expressions, each of them distinct and separate yet magically linked with the others. Whenever he would think back on this night, Peg and Jerry and Gail would appear luminous, as if they themselves were the source of that welcoming light.

"Fate" had often sounded too heavy and glamorous a word for the way life happened; "chance" was the term that Aaron preferred. But for once it felt right to call it fate. Some unseen chart had guided him, some uncanny trick had dropped him here. He had wanted something, had craved it, and now he knew what it was. With the road map in his mind folded and his fantasies swept aside, he wanted to stay in Fox Hill, Maine.

PART TWO

▾ ▾ ▾

Fox Hill

1

▼

High up, a jet winked silver. Aaron watched it cut a white scar across the azure and smiled. In this breezy day, he felt like someone who had parachuted off a storm-lashed mountain and floated down for miles to a country in bloom. Fox Hill had always been here, hidden, far from the screech and flash of cities. It had its own sky, its own pace, its own stories. And all that mattered was that he was here, holding a broom as he leaned in the doorway of Ferguson's Corner Grocery on a blue, breezy Friday.

A green pickup pulled to the pumps. In the past two weeks this truck had become a familiar sight, along with the grizzled little man getting out of it. He gave Aaron a gold-tooth smile. "Goofin' off again, I see. I got a nephew just like you."

"I was afraid you'd show up," said Aaron.

"Ten dollars of the no-lead, de-ah."

Aaron put the broom aside, went behind the counter, and set the digital panel. He couldn't get over this "dear" thing; among some of these old guys like Andy it was a standard address, delivered in that accent which made words slip and skip like pebbles.

Celtic string music played from the radio over the cigarette rack. Aaron looked out the window and watched Andy, hunched with the hose, and felt thankful that humans were so diverse.

From the back room he could hear Jerry opening boxes of canned goods. The digital clock said three-thirty — forty minutes since Aaron had come in — and once again Jerry hadn't left yet. Aaron wondered about Jerry's confidence in him. Wasn't he handling the job? For a hundred under-the-table dollars a week, plus the room up back, he worked Friday through Tuesday from three to ten. He made few mistakes on the register, knew where nearly everything was, and seldom had to check the price or the tax list. Though he had to fight being overly eager, he seemed to be good with people, and this was the nicest, craziest shock so far. He kept the place clean, did the extra work, and above all, kept strict track of money. "My ancestors were Scottish," Jerry had said. "Know how the Grand Canyon was formed? A Scotsman dropped a nickel and went looking for it. That's a joke, pal, but not entirely."

Still Jerry would linger, giving advice and telling him things he already knew.

"Hey, Jerry!" he called. "Slim's waiting for his Alpo."

"What?"

"I said, why don't you let me take care of that back there?"

"Trying to get rid of me, huh?"

"Yeah, I wanna throw a party."

"Don't worry, I'm just checking these. You get to price 'em and put 'em on the shelves."

Tired of pristine harps and penny whistles, Aaron itched to change the radio station. It was better than the mellow mush that he found Peg listening to, when he relieved her on Mondays and Tuesdays, but at least she went home a lot sooner.

Andy came in with his money and asked for a lottery ticket, which Aaron gave him from the machine. "How're things at your junkyard?" Aaron asked, ringing the register.

34

"My high-quality salvage service, y'mean? It's still the-yah." Andy tucked the ticket into his worn hunting jacket. "Tell Fergie I said hi. If he ever starts givin' you grief, let me know. I'll fix him."

"Yes, sir."

Andy left.

Aaron reflected on the people he was coming to know — old and young, male and female. It seemed from small talk that many of them had always known the Fergusons. Apart from these were a minority who reminded him uncomfortably of Stamford — well-dressed professionals who looked out of place among the shelves and coolers. More formal in their courtesy, they spoke less, shopped quickly, and almost never played the lottery. Peg had spoken of the larger, cushier houses that had risen in the past five years or so on the fringes of town, and the families who had come to live in them.

Backgrounds aside, customers were generally polite and easy. There were exceptions, however, and while Aaron could shrug off the occasional brusque professional, he did mind the handful of bedrock Fox Hillers who eyed him strangely.

Peg had been quick to reassure him. "That's normal for some. You're a brand-new face and they just need to get used to you."

Aaron had only grumbled, wondering how they might react to a drag queen or a Rastafarian.

To the sound of fifes, he resumed sweeping as Jerry came from the back room.

"It's all back there," Jerry said. "Stamp 'em and shelve 'em except for the dented ones."

"Okay." Aaron stopped sweeping. "How am I doing?"

"You mean with sweeping?"

"No, I mean how am I doing?"

"I haven't kicked your ass yet, have I?"

"No."

"Then that's good." Jerry lit a cigarette and wandered toward the door.

Aaron bent to use the dustpan. That was the most he was going to get out of Jerry, he supposed. "Can I change the station? Your program's nearly over."

Leaning in the doorway, Jerry looked over his shoulder. "Change the station? And make my grandfathers howl in their graves? Sure, Aaron, change the station. Enjoy your noise."

Aaron fiddled the dial past news, commercials, heavy metal, and synthesized pop, to a station that played a lot of sixties music. Right now it was playing "The Midnight Hour." The song jerked and swooped, and he wanted to turn it up but knew that he couldn't.

"That's not noise," he spoke to Jerry's back. "That's Wilson Pickett, 1965."

"Yes, professor,"Jerry said. "I tell ya, between you and my kids . . . And speaking of which — "

Aaron looked out and saw Gail with another girl, coming toward the store. In her denim jacket Gail swung her handbag as she walked, and called out in her husky but girlish voice. *"Buon giorno, papa!* Great day, huh?"

"That it is. Hello, Dori."

"Hi, Mr. Ferguson."

Gail's friend was freckled and pony-tailed, in a long skirt. They were almost to the door before Aaron saw she was at least a few months pregnant.

"What's up?" Jerry asked.

"Gail just showed me her dress for tonight," Dori said. "Take lots of pictures cuz she's gonna be a knockout."

"I leave photography to the missus," said Jerry.

"Well, she's going to be a dreamboat," said Dori, pinching Gail's cheek.

Gail brushed her away. "Will not! I'll look like Miss Geek and I'll probably trip on the dance floor."

"No offspring of mine looks like Miss Geek," Jerry declared. He moved so they could enter.

"Hey, Aaron," Gail greeted. "You haven't met Dori yet, have you?"

"Hello," he said, trading a smile.

"We saw you go past the school at lunchtime," Dori said.

"Yeah, I pointed you out," said Gail, stepping to the magazine rack. "Some freshman girls said you looked cute from a distance."

"From a *distance*," Jerry spoke.

"Isn't my dad fun to work for?" said Gail.

Aaron smiled at the floor and worked his broom under a cooler. Since his rib pain had started to lessen and Peg had removed his head bandage, he had taken a lot of walks around town and down the railroad tracks. But not until today had he passed by the high school. It looked so different from Chase Academy: plain brick, two stories with big windows, kids sunning themselves on the grass and around the flagpole — and "Class of '87 Get Crazy" spray painted in huge yellow letters along one wall.

"Somebody sure did a job on that wall," he said, and the girls laughed.

"Mr. Higgins freaked!" Gail cackled. "They say he might call an assembly over that."

"Tax dollars at work," Jerry intoned. "Anyway, who's your prom date again?"

"Tommy, of course," said Gail. "Tommy, as in Dryden?"

"Oh . . . right." Jerry ground his cigarette into the ashtray on the counter. "His old man's a good egg, I guess, but that boy I don't know about. I see him working up at Al's Exxon and he looks like something out of the woods."

Gail glared. "Don't be such a snob! He's nice and he's also a good driver!"

"Well, as long as he keeps both hands on the wheel."

Dori chuckled and got a diet drink. Ringing her money up, Aaron tried not to glance at her belly.

Gail bought an issue of *Life* with a cover photo of an Arab family.

Jerry glanced at her. "Other schoolgirls buy *Seventeen* and look at swimsuits. This one wants to spend her time yakking with Zulus and Eskimos."

Clutching the magazine to her chest, Gail answered with dignity. "Pardon me, Dad. I forgot I lived at the center of the universe. I guess I'm the family nerd."

"Now, I didn't say that. No offspring of mine is a nerd."

"She's working at it," said Dori.

"Anyway," Jerry said. "I suppose I should count my blessings."

"Quit smoking," said Gail. "Then you can count another one."

Aaron enjoyed Gail's smirk. Eating dinner with her and Peg last night, he had avoided staring but still managed to observe her closely. Her figure, though slight, was nice to look at, and so was her face. She had her father's chestnut eyes and her mother's fair complexion. Her nose tipped up a little, like Peg's. The origin of her taffy hair was a mystery, as were her teeth — the two front ones a bit big — while the bite-ravaged nails were a touch completely her own.

Frazzled though she often seemed, Gail was capable of sharp insights when speaking of school or of people she knew,

38

and her conversation, peppered with foreign words and phrases, had yet to be dull. Listening, Aaron had checked her for that showiness common to would-be sophisticates at Chase, the ones who made a production of rolling their *r*'s in Spanish class. He was relieved to detect none of this in Gail. She tossed her foreignisms, it seemed to him, like someone who was just too restless to stick with English.

She and Jerry finished sparring and the girls headed out. "Bye, Aaron," they called.

"Have a nice time at the prom," he said.

"I'll be shuffling off too," said Jerry. "If it gets too busy, call the house and I'll come and open the other register."

"All right."

Aaron put the boxes of cans within view of the door and sat on a milk crate, stamping the cans with the adjustable price gun. He liked being by himself, in charge. Stopping to turn up the radio, he thought of how infinitely better this was than the only other job he had held. His reasons for taking the dishwashing job last summer were still hazy — he hadn't needed the money. "I just want to see what it's like," he had told his mother. So between playing guitar with the Gimmix and cramming to graduate early, he worked amid the steam, grease, and yelling cooks of the Black Swan and never grew fond of it. But he stuck it out till August and emerged with satisfaction, knowing that few of his Academy classmates had ever worked a day for pay.

This time his reasons weren't hazy. He was making a living — a thought that made him glad to be busy.

A few people trickled in for gas or single items while the afternoon waned. Finished with pricing, Aaron began stocking the shelves as the radio played its commercials and current hits, with oldies sandwiched in. He was up to the soup cans when a Supremes hit came on. Snatching cans from the cardboard box at his feet, he began a dance step, moving jerkily down the aisle until he heard the door of a cooler open and realized that someone had come in. He hurried to the front, turned the radio off and waited, embarrassed. Wordlessly a wiry, stubble-faced guy brought up two six-packs of beer, paid, and left without taking a bag.

A steady stream of customers ensued and kept Aaron busy for the next two hours. Some he knew by name and he joked with them. Twice, however, he got the strange eye — first from a moon-faced young woman who barely responded when he remarked on the nice day. This he was able to dismiss, but then came the cop. With a slow, deliberate roll, the cop came in and gave Aaron a stony glance. His black hair was precisely short and his mustache precisely small, on a head that widened at the jowls. His body, narrow at the chest but expanding bottle-like to the hips, seemed modeled on the head. When he put a newspaper on the counter, Aaron pretended interest in the front page to avoid the man's prodding, official eyes.

Night had fallen by the time business lulled. Returning from the washroom, Aaron removed the cinder block to shut the door and then finished stocking. He was brooding over the magazines when Peg dropped in.

"You look perturbed," she said.

"I met Officer Friendly."

Peg laughed. "McDonald! He's the one who ticketed Jerry. The fella's kind of a legend in his own time. Gail calls him the Pear with a Badge because of how he's shaped."

"I'd call him something worse."

"Jerry sure does. But that doesn't mean you have to mind him." She handed him something in a small paper bag.

40

"Here's some sandwiches. Young people on their own tend to waste away."

"Thanks, Peg. . . ." He stood crinkling the bag, then put it on the counter. "But jeez . . ."

"Yes?"

He ran his fingers through his hair. "You patched me up. You gave me this job. You gave me a place to stay. You've had me to dinner twice already."

"So what else do you expect from wonderful human beings?"

Smiling, he looked out the door. "Yeah, well — I just don't want you to end up feeling saddled."

"I swear!" she breathed. "You're so hyper and serious! Look, you're saving us money by working here, and besides that you're interesting to talk to. You're different, and around here you get tired of hearing the same voices all the time. And once in a while it's good to have a substitute guy at dinner, with Jerry and Doug off doing their things."

Glad though Aaron felt for Peg's assurances, he wanted her to stop. But she continued. "You're nice and you're responsible. I mean, you're working out better than our own kids. Gail would have jumped in if we'd gotten desperate enough, but she talks too much with customers. And Doug . . . well . . ."

Aaron seized the chance to change subjects. "I guess it must have been weird having their dad for a boss."

Peg rolled her eyes. "I guess! That's sort of why Gail went and lined up a summer job at the print shop. For years the kids had their turns here, working weekends. But when Doug graduated last year he started full time, and I suppose we should've seen what was coming. He and Jerry can get like roosters in a pit."

41

"That's too bad."

"Well, they might have done all right except that Doug started with this rock band."

Aaron cocked his head. "Doug's in a band?"

Peg nodded. "With some buddies of his. He took night guitar classes up at the school, and then he was practicing in his room a lot and waking the dead. Then came the group, and he got involved to where Jerry got worried — about Doug's future, I mean. One day — get this — he brought his guitar and amplifier in here, for when business got slow!" She tittered. "Then he started showing up late from practice, and Jerry would hit the roof. Just before Christmas they kind of agreed to disagree, and Doug started washing dishes at the Briar Patch."

Aaron nodded. A band, he thought, here in Fox Hill. Since that first dazed evening at the Fergusons', he had seen Doug only one other time, while out walking. Doug had said hi and strode purposefully on, seeming more absorbed than unfriendly. Peg and Gail would laugh or roll their eyes when they mentioned him, but Aaron couldn't bring himself to ask why without feeling nosy.

"Like you say," Peg went on, "it can be rough working for your father — a father like theirs, anyway. But sheesh! Nowadays I only see Douglas when he gets in from the restaurant. For instance, last night at dinner time, where was he? Jamming with the guys."

Aaron checked the urge to probe further, just as a carful of young workers from Hale Construction pulled in. Ringing up some cigarettes for them, Aaron observed Peg looking through a magazine and wondered why she hadn't taken the opportunity to leave.

Once the men were gone, Peg remarked, "Probably on their

42

way to Milo's or the Patch to get tanked. This town, I'm telling you . . ."

"Well, I like it here," said Aaron.

Peg put the magazine back. "I had a couple of questions for you. And they're the none-of-my-business type."

Aaron had expected this to come sooner or later, but he hoped that she wouldn't be point-blank about it. "Shoot," he said.

Pocketing her hands, she looked at him thoughtfully. "It's just . . . you've said really little about yourself."

"Maybe I'm not as interesting as you think."

"Go on. See, this is what I mean. I start asking about you and then you turn it around. I'm just concerned cuz I'm a mother, I guess. And all I know is that you're eighteen and you're from Connecticut. I'd like to . . ." She pulled a hand out and waved it. "Of course, you know you don't have to answer any of this."

He shrugged.

"First," she said. "About school — did you drop out or what?"

"I graduated a semester early. During junior year I buckled down."

"I'm impressed."

"Don't be. A lot had to happen before I straightened my act out. Anyhow, I busted my tail to do that and I'm not thinking about college yet."

She nodded. "What about your parents? Aren't they worried? Shouldn't you be in touch?"

He replied with care. "My folks are split up. I told my mother I was hitting the road and I'd be back. And . . ." He tussled with the thought. "And I will, when I'm feeling ready. Whenever."

43

"Have you contacted her once yet?"

"No, but I will soon."

Peg looked down. Her wry smile relieved him.

"Okay," she said, and gave a brisk sigh. "Well, I have knitting to do. And waiting up for Gail." She started to the door. "She and Tommy looked cute for their pictures. Nothing like that to make a lady feel ancient."

"You look plenty young to me," said Aaron.

"Right. Butter me up."

He thanked Peg for the sandwiches, and she said they would have him over for dinner again next week. Then she left, and he watched her cross the lot and turn down the sidewalk.

Musing about Doug and his band, he ate his sandwiches and waited on a few more customers. Shortly before ten a pair of younger guys came in, all grins and greetings. One got a six-pack, and Aaron asked haltingly for an I.D.

"Uh . . ." The boy shrugged. "Listen, guy — give us a break this once, okay?"

Jerry had been especially clear on this point. Aaron shook his head. "Sorry, I can't. There's no way."

"C'mon, man," the other guy pleaded. "They turned us down at the Seven-Eleven."

"We'll give you one," said the first.

Aaron told them no and they left muttering. Feeling sour, he put the beer back. This I.D. issue was one part of the job he could get to hate.

But it was closing time. He flicked off all the lights except the one above the counter, then turned the radio on low. Jerry would be here any minute to total the day's cash, but Aaron decided to save him the trouble. Neatly he separated bills and change by denomination, then got out the pad of carbon deposit slips and tabulated with a pen.

This he liked — not the money itself but the fact that it mattered. Dollars, quarters, and even pennies mattered and somehow made other things feel more important: Jerry's trust, Peg's sandwiches, his room, and just being here. Adding up the money, he sensed a firm connection between all of these things. It made him feel invigorated.

He jotted the total, put the money and copy slip into the canvas zip bag, and waited. Jerry was taking longer than usual. Gazing out at the silent street, Aaron thought about Gail's class prom. Maybe the Chase Academy prom was going on tonight also, down there in Connecticut, but that was no loss to him. There was no girl he would have been hot to ask, and anyway the event would probably feature more coke than dancing.

An old hit by the Shondells came on the radio, with a tremulous descending guitar. Right now, the senior class of Fox Hill Regional High was partying to some covers band at a ski lodge in Bridgton and probably having a good time, a time to remember. Abruptly he longed to be there, to be one of them, and just as abruptly he wished that he could have seen Gail in her gown.

When Jerry showed up out front Aaron switched off the radio and the remaining light, then stepped out and handed him the canvas bag.

"Oh . . . You made the slip out already, huh?"

"Yeah, since I had the time."

Jerry grunted and unzipped the bag.

"What's the matter?" Aaron asked.

"Aw, nothing." Jerry put the slip back in and rezipped. "I've just got a thing about doing it myself."

Aaron gave an impatient sigh. "I thought I was doing you a favor."

45

"Naw, naw — that's okay." Jerry patted his arm. "I'm sure your math's fine. So how'd it go tonight?"

"All right."

"Good." He jingled his keys out and locked the door. "Guess I'll have Peg make the bank drop in the morning. I feel about ready to drop, myself."

Aaron felt like walking and accompanied Jerry to the corner of Lark. "I bid you good night," Jerry said, turning down toward the house. Aaron watched his dark bulk move away, the bag in one hand and the orange spark of a cigarette in the other.

As Aaron continued down Main, his footsteps and the rustle of trees were the only sounds. He looked at the cozy light of the houses, the signs and darkened windows of Talbot's Hardware, Newton Drug, Molly's Flower Shop, and the *Fox Hill Weekly Advertiser*. The breeze on his face had a liquid quality, smelling of buds and bushes, and he felt light.

He passed an elderly man who was walking his collie, and smiled hello. At the hushed square he sat on a bench and watched a few cars go by. A young married couple whom he knew as customers ambled past, and he swapped greetings with them.

On a pedestal across the square, a tarnished Union soldier stood on permanent sentry duty: For Those Who Served and Died in the War to Save the Republic. To the right of that was a small cannon with a welded stack of cannonballs. Yesterday in a moment of indignation, Aaron had dug a year's worth of wrappers, tissues, and crushed cigarette packs from the cannon's muzzle. He liked monuments and their solid, silent proof of great causes. He liked almost anything that was old. Back in California he had collected rocks and fossils, and despite his feelings about Chase, he had liked its vines and sculpted ledges. Old buildings, museum exhibits — he could gaze upon them and feel peaceful, musing that maybe these dusty, weathered tons of workmanship had a point in lasting so long, and that maybe the world itself had a point to it. But this had been a rare hope, a rare consideration until lately.

He envisioned the fractured sprawl of Los Angeles — its hills and flats, beaches and freeways, and the endless streets that became a light-studded labyrinth by night. Then he conjured up New York — crammed, towering, and more frantic with its own importance. Walking alone there after dark, he had tempted harm and not known why.

These places were other planets now. Nothing cruel crouched in the shadows around him.

Spreading his arms across the bench's back, he stared up at the clock in the town hall's dome. What would it have been like to grow up beneath those crafted iron hands? He looked down beside his thigh where an arrowed heart, well faded, had been carved with jagged initials: J.H. + M.L. 1980. What would it have been like to grow up knowing each face, street, and building? How would he have felt and seen things now?

He got up, crossed the square, and headed for a side street called Ash Road, where yesterday he had discovered the bridge and stream. Reaching the corner, he saw a blue light pulsing farther down Main, past the rail crossing. He chuckled — probably Gail's Pear with a Badge keeping busy.

The log bridge was at a wooded part of the road where there were no houses or street lights, only stars for seeing. He leaned against the rail, staring down into a darkness thick with crickets and the bass twang of bullfrogs. The stream washed by in black eddies. Watching the water curl about the boulders, he felt a small ache, and the ache became a sweet, dizzy expectancy that welled with the water's gurgle. He was thinking of Gail again — her eyes, her laugh, her bitten fingers.

Then, resting his chin on his forearms, he pushed her gently from his mind. Given the situation, he thought, this was one daydream that he could not afford to dwell upon. There was plenty else he could enjoy here, risk free.

On his way back toward the store and his room, he wondered again about Doug and this band of his. How good were they? And what did they play, exactly? Curiosity scratched as he lay on his mattress, watching the black and white portable that he had bought used at Talbot's. He hoped to meet Doug again soon.

2

▼

Wednesday it was dinner at the Fergusons', and once more Doug wasn't there. Hiding his disappointment, Aaron cut his roast beef and listened to Peg.

"A radioactive waste site," she repeated, "right around Lake Sebago. That's the major water supply for the region." She smiled blandly.

"So let me guess," he said. "You got upset?"

Gail laughed, eating her peas. "Should've heard her at the town meeting!"

"And at the hearings too," Peg said. "All that spring we gathered signatures, wrote letters, and basically howled till they dropped the idea. Their ears must still hurt."

"Congratulations," he said.

"Well, we can't keep patting ourselves on the back. I've read stuff about chemical dumping in Maine that'd curl your hair." With her fork she motioned to the stack of pamphlets on the counter. "So I'm doing my bit."

Lured by the foodsmell, Slim made a timid approach. Aaron slipped the dog a piece of meat before Peg ordered him back to the doormat.

Afterward Peg made two beef grinders to bring over to Jerry at the store. "Stick around and watch TV if you like," she told Aaron as she went out.

While Gail did the dishes, he wandered into the living room and looked at some family photos. A black and white picture of Jerry, young and solemnly handsome in his army uniform, was propped next to a gold-framed wedding portrait on the coffee table. Standing close, the newlyweds beamed — Jerry looking sharp and much trimmer in his tux, Peg slim and petite, with raven locks beneath her veil. Last year they had celebrated their silver anniversary.

Mounted in a single large frame on the wall were other photos, mostly of the kids at various ages: Doug and Gail, chubby and small, holding hands by a sandbox; Doug, about ten, opening Christmas presents; Gail, about the same age, holding Slim as a pup and flanked by fawning grandparents; and Jerry Jr., the eldest, a grinning, crew-cut boy in a sweater. Jerry Jr. was now twenty-four, Peg had said. He was single and lived way up in Millinocket, working as a ranger in Baxter State Park. A center photo showed him in his high school graduation gown and arm in arm with Peg and Gail. Despite the beard, there was more than a trace of Jerry on him — the deep-set eyes, the faintly amused look.

After another minute of gazing at the happy collage, Aaron returned to the kitchen, where Gail was drying the last few dishes. The mellowing light from the windows meant sundown. He put his hands in his pockets and felt suddenly awkward.

"*Mash* is going to be on soon," Gail said. "Wanna watch that?"

"Sure. So, uh . . . Your brother's off practicing with his band?"

"Yup. Makin' noise with the boys."

"Are they good?"

"Kind of rough, but yeah. Some poke fun at them but most people like 'em. They played a couple of dances at school, and at Milo's, and Randy's Roadhouse, and a couple of times in Bridgton. Dori and I snuck in when they played Randy's. It was a pretty fun time."

"What's their name? What do they do?"

"They call themselves Toy Soldiers. They do a lot of stuff off the radio, and some of their own songs. Doug's written a few." She dried her hands. "Doug's funny. I think he expects they're all going to be stars."

"There's no telling."

"Yeah, more power to him." Chuckling, she undid her apron. "I tell you, though, it'd sure be better if Douglas had his own place. Like last night he gets home and decides to practice a little in his room, and in a minute Dad's yelling, 'Put that thing away or it's going into the furnace!'"

Thinking of how he had usually taken praise for granted, Aaron felt sorry for Doug.

He sat on the living room couch as Gail turned the TV on. Slouching in her father's chair, she chewed a thumbnail and pondered aloud. "I guess I have to respect Doug for hanging in, but I can see how it's a thorn in my folks. He'd be better off living in Portland with a half-decent job, but that'd mean giving up Soldiers." She sighed. "Around here I just try to stay clear of the whole thing."

Aaron nodded. "Uh-huh."

Gail glanced at him. "You play an instrument?"

"I play guitar some."

"Ever in a band?"

"Once, not long."

"Really? Well, you and Doug could bend each other's ears, I bet."

Peg got back from the store.

"How's Dad?" Gail asked.

"Perturbed," said Peg. "The gas dealer didn't show up and the unleaded went dry."

Donning glasses, Peg took her typewriter to the kitchen and began tapping out a letter — to a state rep, she announced, on the toxic waste issue.

The *Mash* episode wasn't one of the better ones. As their attention flagged, Gail asked Aaron how he liked Fox Hill.

"Fine, great," he said.

Gail's skeptical look made him feel curiously challenged. "You don't believe me?"

"Oh, I believe you," she said, looking at the TV. "This place has its good points." She giggled. "Don't ask me to name 'em, though!"

He opened his mouth, but she flicked the air with her

51

hand — the exact gesture he had seen Peg use to dodge a subject.

"Don't mind me," said Gail. "It's just my senioritis, I guess. *La maledad del cuarto año.*"

Aaron tried to think of some half-funny reply in Spanish but couldn't remember the right words. They kept talking. Gail said that she had been accepted at the University of Southern Maine in Portland, and that she was thinking about an Education or a French major. But this depended on a state scholarship that she had applied for, and a bureaucratic delay had left this uncertain for now.

"Eventually I'd like to be average to good in five or six languages," she said. "A few of the major ones and one that's more obscure, like Tibetan or something."

"Hey, I never would've guessed," he said. "So in the long run you'll be teaching?"

"Oh, probably. But I wouldn't mind being an interpreter. I could cash in at the Olympics." Drawing her legs up, she gave him a crafty gaze. "Plus there are these little power trips you can pull, if you need to."

"How do you mean?"

"Well, imagine being able to insult somebody in Korean or Hebrew."

Aaron smiled. "Um . . . Never thought about it."

"Think." Gail's fingers came up, tickling the air as she spoke. "Say someone's giving you grief, someone you can't afford to scream at. Like a customer at the store — some bonehead who's out to make you miserable. In Korean you tell him, 'You know, I've seen road-killed toads that weren't as ugly as you.' Or in Hebrew you say, 'May the manure heaps of Mesopotamia fill your refrigerator.' "

Aaron broke out laughing.

"I mean, picture it!" Gail went on. "Instead of more trouble they just give you this totally confused look. Like when McDonald gave Dad his ticket, Dad could've said in Tibetan, 'McDonald, you useless piece of last week's garbage, if brains were illegal you'd be head of the FBI.' "

Laughing, Aaron flopped back against the couch pillows. "You keep a list of those?"

"Sure do. Call me nasty, but before I die I'm going to use every one of 'em."

"Well, I hope you don't meet that many boneheads."

Just then they heard the back door slam, and Peg's typing ceased. "Hi, stranger," she said, and Aaron perked up.

"Mind if I play this, Mom?" It was Doug's voice.

"Soon as I'm done with this, and as long as Gail and Aaron don't mind."

Gail leered at Aaron and cupped her hands to her mouth. "Incoming wounded!"

Carrying a guitar case and with a record album under his arm, Doug entered the living room and nodded to Aaron.

"Hi," Aaron said.

"Short practice tonight," Gail remarked.

Doug put his case down and sat at the other end of the couch. "Yeah, Neil's mom had company," he mumbled. "But I think we got another date at Milo's."

"C'est magnifique!"

Doug sat forward, flipping the album in his hands. Though stocky of build he was more obviously Peg's son, dark and fine-lipped.

"Neil lend you another hot one?" Gail asked.

"Uh-huh. You gonna watch anything after this?"

She looked to Aaron, who quickly shook his head and eyed the album.

53

"That must be their latest," he said.

Doug looked at him. "It is. You like the Del Fuegos?"

"I have their first one back home. Their sound has a real edge to it."

"Yeah, nice and raw," Doug said. The mumble was gone.

"Guess I lead a deprived life," said Gail with a yawn. She pointed to Aaron. "He used to be in a band."

Doug blinked at him. "Oh, yeah?"

"Gail was telling me about yours," Aaron said.

Peg called. "Okay, Doug. But not too loud, okay?"

Gail turned the set off and left the room as her brother took the record to the stereo. "Check this out," he told Aaron.

They stood over the turntable as the drum punch and banshee vocals started. Doug smiled, bobbing his head, and Aaron felt both at ease and excited. Gail was right: there would be a lot to talk about with this guy.

The phone rang and Peg answered it, then called upstairs. "Phone, Gail. It's Tommy." She signaled Doug to lower the volume and he sullenly complied.

After Gail came down Aaron glanced a few times to the kitchen, where she sat coiled with the phone cord. Her face was turned away.

"You play guitar?" Doug asked.

"Yeah. What kind do you have?"

Doug got out his guitar, an old Fender Mustang. Aaron stroked its face and fingerboard. Old and duct-taped though the instrument was, he grinned as he held it. "So you play around the area?"

"Not as much as we'd like," said Doug. "We might get a few nights in Portland this summer, if they don't ask our ages."

Their talk skipped along through music and performers.

54

Springsteen was high in Doug's constellation of heroes. "My brother Jerry and I saw him in eighty-four at Saratoga Springs. Man, it was like Christmas in July!"

"I caught him in New York City that year. He was unreal." Aaron had to suppress another tidbit — his friendly handshake with Springsteen in a Columbia Records building when he was twelve, during a visit with his father.

Aaron told Doug of his feeling for rockabilly and the great sixties singles. Though Doug stayed enthusiastic, his pre-seventies knowledge appeared spotty at best. Aaron thought of his own record and tape collection and how much he would have liked to keep Doug up all night, listening to everything from the trashy to the classic. But those were all back in Stamford, and Stamford might as well have been Antarctica.

It was a while before they realized the record had ended and Doug went to turn it over. As he did, they heard the back door open. Doug's face went somber.

"That kills that," he said.

Jerry's voice was in the kitchen with Peg's.

"You closed early?" she asked.

"Yeah. It was slow all day and I was just too damn ugly about the gas people."

"Want some decaf, hon?"

Doug put the record into its sleeve, and Aaron thought of the time. He didn't want to push his welcome.

"Guess I'll be going," he said.

"Listen," said Doug. "Drop by sometime tomorrow, all right?"

"Sure."

Doug took his case and headed upstairs. "See you then. I'll let you play some on this."

Walking to the kitchen, Aaron saw Gail still on the phone. Jerry was seated while Peg stood rubbing his shoulders.

"Repeat after me," said Jerry. " 'Life is a bitch.' Can you say that, kid?"

"Never mind," Peg said. "Let Aaron get cynical on his own."

Aaron was glad to see them looking like one of their old photos. He thanked Peg and said good night.

The elation of talking with Doug hung on as he kicked about the quiet streets, and his hands anticipated the feel of a guitar.

3

▼

Doug adjusted the shoulder strap and started tuning. "I can thank my brother for getting me into music. It was sort of by accident, just from listening to his records. After he left, I inherited all of 'em."

Kneeling before the cardboard box by Doug's bed, Aaron thumbed through the worn albums. They included a fairly standard slice of the seventies, minus any disco.

Doug struck a sharp chord. "Bet my dad would've made a bonfire out of those, if he'd known it would lead to this."

"Your dad's a good man," Aaron said. "He just worries a lot."

Doug shifted position on the bed and played a few notes, which sounded fuzzy through the cut-rate amp. "This amp's a joke. Over at our practice space we have a Fender Twin — great for reverb and everything."

Wondering when he would get to try the guitar, Aaron kept looking idly through the records. Then he tipped back a Bob Seger album and his hand went still. From behind bars on the cover of *Rattle the Cage,* his father stared out with a face eight years younger. But the eyes were the same, and so was that stolid expression which could leave anyone guessing. Aaron knelt there, staring as the room grew hotter.

A series of deep, loud chords broke the trance and he looked up at Doug, who was on his feet and showing great concentration. Aaron stood up and listened. It was a stiffly correct rendition of a Springsteen song. Doug stopped to fiddle with the knobs, then played a winding, stinging progression that Aaron didn't recognize.

"Came up with that last week," he said when finished. "It's called 'Scene of the Crime.' Wanna guess the place that it's about?"

Aaron seethed to play, to blow away the face now looming in his brain. "So, you guys do originals?" he asked.

"I write some and so does Neil," Doug replied. "He does keyboard and lead vocals. But in clubs we gotta do mostly covers. You know how it is — people want to hear stuff they know." Handing Aaron the pick, he unslung the guitar. "Go to it, guy."

It took all of Aaron's restraint not to seize the instrument like a stolen toy. Feeling it out, he picked notes and tried a few chords.

"Like I said, I'm probably rusty," he told Doug, and unleashed the smoking intro to a Dire Straits song, swaying on

57

his feet as he played. The amp's fuzziness annoyed him, but when he finished, Doug looked excited.

"Jeez, not bad!" Doug exclaimed.

Aaron did some quick tuning. Then, working the pickup controls, he whipped off a dance song of his own. In the middle of the song's bucking bridge he glanced at Doug, who was seated on the bed and tapping his knees. Aaron wound up with a flourish.

"What was that?" Doug asked.

"I call it 'Suburban Stomp.' "

"You write your own too? Great! Keep going."

Yearning for a good amp, Aaron played on while Doug sat absorbed, tapping his knees. Aaron laid into another song and thought how natural it felt, like a fast car ride. Just then the barred face reentered his mind and he missed a note. He cursed under his breath, upped the volume, and worked his hands faster.

At the end of it, Doug sat up smiling. "Shit, you're not rusty! I still have trouble working in a rhythm line. You make it look easy."

Aaron wiped sweat from his brow. "You just need to be loose. Concentrate but relax."

"Was that one yours too?"

"Nope. Elvis Costello."

"Oh. I'm not really into him, but Neil is. Speaking of Neil, you should meet him and the other guys. We're practicing this evening."

"Good. Okay." Aaron handed back the guitar, then leaned against the wall by the closet. He looked out the window and across the road, to the yard of Hale Construction and the woods beyond. The sight settled him, reminding him of where he was.

With the guitar in his lap, Doug picked through a slow song and kept talking. "Neil should be at his house in an hour or so. His garage is our space. He works days as a bus boy at the Patch."

"Yeah, I'd like to meet him," Aaron said, and glanced into the open closet. Behind a pile of dirty clothes was a stack of *Rolling Stone* issues. He reached in and took the top one, which had Sting on the cover. It was four years old and tattered. "Mind if I look through these?" he asked.

"Go ahead," Doug said. "More of my bro's junk."

Aaron pushed the clothes aside and started rummaging through the magazines. The covers were a musty slide show of celebrities — some still active and talked about, others not.

"Some of these'll probably be collector's items someday," he told Doug. The remark was barely out when he brushed another *Stone* aside and came upon his father's face — faded yet every bit as cryptic, with his strong chin and blue-eyed gaze, bordered by collar-length black hair: the face behind the songs and the fierce guitar. Even without the renown it would have drawn people, just as it drew Aaron's gaze. Reportedly it had attracted a swarm of women since way back. Twenty years ago it had drawn Aaron's mother.

"Danny 'Spider' Webb," it said underneath. "The Trials and Triumph of Rock's Darkest Prince."

Shoving the other magazines back on top of it, he stood up and leaned against the wall again. Doug kept playing, eyes lowered as he murmured the words. Aaron didn't listen. Looking out the window once more, he could see only the lingering stare. He had forgotten about the 1979 cover story. Like a heat-seeking missile the face had found him in this distant hideaway, in this room that was suddenly too small. He felt like punching the plaster.

"Doug?"

Doug stopped playing.

"Mind if I go listen to that Fuegos album again?"

As they left for Neil's they saw Gail and Dori coming down the walk, graduation gowns bundled in their arms.

Gail looked up from talking. "Gee, Aaron. You hang out with *any*body!"

"I was just gonna say the same thing to Dori," Doug spoke.

Picking up their conversation, the girls passed them. Gail had done something nice to her eyes — darkened her lashes or something. This guy Tommy had reason to be happy, Aaron thought.

The day was warm and buzzing.

"Don't mind my asking," said Aaron as they walked, "but isn't supper time a weird time for practice?"

Doug's bland expression didn't change. "We don't usually start playing till seven or so, after we're all there. I usually eat something with Neil and just mess around the garage until then." He shrugged. "Besides, I'm not big on the whole family scene."

"Man, I *like* it at your house!"

Doug croaked a laugh. "That's because you don't live there. I mean, when I'm stuffing my face, the last thing I want to hear is my mother asking about my goals, or Gail bitching about school and talking French, or Dad . . . Or Dad, period."

Objections jammed in Aaron's mouth before he could speak them.

"Tell me about this band you used to be in," Doug said.

"They were called the Gimmix," said Aaron. "I just answered an ad in the local paper. The other guys were a few years older. We did a lot of gigs, mostly along the Connecticut shore. Anyway, I had disagreements with our front man. To him I was always the new kid and I got tired of being diplomatic. So they ended up bouncing me."

Doug sniffed. "Diplomatic . . . I know what that's about."

Soon they came to a rust-colored house with a terrace, a second-story veranda, an adjoining garage, and a red Nissan Sentra in the driveway. "Neil's mom usually leaves us alone till about ten," Doug said. "That's the great thing."

A flagstone path led them to a carved door, and Doug rang the bell. Inside, a boozy George Thorogood song was playing.

"Come on in!" came a yell.

Upon entering, Aaron saw a thin, shirtless guy with sharp features, drying his hair with a towel at the foot of a staircase. A silver earring gleamed on one of his lobes.

With Thorogood's gritty growl at full volume, Doug had to shout the introduction. "Neil, this is Aaron! He's going to hang out while we practice!"

Neil gave a quick handshake and tossed the towel in a chair, then strode to the hi-fi and turned the radio down. "I'm gonna have a beer. You guys want one?"

They nodded and Neil brought three beers from the kitchen. His movements were quick and haphazard, his aquiline face intent. With his brown hair spiked wet, he looked crazed or shocked. He threw a shirt on and they sat in the living room, which was expensively decorated but cluttered with papers and magazines. Doug asked his friend how work had been.

"Sucked, but what else is new?" Neil replied, and gulped his beer. "They're talking about putting me on nights again. They try that, I'll quit."

"Yeah, that would screw us up good," said Doug. "Anyway, you hear anything more about Milo's?"

"I called and he has us booked for the eighteenth. That's

three weeks. We have to get at least a few new songs down by then."

The conversation turned to the top-forty radio station that Doug and Neil were forced to endure in the Briar Patch kitchen. Aaron said little and when he did speak, Neil gave him a token glance and swigged his beer. Aaron was just intrigued enough not to take offense.

Doug suggested that Aaron get a look at Neil's album and cassette collection, which filled a large cabinet against the wall. Neil shed his preoccupied manner, pulling out one record after another for eager mention.

A car door shut outside. A smartly dressed older woman came in, carrying folders and a briefcase. She squinted a smile.

"Gentlemen," she said, her face half concealed by stray hair.

"Hi, Mom," said Neil.

"I'm just here to change. I'm meeting a client for dinner." Headed toward the stairs she stopped, looking crestfallen. "Aw, Neil — you still haven't tidied up the living room!"

Neil looked surly. "I'll get to it."

She proceeded upstairs.

At Neil's suggestion they made sandwiches in the kitchen. They heard Neil's mother leave and start her car, then they went out to the garage and Neil turned on the ceiling light. The garage was admirably spacious and dry. Stepping among the wires, Aaron examined the mikes, amps, and drum kit. Doug plugged into the Fender Twin for tuning up and Neil fussed with the sound board.

"Ben and Mike'll be here soon," Doug said. "Hey, Neil. Aaron plays guitar and he's good."

"Yeah?" said Neil, without looking up.

"I'm going to let him play some later on. You ought to hear him."

"Do some treble for me."

Frowning over the board, Neil set a switch as Doug tested his treble. Aaron smiled to himself and inspected the Vox organ, hooked up to a Leslie speaker at the center of the space. "Nice," he said.

Neil looked up and nodded proudly.

When a knock came at the garage door, Doug raised it to admit two other guys, whom he then introduced to Aaron. Ben, carrying a bass, had curly black hair and glasses and seemed quiet. The drummer was Mike, shaggy-blond and affable, with rugged arms; Aaron remembered selling him junk food at the store. Mike lost no time in fetching a beer for Ben and himself before getting his drumsticks. He sat on a stool behind the kit, thumped the bass pedal a few times, and did a flailing solo.

"Okay, Conan," Neil said, and did a flashy run on his organ.

Discord filled the garage and Aaron watched with mounting interest, wishing that they would start. It was another ten minutes of sound checks, beer guzzling, and trips to the bathroom before they banged into a song. The clashing drowned Aaron's thoughts but halted with a head-shake from Doug, who then took a minute to work out a chord change.

There were other false starts. Neil undid his sleeves and looked peevish, leaning on his organ. But the number eventually fell into place. Neil put his hands to inspired use, and his aggressive midrange voice wasn't bad either. Supplying harmony, Doug's voice was thinner but distinctive.

Other songs were fumbled with, hammered into passable shape, and cast aside, and Aaron saw that Gail's appraisal of the band was correct. They were pretty rough. Neil, obviously the ablest, nevertheless lost himself while singing and got sloppy on the keys. Mike, though fun to watch, tended

63

to be ham-fisted, and Ben's playing proved no more supple than Doug's. Defects and all, however, they achieved a kind of fluky charm. Instead of sounding like direct copies, the covers bore the band's own stamp — clumsy, surprising, and headlong. The Gimmix, although more proficient, had never boasted such a gift, and it made the memory of them all the more distasteful.

The evening clipped by. Aaron watched their faces, wanting to be up and playing with them. Then, as another song ended, he heard the front door of the house open. He scowled. At that moment Doug looked at him and offered the guitar.

"All right, Aaron."

Nearly springing off the steps, Aaron took the instrument. "Will your mother mind?" he asked Neil.

Neil made an offhand gesture. "Never mind her."

Aaron flexed his fingers, took the pick from Doug, and went down the scale, relishing the clear sound from the amp. He took a deep breath.

"Do the one you did for me," Doug urged. "The one you wrote."

Aaron did "Suburban Stomp." Hitting the bridge section, he bent back and launched it to the rafters. In his mind the walls and four faces dissolved and he was by himself, spewing chords like jets of color from a pinwheel. Improvising, he extended the song, bending the notes and spinning the melody until he could do nothing more with it, and stopped.

From a corner, Ben blinked behind his glasses.

"All right!" Mike said.

Doug grinned to Neil, who stood staring.

"Pretty good," said Neil. "Can you do something we can all play?"

Suggestions were tossed around and they settled on the

Kinks' "All Day and All of the Night." Aaron began the whiplash riff and kept it going as Mike and Ben came in solidly. Neil held the microphone, waited, then began singing. "I'm not / Content / To be with you / In the daytime . . ."

With an upward shift, the song coiled tighter as Doug stepped to his mike for harmony. Aaron churned the riff out. And in a crescendo that wasn't quite on key, they were all shouting the title chant.

The two of them were halfway back toward Main when Doug pointed out the moonlit, shrub-studded hill on their left. "This is a short cut."

They jumped the ditch, groped through a cluster of trees, and sprinted up the slope. Slowing to a trudge, Aaron looked up at the moon's bright hook. His ears were still ringing. Surrendering the guitar had given him a naked, sinking sensation — the same thing he had felt when he sold his Stratocaster, just after the Gimmix axed him. But he was glad for having had the chance to play, and he felt wide awake.

Doug was a few strides ahead of him, lugging the case. "Let me carry that," said Aaron.

"Thanks," Doug said, and turned to hand it over.

Aaron gripped the handle and they fell in step. "That was a good time," he said.

"It's not always that fun," said Doug. "We'll get you over there again soon. . . . Hey, look!" Doug pointed.

Aaron caught sight of two deer bobbing away toward the black bulwark of the woods, where they vanished.

"When I was a kid, this was my secret place," Doug said. "Used to come here to eat blueberries and watch for deer. Played war by myself too — a lot of Nazis and cannibals ate lead here."

Gazing across the bushes and brown grass, Aaron thought what a fine place it would be for daydreams and being alone. The slope was gentler now, leveling, and he saw a picket fence ahead.

"Somebody's yard?" he asked.

"Sort of," said Doug. "But these folks are pretty mellow. Let's rest for a minute." At the fence, he hopped over, reached back for the case, and grinned.

Aaron hopped over, took three strides, and stood still. Several trees cast cool shadows, and in the moonlight between them were headstones of all sizes, some of them listing. Farther down the hill, the stark white steeple of the Presbyterian church pricked skyward, with the muted glow of Main Street beyond.

Doug laid the case by a headstone, unlocked it, and took two beers out.

"Two for the road, from Neil," he said, and handed one to Aaron. "Careful, they're probably half foam by now." He squatted with his back to the stone.

Aaron twisted the cap off, let the foam flow down his hand, and sat under a tree, facing Doug. He took a swig and sighed. "So how'd you get to know Neil?"

"He moved here from Brunswick our sophomore year," Doug said. "We both had detention a lot for cutting class, and we just got to talking — found out we were both heavy into music." He took a gulp. "He can be a pain in the ass but he's all right. If it wasn't for him there never would've been a band. He paid for most of that equipment. He even came up with our name."

"He seems kind of down on his mom."

"He is, and that sucks cuz she's a cool lady. Daffy but cool. She and his dad divorced about a year ago. I guess it was rough, but at least they're not hurting at the bank. She does

66

real estate in Bridgton and his father's some kind of engineer."

Aaron raised the bottle to his lips but didn't drink. He set it between his knees. "What about the other guys?"

"Mike I've more or less known since grammar school. I'd drop by his house and he'd be banging on his mom's pots and pans. His dad owns the produce market and Mike still works there. Good guy. I used to get pissed off at him cuz he wouldn't show up for practice, but he's better about that now. And Ben — he moved here a few years back, I think. He's in Gail's class. His father's a dentist. Kind of quiet, but when we found out he was learning bass, we grabbed him." Doug took another swallow and burped loudly. "I don't know. It's dumb, but sometimes I picture us making it out of here, cracking the big time. Cash, cars, babes — the whole stupid nine yards. I can't help it, y'know? We're no great shakes, but it's fun to think about."

Using his thumbnails, Aaron began peeling the bottle's label. He shook his head. "Man, I envy you."

Doug rested his back against the headstone. "What?"

"I mean, I wish I'd grown up here."

Doug's shoulders started pumping and his laugh danced through the quiet. "That's . . . That's too much!"

Aaron put his bottle aside and stared at Doug until he finished laughing. "It feels nice in this town," Aaron said. "The way people all know each other. . . ."

"Yeah," Doug chuckled. "Sure, but listen . . ."

"Your mom's a great lady."

"Yeah, she is." Doug stopped smiling, and nodded. "She nags, but I know she's great."

"And Gail's a nice girl."

"Well, sometimes I don't know what wavelength she's on, but she's a good kid."

"And your dad . . ."

Groaning, Doug wagged his head. "Look, he's my old man so I gotta look up to him, but you don't know what it's like to be on his hot seat. He gets this friggin' *look* on his face and drills me about whether I'm going to fart around my whole life — I mean, as if I don't ever wonder about that stuff on my own! Like it doesn't bug me!" He sucked his beer almost empty and gripped his knees. "It stunk when I had your job. Later on I figured out that I screwed up on purpose. I can't work for the guy. Shit, I can barely live in the same house!"

Aaron looked at Doug's pensive mouth, and confusion scattered his arguments. "Didn't mean to get you bummed about it."

"I know," Doug muttered. "Guess I shouldn't bitch so much — I sound like Neil." He stuck his legs out and knocked his sneakers together. "It's my choice to live here, pretty much. For the time being. College was out for me cuz I didn't have the grades, and anyway I wasn't hot on the idea. Gail's more cut out for that. There's trade school but I get depressed just thinking about it. But mainly it's the band that keeps me here. Who knows? We could hang it up tomorrow, but I want to see how far we can take it."

"I hear you," Aaron said.

"Meanwhile, my folks think I'm going to end up another Fox Hill mutant, washing dishes and raising hell at Milo's five nights a week. It's a drag." Doug put his bottle on the ground and got to his feet. "Gotta take a leak."

He stepped around to the tree's other side, and Aaron looked at the headstone. It was brown and tilted slightly forward, with lichens blotching it like disease. Chiseled crudely at the top, its angelhead bas-relief kindled his interest and he leaned forward to read the inscription: Samuel Augustus Simpson, b. Dec. 14, 1782, d. Feb. 20, 1802, aged 19 yrs. 2 mos. He squinted to read the verse underneath: "Though fresh of face / and young of years / thy soul hast quit / this vale of tears."

He read it again. Nineteen years, two months. Then his eyes drifted past the headstone to a row of smaller markers, stunted-looking and unnaturally white before the moon. Less worn, these bore clearer, briefer inscriptions for various Simpson children: Sarah Fuller, died 1840, age three; Ezra James, died 1859, age five; Julia Elizabeth, died 1882, age eight months. There were others.

Aaron got up, stood over the graves, and felt cold on the back of his neck.

Doug came back around. "Finish your beer?"

Aaron plucked the bottle up and drained it, as Doug did his before picking up the case. On the way down toward the church, Doug lazily hummed a Springsteen song until he noticed Aaron carrying the empties. "Civic-minded guy, huh?"

"There's a nickel deposit on these."

"You've been hanging around my father too much."

They dropped over a masonry embankment to the church parking lot and saw the police cruiser parked there, facing the street.

"McDonald," Doug murmured. "Laying for speeders."

They hadn't gotten far down the sidewalk when a flat tenor voice called after them. "Having yourselves a party up there?"

They stopped and turned. Aaron saw the jowled face with the exact mustache, peering at them over the cruiser's roof.

"We were serenading our friends," Doug said.

"That so?"

"No, not really. Matter of fact, I'm pullin' your leg."

"What's in your hands there?" McDonald snapped.

Upending the bottles, Aaron held them out and shook them. "Just helping out with the litter problem," said Doug.

McDonald let a moment pass. "We've been asked to keep you kids out of the cemetery," he barked. "If I catch you, you're gonna wish you were planted up there!"

Doug saluted as they started away. "Happy hunting!"

Once out of earshot, Aaron gave Doug a grin. "The Pear with a Badge."

"Conehead," Doug corrected. " 'Pear' sounds like he's the host on a kiddie show. Once, a few years back, I was out playing hooky from school and he pulled up and grilled me about some broken windows at the town hall. I wised off to him and he shoved me against a wall. Ever since then, he's been Conehead McDonald to me."

They said good night when they got to the corner of Lark. The Ferguson home was dark except for the kitchen windows, and Aaron watched Doug walk toward it, carrying the guitar case like a cumbersome gun.

Outside the store, Aaron dropped the bottles into the trash barrel and went up the back steps to his room. He got some leftover spaghetti from the mini-refrigerator that the Fergusons had lent him, then sat on his mattress to watch TV. The late news reported President Reagan denying prior knowledge of the Iranian arms deal and the related funding scheme for the Nicaraguan contras; there were highlights from the day's investigative hearings. In a Baltic port, Secretary Gorbachev spoke with a crowd of dock workers; a brief clip showed rebels in Afghanistan aiming rocket launchers at Soviet gunships. There was an update on AIDS research and the rise of the disease among intravenous drug users; sunken eyes looked up from beds in a crowded New York hospital. The final item featured an elderly Missouri man who made small animal carvings and gave one to every child he met.

When Aaron turned the TV off and got under the covers, he thought about tonight at Neil's. He smiled. Then, gliding toward sleep, he saw his father's face behind the bars of the album cover.

4

▼

At the store, Jerry did his usual hanging around but didn't bustle or instruct, and Aaron wondered whether spring was finally working its optimistic spell on his boss. Whatever it was, Jerry seemed almost whimsical as he leaned against the doorway and mulled about having the store painted.

"Maybe just some trim on it. Red would look nice. Or tan." He nudged his baseball cap higher on his forehead and shielded his eyes. "Hey, it's . . . Take a look at this."

Aaron discarded the empty bread cartons and walked over beside Jerry, who pointed to a clump of bushes at the lot's edge. A pair of tawny crested birds flickered about one bush, one of them dabbed yellow on the tail-tip.

"Waxwings," said Jerry. "I don't think I saw any of those last year."

Aaron listened to their reedy chirps. "Wish I knew more about birds," he said.

Jerry puffed his cigarette. "Well, growing up in a city you're stuck with sparrows and pigeons. I learned about them from tramping around the woods with my father. We went hunting a lot. He taught me their calls, too, but I forget most of them."

A grade-school brother and sister came up the sidewalk and crossed toward them. Aaron went back in and Jerry greeted the kids as they entered. Quietly serious and clutching coins, they picked out some candy and brought it to Aaron, while Jerry continued thinking aloud.

"I could get the Harris brothers to do it but they're kind of slow." He moved aside for the kids to leave. "Suppose I could do it myself. It'd take maybe . . . Aaron, was that an earring? On the boy?"

"Yeah. One of those little plastic jobs."

Jerry tugged on the bill of his cap and rubbed his cheek. "I just don't know."

Smiling, Aaron reached for the cloth and the bottle of glass cleaner. The front window needed cleaning and he wanted Jerry to see, for once, that he could stay on top of things without the prodding. Outside in the warm breeze, he sprayed and wiped while Jerry whistled to the Gaelic jig from the radio. Aaron tried to imagine life through the big man's eyes.

"Jer, how long have you had the store?"

"Oh, since bread was about thirty cents a loaf, if that's any clue. Or since my pants were five sizes smaller." He laughed, then crushed his cigarette on the door frame and tossed it in the barrel. "It was sixty-two, I think. . . . Yeah, the year after we tied the knot."

"What did you do before?"

"I was a pipe fitter with the Portland public works. That was after the army."

"And how'd you get this place?"

Jerry hesitated, as if thinking back was an effort. "Well, I heard that old Nichols — he'd built it right after the war — I heard he wanted to sell. Peg and I batted the idea around and I took out a loan." He looked thoughtful. "Jeez, when I think of it . . . Twice they nearly foreclosed on us. It helped when Peg got the library job but by then the diaper brigade was coming."

Aaron stopped wiping as Jerry went on.

"Was ten years, I'd say — that long before I knew it'd be okay, and I put in the gas pumps and built the addition. Before that I almost sold the place a few times." Jerry folded his arms, and there was a glimmer of pleasure on his face. "I'm glad I didn't — that's easy to say now. See, I used to come here as a kid, and there'd be old Nichols behind the counter. Nice old fella, but his face was paralyzed on one side and we were all scared of him . . ." He broke off, chuckling.

Aaron resumed cleaning, and his reflection showed more clearly on the pane. "Well, you came through."

Jerry gave a nod. "That we did, with some pissing and moaning along the way. I just wish the damn insurance wasn't so high. That's what I have to go take care of now." He tugged at his cap. "Carry on. If it gets too busy . . ."

"I'll ring you."

"Right."

As Jerry walked away whistling, the green truck pulled up and Andy, the junk dealer, got out and called to him. "Thank God there's somebody around here who's uglier than me!"

Jerry grinned and stepped over to talk.

Aaron went back inside and changed the radio to his station, but he didn't really hear the music. Without Jerry's voice his mind drifted to Toy Soldiers and how it had felt last night.

Through the evening, underneath his work scramble, some kind of excitement quivered.

McDonald came in for a newspaper during a busy period

73

but Aaron betrayed no special notice of the cop, who looked ill at ease among the other customers. As the cruiser drove off, Aaron snickered. Shopping was a great equalizer.

Jerry arrived just as Aaron was turning the lights off and he seemed pleased with the day's take. Watching him pick at his pocket calculator, Aaron felt pleased too.

The store was Jerry's passion as well as his curse, its problems like a hoarse, orbiting flock of ravens that no spring day could scatter. It was funny to think of it as a passion, since when it came to self-expression Jerry's sense of economy won out. If feeling showed at all, it meant something; if nothing showed, that could mean something too. His tangents that afternoon had been an exception. As a rule the rocky face made no overtures and kept Aaron guessing.

Aaron watched him concentrating on the numbers, and all at once he saw his father's face.

Up in his room, however, he forgot the sudden image and lay down to watch TV. He glanced around the room, which still looked bare. The old hot plate that he had bought at Talbot's sat on a scratched table from the Fergusons' attic, and the TV on a smaller table that Peg had scored at a flea market, along with a chair. "How else are you going to write letters to your mother?" she had jabbed. Considering the cracked window, he thought of getting curtains.

He stared up at the light bulb and its erratic white moths. Their flutter seemed one of strange anticipation, like the quiver he had been feeling all day. As he lay still it grew stronger, and he was barely surprised when the knock came.

"Come on in," he said, guessing who it was.

Doug stepped in, sweaty in his Springsteen T-shirt, his denim lap soaked dark.

"What's up?" Aaron asked.

"Just got out of work."

"I couldn't tell. Take a chair — any chair."

Turning the chair around, Doug sat and clapped his damp thighs, then glanced at the TV. "What's on?"

"*Magnum*. A rerun." Aaron sat up and waited.

The dank smell of dishwater drifted across the room, but Doug didn't seem tired from work. He looked stiff in his seat. "I stopped by to, uh . . . Whao! Check it!"

Aaron looked at the butter-smooth bikini girl crossing the screen. "Well, that's Hawaii," he said.

Doug nodded gloomily. "Yeah. This is Maine." He looked back at Aaron and leaned forward. "I was just saying . . . I didn't want to spring this till I checked with the other guys, but I called up Mike and Ben and I talked with Neil at work, and . . . we want you in the band."

Aaron pulled his knee in and puckered his mouth. "What would I be doing? Rhythm?"

Doug shook his head: "You'd be lead. I can do rhythm, and anyway you're better than I am." Spreading his hands, he hunched farther forward. "Look, you have the same days off as me, so practice wouldn't mess you up. I know getting a guitar'll cost you, but Neil says he might help you out, and maybe you could get a good deal. With you, we might get somewhere. Maybe we could finally play Portland. We could use some of your material. And that's not all."

"What else?"

"The Annual Battle of the Bands. Some radio stations and businesses got together and started it last year, at the Expo building in Portland. They sell tickets for it and bands come from all over the state — about twenty-five or thirty of 'em this year. The age limit's twenty, so you don't compete with any real pros. So the groups come and play for the crowd, and they have judges who rate you. It's not till two months yet, but Neil's already paid the registration fee."

"And the winners?"

Doug clapped his thighs again. "Five hundred, top prize, plus a chance to record a demo at some studio."

Aaron gazed across the room.

"Not to mention getting their name around," Doug added. "If we snag that, we won't be just world-famous in Fox Hill." He chuckled nervously. "That's what Neil calls it — 'world-famous in Fox Hill.'" Sitting back, he eyed Aaron with uncertainty. "So what d'ya say?"

The look on Doug's face made Aaron feel guilty for his cautious façade, and he smiled. "Okay."

"All right!" Doug slapped his hands together and got up. "Listen, I'll call Neil in the morning. He's off tomorrow and he could take us to Portland to check the music shops."

"After hitting the bank, of course. I think I can swing the price on my own."

"Good enough!" Doug put his hands in his pockets and rocked happily on his soles. "Wish I'd brought us a couple of beers to celebrate."

"Wanna stay and watch tube?"

"No, thanks. I feel like a slime bucket in these pants."

"Okey-doke." Aaron lay back with his hands behind his head. "Thanks a lot, Doug."

Closing the door, Doug gave him a thumbs-up sign.

Aaron looked up at the moths, giddy in their light-bulb dance. He started to get sleepy. "So," he thought, "you're in a band." It would be different this time. However many hassles awaited him, it would be different.

5

▼

In the back of Neil's car Aaron stretched and enjoyed the sea breeze from the rolled-down window. The sun along Portland's main drag had brought out a spectrum of people, not as varied as in a big city but still interesting: scruffy street kids, striding business people, bent old men and women, girls with perms and sunglasses, boys on skateboards, and mothers shopping with children. And thanks to an imminent Grateful Dead concert at the Civic Center, the rainbow colors of Dead fans could also be seen. Decked in beads, turbans and headbands, in gypsy vests and tie-dyed shirts, they brightened the traffic and greeted each other with glowing good will. A few on curbs and corners held cardboard signs aloft, pleading for tickets.

Aaron thought of his mother, who loved the Dead and had seen much of them back in the Bay Area. Whenever she had spoken of them or of the communal bliss they inspired, he had turned sarcastic. Similarly, whenever she had lamented her missing out on Woodstock, he had branded it Woodcrock to quiet her. But he hoped that he hadn't sounded quite as nasty as Neil did now, from the driver's seat.

" 'I need a ticket,' " Neil quoted a sign. "Gawd, what they all need is a lobotomy!"

Beside him, Doug stopped tapping his hand to the radio. "I don't know. Better Deadheads than skinheads — at least they're not out to stomp anybody. And there's a lot worse music around."

Aaron watched a newspaper girl in a bright-striped shirt, striking ballet poses as she waved a paper. He was glad to hear Neil's sneer challenged.

"But it's stupid!" Neil pressed, braking for a red light. "It's like they're getting off on something that's not real anymore. If it ever *was* real." He glanced back at Aaron. "What's your opinion?"

Again Aaron heard that new, awkward tone of respect in Neil's voice, and put on a smile. "Opinions make my face break out."

Holding the red and white Telecaster, Aaron struck a note, adjusted the tone, and spread his feet. His mind was made up within the minute but he kept playing, filling the store with the guitar's cry and jangle. When he finally stopped, Doug grinned at him and Neil nodded.

Steve, the tall shaggy-haired proprietor, looked on patiently. Doug turned to him. "Uh . . . Price is still a tad heavy. Knock 'er down to three hundred and it's cash in hand."

Steve fingered his wraparound shades. "Jeez, though — as is, it's the steal of the century. Practically mint. Case included."

"Let's shop around some more," Neil spoke on cue. "We can come back if . . ."

"Well," Steve said. "I'll say three-fifty, but . . ."

"Three twenty-five," Doug said. "And we'll tell everybody what a cool guy you are."

Steve sighed, then bent to pull the cord from the amp. "What a cool pushover, you mean. All right."

"Seriously," Steve said as they left. "You're making out like the bandits you are." He looked at Aaron. "By the way, you play really well."

There were a couple of hours left before work, and Aaron wished that he and his new possession could be teleported to Neil's garage. But the other two wanted to hit a nearby record store.

It was there, looking absently through a cutout bin, that he raised his eyes and saw the poster tacked up behind the cashier's station. In jeans, a leather jacket, and beat-up sneakers, his father stood against a Cyclone fence and scanned the distance as lightning cracked the red clouds behind him. "The Spider Returns," it read at the top, and underneath that, "*Thunderhead* — new from Danny Webb and the Red Sky Band — on Columbia Records and Tapes, also available on compact disc." Along the bottom were schedule listings for the "1987 Reunion Tour."

Aaron picked up his case, squeezed past the other browsers, and stood by the door, where he tried to concentrate on the street outside. An old man in an oversized coat hobbled past a tie-dyed Deadhead holding a sign. Two boys in a knot of street kids practiced karate moves on each other.

It clouded over and started to drizzle as they left Portland. Neil and Doug gabbed about the albums they had bought, and about how much they would rather live in a city. Slouched in the back with the case across his lap, Aaron thought about the poster and wanted to laugh. This was getting ridiculous.

Then he began to worry about the time. Annoyed by the bumping of the wipers, he rapped his knuckles on the case and pictured Jerry checking the clock.

Neil's Rolex said three o'clock when they arrived at the store. Aaron got out with his guitar, said goodbye, and jogged to the door. Inside, Jerry was doing a newspaper crossword.

"Maine weather," Jerry said. "Full of surprises."

Aaron wiped water from his face. "I noticed."

"Well, thought I'd go catch the Red Sox on TV." Jerry folded his paper. "Listen, we got a goddamn leak back there over the dairy cooler and I put up a tub to catch it. If you could keep an eye on it and . . ." He was looking down at the guitar case. His lips parted, then pressed together as static burst from the radio.

"Yeah, Jer?" Aaron said.

Scratching an ear, Jerry turned his gaze to the trickling glass door. "Just . . . keep an eye on the tub and empty it when it gets full, okay?"

He pulled his cap on, took his newspaper, and came around to the door. He paused with his back to Aaron and lit a cigarette. "Keep up the good work," he spoke flatly. "Know what I mean?"

"Sure. Why wouldn't I?"

Zipping his jacket, Jerry stepped out into the rain. "See ya, pal."

Aaron looked down at his black case, glittery with droplets, then took it behind the counter and set it down. Leaning on his hands, he sighed. It was a while before he thought to change the radio station.

PART THREE

▾ ▾ ▾

Toy Soldiers

1

▼

Webb's few comments about his son and ex-wife are terse. Of Aaron, now ten and whom he sees as regularly as career demands permit, he speaks with hope. "He's a sharp kid. We have a good relationship, I think." He hesitates, reflecting. "Aaron makes me think that kids have more toughness than we give 'em credit for. . . ."

There was a lot more, but Aaron stopped reading. His thumb played with the page's crumbling edge as he looked at the pictures. There was the bleary, aloof portrait of his father, open-shirted and holding his drink. Another photo showed him on stage with Red Sky in the mid-seventies. But Aaron looked longest at the grainy black and white one taken in 1967: the fresh-faced young man holding his guitar in an awkward pose, dressed in a tassled jacket with patterns of the sun and moon. Aaron tried to penetrate the face and its quizzical half smile.

Los Angeles and the canyon shimmered like heat waves before him, with the housekeeper dusting the furniture. His daddy would be home tonight, she told him — tonight for sure.

Aaron flung the magazine across the room and sat with his arms folded. He'd had to go and do it — borrow it from Doug and bring this snarl to his stomach. But in a moment his thoughts turned to his father's father, the long-dead man for whom he was named. The interviewer had gotten more details than Aaron ever had:

> Webb chuckles. "My old man . . . He'd invite me down to the Whitewall Pub and once he got past his second beer, he'd interrupt one of his war stories and turn to his buddies and point at me — 'See this guy? They tell me he's my son. He's the one who wants to get rich makin' bug-noise on a guitar and wearin' a pink jacket!' " The laugh winds down and he clinks his ice. "After a while I stopped going down there with him. Man, you better believe when I heard the Animals doing 'We Gotta Get Out of This Place,' I just said, 'yeah!' "

Aaron's grandfather had dropped dead of a heart attack at the age of forty-five, while on a picket line outside his Flint, Michigan auto plant. That was three years before Aaron's birth. A framed portrait at Grandma Webb's had presented a man whose smile resembled that of his rock-star son, but whose squarish cheeks and forehead did not. "Everyone loved him," Grandma would say. "Everybody." Grandma Webb, four years dead, was someone whom Aaron had loved. With her forthright pixy face, she had been one of his all-time favorite adults, and any thought of her made him smile. Among his first memories was one from a rare visit to Flint, of Grandma denying him a second molasses cookie and then giving in.

Aaron rose, walked to where the magazine lay splayed on the floor, and picked it up. Some of its pages had come loose and he carefully put them back, then placed them on the pile of other borrowed *Rolling Stones*. He paced to the window, looked out at the night, and then at the raspberry-red curtains he had bought at North Star Discount. They had pleased him before but looked dumb now, out of place. His mind kept turning.

All those things . . .

All those things had transpired while he had played on the floors of that house, or in the glades of that canyon neighborhood. . . . Until he reached some point of awareness, before his mother's behavior took an ominous turn, he had been as happy and unencumbered as any small kid. Life fit all notions of what it ought to be. Yet thinking back to that earliest time was like staring through a series of shattered, sun-blinded windows, or hearing a wayward needle's scratch across a record. Even then, judgments were being pronounced on him as well as his mother. Vague punishment for vaguer crimes, right from the start.

Remembering his dirty dishes Aaron washed them in the bathroom sink, then pulled up his chair to watch TV. But he couldn't concentrate on the program.

Bob Dylan had children, including a son who was about Aaron's age. Keith Richards had one too. And there was Julian Lennon, whose father was dead. How had they all done? How were they doing? Were their mothers anything like his? And were their fathers anything like his? Mythical figures, swooping down once or twice a year from a private Olympus, to grab them, soar high, and then drop them back where they had been?

At Chase there were kids who recalled their parents' divorces as a great relief, and Aaron had no trouble believing them. For some it had been a tale of gradual deterioration, for others a war in which they played a hapless civilian role. A few went on to say how well their mothers and fathers had done since the split.

Aaron didn't know what words applied to his parents' unraveling — it didn't seem like any other. And he wondered whether what he felt about them could be called regret. Could you really regret anything that was total and irreversible, especially when you'd had this much time to get used to it? Faced with a fact so large, his emotions didn't know where to begin. And even if regrets were possible, they would still be pointless — their pointlessness spelled out in magazines, in record stores, on the radio, and in all reminders of what his father was. The best you could do, Aaron thought, was tell yourself how inevitable it had been. The best you could do was shrug.

Yet repeatedly, in recent days, he had asked the walls and window why it couldn't have been different — why his father couldn't have had some other job, keeping music as a week-end hobby instead of a gale-force career — why his mother couldn't have known the shelter of better friends in better places, with a man whose love brought happiness instead of lasting damage. Had it happened this way, would the three of them have stuck together? Would he have had brothers and sisters? Would they have become anything like the close, crackling circuit of the Fergusons and be living in a place like Fox Hill?

With a twitch he realized that this was the whole stupid mirage again, and he banished it. No, there were plenty of reasons for how it had turned out — endless reasons. People were the way they were, and events went on from there.

With the light out and the TV off, Aaron attempted sleep. But old, loud music tumbled through his head. He was envisioning the sixties — their color and shadow, their clamor and spark; the flags of warring sides, and great events both dirty and noble. Had he been born in time for that decade, maybe by now he would have found a way to be and a part to play. In spite of his put-downs, maybe the storm of those years would have done it for him — carved him into a simpler, more definite personality. Then he might have known where he fit in the world.

But in the midst of this he saw his mother, and his fancies dribbled away until only a song remained, echoing: "Eyes in the storm / In a wind that's never warm / Your eyes they cut like starlight through the cold." It was bizarre to think that he had once loved that song, the one written for her. In the year of his birth it had received modest radio play. And somewhere tonight the Spider was probably doing it for an encore, keeping some audience happy.

2

▼

On Neil's signal they kicked off a song by REM. Aaron was getting the riffs down well, and the number chugged along until Neil threw a hand up. Looking disgruntled, he said it was too fast. Then Doug complained of trouble in getting his whammy bar to do what he wanted. Aaron checked to see whether the bar was loose, but finding that it wasn't he had Doug toy with it for a minute while he watched. Behind him, Mike sat with his sticks crossed and Ben looked on attentively. Neil leaned on his Vox, patting it to hurry the seconds.

Aaron got Doug to press the bar more lightly, and it worked.

Neil swigged his beer. "Okay?" he asked.

Slowing the tempo, they made the song respectable before moving on.

Whenever they broke to confer, which mostly meant listening to Neil, Aaron was thinking hard. He liked the band's roughness, but knew that they would have to temper it and channel the energy better. To get anywhere, they would simply have to be better with their instruments.

Doug was hard-working and eager. Ben seemed quietly committed and Mike too had a willing nature. Though crude musicians, these three were good listeners and showed potential. But Neil, looming with that inward glower above his keyboard, presented a snag. This, even though Aaron shared his fondness for the Ramones, Three Colors, Echo and the Bunnymen, and other bands whose material wouldn't pan out in a small-town bar. Already today Neil had torpedoed suggestions from the others. Aaron knew that with a guy like this in the group, he would have to watch his step.

It was seven weeks till the Battle of the Bands and only two till the gig at Milo's. They needed to improve by then. Yet the shortness of time helped to fuel Aaron — that, and his new Telecaster. Soaring through a solo, he felt a hope growing warmer.

3

▾

The railroad tracks sliced cleanly through the trees and vanished at a curve a half mile ahead. It was quiet except for the birds. Despite practicing till eleven last night, Aaron wanted to be back at it. But it was fine out here and he could wait the few hours till he would be in Neil's garage again.

Walking along one rail he tested his balance, arms out and his feet quick and careful. At a crosstie, he wobbled and hopped off. A woodchuck whistled from the bushes and scuttled under a rotten log.

A typical Fox Hill day — a bright day with the sense of dancing in the air. The tracks were his secret place, he had decided. It was never too late to have a secret place.

He walked some more and stopped to pitch stones, then turned back. After the town dump, with its crow-caws and smoking rubber stench, he came to the Ash Road crossing and went right, past widely spaced houses and then the elementary school. Some kids were out playing kickball, supervised by a young female teacher who was a regular at the store. Aaron waved to her and she waved back. At the bridge he stopped to watch the water, then continued to Main Street. A passing car honked and he waved, not knowing who it was but glad for the greeting.

People on the street and in shops, others playing Frisbee on the square, a little league game starting on the field behind the library — each sight tickled him, lifted him, and made it easy to pretend that he had lived here for years.

On an impulse he jogged up the steps of the library. Peg was working there today and he needed to talk to her. Edgy as he opened the door, he relaxed when she looked up from her desk and smiled.

"Fancy meeting you here," she said. "You want a book?"

"Only if it has pictures," he said. "How's it going?"

"Good question." She placed a card in the catalogue drawer before her and sat back. "After this I have to go home and stuff envelopes for the Maine People's Alliance. I've been at it all week, sending out fliers."

"Tough being a hell-raiser," he said, and pulled up a chair. "So is that why you've been rushing off so fast?"

She looked perplexed.

"Monday and Tuesday," he said. "When I switched with you at the store?"

"Oh . . . yes," she said. "I guess I was in a hurry."

He looked at his knees. "I thought it might've been because you were trying to keep something to yourself. About recent happenings."

"Ohhh!" A knowing look crossed her face. "You and Doug's band? Don't worry your head about that."

"I just pictured you thinking I'd get too wrapped up. That I'd go slack or something."

"No, no," she said, and flicked a hand. "No, we'll stick to fretting about Douglas."

Aaron felt clumsy but relieved. "Jerry, though . . ."

"I know. All I can say is don't mind him." Removing her glasses, she rubbed an eye and winked at him, but behind her placid brow he sensed restraint.

"Think I'll look around," he said, and got up.

He spent fifteen minutes among the stacks of the tidy but cramped library. The only other person was an old man nodding off at a table in the archives section. Aaron found a book on the Vietnam War and brought it to Peg, who stamped it, and they said goodbye. He headed for the door but then turned around. This was a day of impulses.

"Listen, how 'bout if I talk Doug into dinner at the house? Next week, say?"

Peg peered up from under her glasses. "You a miracle worker?"

"No, but I can always drag him. How about it?"

"Pull that off and you get seconds on dessert."

"Fair enough. So long."

Holding his book, he hopped down the steps and was happy again.

Practice went more smoothly through most of the evening. Mike's girl friend Laurie, a cute eleventh-grader with short red hair, arrived with him and stayed awhile. Her quiet presence seemed to have a calming effect as they worked. When she had to plug her ears a third time, she decided to leave and gave Mike a parting smile. It was the kind of smile that Aaron would have liked a lot from a girl.

Then Neil's mother appeared at the kitchen door, baggy-eyed and with a lime-twist drink in her hand. She asked whether they wanted some lemonade and all except Neil said yes. Returning with a tray of glasses, she chuckled listlessly. "So, you guys are sounding good tonight. Gonna knock 'em dead, aren't you?"

Neil leaned silent against the garage wall and folded his arms. After his mother left, he paced until they had finished their drinks and gotten ready again.

4

▾

The next afternoon, Jerry was the same as he had been since last weekend. On nightly cash pickups in particular, his bearing had been polite but apathetic. His eyes would stray, and rather than converse he would whistle to himself. Right now he was whistling to a female folk singer whose lullaby cooed from the radio.

Aaron stood ready behind the counter. However much it took, he would stay on his toes. This whistling, wide-chested sphinx in a baseball cap was not going to get to him.

Whistling, Jerry dropped two string-tied stacks of the *Weekly Advertiser* in front of Aaron. Aaron got the jackknife from the drawer, placed the stacks by the magazine rack, and cut the strings. Jerry's lingering was mercifully brief this time. He propped himself in the doorway, scanned the sky, and cleared his throat. "Carry on," he said.

"Will do," said Aaron.

Jerry ambled away, and Aaron breathed easy as the whistling faded. He changed the station and stood outside the door, half listening to a beer commercial and then a song. Halfway through the song, at the fast strumming of the bridge section, he realized it was "Dead-End Dancer." He turned, walked inside, and stood before the radio. He listened to that younger, more nasal voice of his father, struggling in the muddy cocoon of an old recording studio.

> Sparking down the dirty ice
> Of a dead-end evening street

92

The dead-end dancer celebrates
On fast electric feet.
He knows the war's as good as over,
Knows the plague's as good as gone . . .

"Dancer" segued into a cut from *Thunderhead,* and the voice's latest version — deeper and fuller, with a slight rasp, and Red Sky ramming behind it. Time shut off and Aaron found himself caught in the old sensation, knowing the voice right down to his core, along with the fact that he was only one of multitudes listening. Many thousands of strangers were all hearing the voice and maybe admiring the guitar. Apparently his father still lived up to the nickname, playing like an eight-limbed creature. Half man, half spider.

The song ended and the deejay came on: "Danny 'Spider' Webb, yesterday and today! Back to back, that was 'Dead-End Dancer,' recorded with Kamikaze back in 1965, and 'Racing the Fire,' from his new *Thunderhead* album. There's a man who's come a long way, and we hope he'll be around a lot longer. Coming up, another half hour of uninterrupted music, starting with . . ."

Aaron lowered the sound and rested against the counter. Maybe he would just have to resign himself to ambushes like this, he thought. Then he smiled — his story had to be one for the books. He might have laughed wildly if a man hadn't walked in for cigarettes.

A few other customers came, and Aaron was going through the motions when Gail wandered in. A young woman brought up milk and bread, and as she dug through her purse, Aaron glanced at Gail. From behind a copy of *Vanity Fair* she was playing peekaboo with the woman's little boy and girl, elfin preschoolers in overalls. Aaron rang the total up wrong, apologized and did it over, then bagged the items.

Gail got return waves from the children as they left with their mother. "Muffinheads," Gail spoke.

"What?" he asked.

"Muffinheads," Gail repeated, crossing her eyes. "That's what I call 'em if they're between two and six."

"Oh." Aaron shoved the drawer in. "Where's your side-kick?"

"Dori, you mean? She's at the doctor's." She closed the magazine. "So how's life as a Toy Soldier?"

"Fine, but . . ." He hesitated, wondering how open he should be. "I don't think your father likes it too well."

She laughed. "Yeah, well, the thing with him . . . Wait a sec — say 'father' again."

He looked at her. "Father . . . Why?"

"You said it like a Down Easter the first time. We're starting to rub off on you, huh?"

He grinned, wondering why he was blushing. "*Fa*-ther," he repeated.

"I was saying," she went on, "if the band fell apart it'd be enough to make Dad go back to church. He figures it'd make Doug get serious — *his* kind of serious, of course. But here's Doug coming home raving about how good you are, and it's like you've given them a new lease on life. And Dad . . ." She shrugged. "Dad needs to adjust, that's all. He's had all these times when things haven't gone his way, and now he feels he's earned a few breaks. That's how Mom explained it to me once. She said that's how a lot of people get when they reach a certain age."

Aaron looked at the counter top.

"I wouldn't worry," she said. "He likes you and you're a good worker."

He nodded.

"Hey, wanna see my yearbook?" Putting the magazine aside, Gail stepped to the corner of the counter where she had placed her handbag. From under it she took a blue yearbook with a pine tree design on the cover, then opened it between herself and Aaron. He tilted his head to look.

She guided him through the senior class portraits — a gallery of happy and serious expressions, some in the studio and others outdoors, with quotes and activities printed beside them. Robust-looking boys, girls with graceful necks — all of them summoning charm and confidence for the camera. Aaron had seen some of them at the store.

"Some of these people I never really knew," said Gail. "Isn't Dori's nice?"

Dori's portrait was a cheerful outdoor one. With no swell in her stomach, she leaned against a wooden fence amid dead leaves. Another graduate caught Aaron's notice — a somber, frizzy-haired guy dressed not in a sportscoat but a parka, with a snowy landscape behind him. Aaron had seen him here a couple of times. "Thomas P. Dryden," it said to the side — Gail's prom date.

She turned the page and tried to get past her own portrait, but Aaron stopped her. It was a striking picture: with head turned, her soft eyes gazed past the camera. Her combed hair appeared darker against the studio backdrop. She wasn't smiling but her lips were parted, and the look was subdued but assured. Her quote was from Helen Keller: "Life is either a dangerous adventure — or nothing."

"That's real nice," he said.

"Bull. Me and my rabbit teeth."

Ben the bassist appeared two pages later, darkly dignified and minus his glasses.

They continued through underclassmen, teachers, sports

events, clubs, and activities, but Aaron's attention sagged beneath mental images of Chase. Four years, mostly spent hating things. A drug-garbled sophomore year with a string of weird incidents — cackling in class, chiding a teacher to rage, sessions with the headmaster. Four years of bouncing between hate, indifference, and a huge desire to be anywhere but there. He could live to be ninety, but no nostalgic mist would ever settle on that time.

He glanced a few times at Gail, who laughed over candid shots of kids and teachers, stopping to mention who was nice or smart, a snob or a jerk. He liked her husky, surprising voice. He liked her striped, ruffled shirt and gently falling hair. And he wanted to reach across the foot of space and touch her.

Coming upon a picture of the student council, she scowled. "Wicked snobs. All of 'em — the real ignorant kind. God, that's what I can't take about this town!"

The way she bit the last word off stung Aaron from his haze. He straightened up and tried to sort out a response. "I don't think that's . . ."

She looked up and he cleared his throat.

"Well," he said, "you might get some of that, but one way or another you get it anyplace."

"Sure, but come on," she scoffed. "Some places are just more ignorant than others." She closed the yearbook.

"What do you mean?" he asked guardedly.

She spread her hands and sighed. "Last year our French club went on a bus trip to Montreal, right? I looked at all those people there — all sorts of people looking, talking, acting different from one another — and it hit me how much is out there. I mean, it's scary how much you miss! Everything was so open compared to here. I spent half an hour gabbing in French with a Pakistani shopkeeper. I couldn't get enough of it, but when we got back here some kids were saying, 'Man, that place is weird — I could never live there.' Well, I could!"

Aaron shuffled his feet. "All right, but it still depends on what you mean by ignorant."

"Okay, okay," she said. "I suppose that makes *me* sound snobby. I mean, I don't know what it was like where you grew up, but let me give you some idea about this place. . . . Ben Katz, your bass player?"

"Yeah?"

"Nice guy, right? Sort of keeps to himself? But that's not why he gets picked on. He gets picked on cuz he's Jewish. And then . . ." Her voice fell. "Then there's Tommy. He's shy too, and his family's about the poorest in town, so some creeps get on his case for the fun of it. He takes it but I can tell it hurts him. And Dori . . ." Her tone hardened again. "Dori's pinhead boyfriend gets her pregnant, then takes off out west and joins the army. She's not the first and she won't be the last, so you'd think people would learn how to handle it right, but no! At school she gets these insects, including some of her so-called friends, talking behind her back and looking down their long, stupid noses! And of course she gets the other airheads who're just tickled pink about it and ask her all kinds of questions — that's another sick part of it. But here she is, going through with it by herself, and all she gets is shit! For one thing, she's barely going to graduate. Her parents are down on her, her dad especially, and she spends more time at our house than she does at her own. As long as she lives here, nobody's going to let her forget she messed up. And of course no one asked her to the prom. . . ." Faltering, Gail let out a breath and flicked her hand. "Sorry to get on the soapbox, but it just gets me so ugly."

"It's okay," he said, gathering himself. "But look, show me a place that's perfect. It's a tradeoff."

"I know, I know. But there are a few things here I wouldn't mind trading off." She chewed her thumbnail and looked down. "It's such a crock. Kids who've grown up here zapping the newer kids, and vice versa. In the cafeteria you hear some dork bragging about blowing away a rabbit or a woodchuck with his shotgun, or some rich bitch going on about the car that Daddy just bought her. I'm just wicked glad to be getting . . ."

A guy stepped in the door. "Gail?"

It was Tommy, tall and gangly in a sweatband and tattered vest. Gail looked up in surprise.

"Been looking all over for you," he said. "That party at Rick's starts around nine."

"Oh . . . I don't know if I'm going."

"Why not?"

"Well, just a sec." She hoisted her handbag and got a bag of cashews.

From the corner of his eye Aaron saw Tommy look at him. Gail made a quick introduction.

"Hi," Aaron said, ringing the register.

" 'Lo," Tommy mumbled.

Gail's eyes went wide. "Seventy-five dollars?"

Aaron had punched the wrong key again, and he hurried to fix it. "Senile already," he said as Gail laughed.

She took her change. "So I hear you're going to talk Doug into having dinner with us."

"I'm going to collar him about it tomorrow."

"I'll believe it when I see it." She tucked the yearbook under her arm. "Good luck."

Gail and Tommy left as three boys in little league uniforms came in. From then until ten, when Jerry came whistling out of the dark for the day's cash, Aaron was busy enough to avoid thoughts of Gail or what she had said. But that night he dreamed of luxurious sex with her on an embankment by the railroad tracks. He dreamed of caressing her face as they lay there.

5

▼

Aaron pulled his clothes from the dryer, piling them on top, and grimaced at the smell around him. The assaulting odor of skunk filled the Fergusons' cellar, to which Slim had been banished two nights ago before his carrot-juice bath. Aaron rolled his sock pairs together, made a token effort at folding, and put the clothes in a plastic basket. Once back upstairs, he exhaled gratefully and put the basket by the door, with his guitar case.

"Thanks for the facilities," he said.

"You're welcome," said Peg. "I'm surprised you didn't suffocate down th . . . Gail, you're making me nervous!"

Wrapped in a hair-sprinkled bedsheet, Peg sat in the center of the kitchen as her daughter snipped carefully with scissors.

"I can't (hic!) stop them," Gail said. "I tried (hic!) drinking water."

"Wait a minute," said Aaron. He got a teacup from the

cupboard. From a pot on the stove he poured some tepid tea and stuck a spoon in, then handed the cup to Gail. "I know this sounds lame, but drink this with the spoon handle against your forehead and the hiccups'll be gone before the tea is."

"How could that . . . ?"

"Don't know, but it works."

"It isn't even (hic!) hot."

"Give it a shot," Peg urged. "For the sake of my nerves."

"This (hic!) feels silly," said Gail. She drank the tea with the spoon handle resting between her eyes.

Aaron took the cup and waited as she stood blinking. She put a hand to her chest and smiled. "Wow!"

"Told you," he said.

"What a guy," said Peg. "Now could we finish this? That casserole's due out real soon."

Gail resumed trimming. "You sure Doug's coming?"

"It took some doing, but he said he'd be here," Aaron replied. "I ran into him on my way here and he was going to get a new bicycle chain."

"I invited Dori but I don't know if she'll show. She wasn't feeling too great."

Holding still, Peg eyed Aaron's basketful of clothes. "You a cat burglar in your spare time?"

"What do you mean?"

"You're big on black. I was thinking there are some old shirts of Jerry Jr.'s around here. I'm sure they'd fit you."

Aaron hesitated, then shook his head. "No, thanks. You've lent me enough stuff."

"It's not like we need 'em."

"Naw, that's okay."

"All right, Darth Vader."

Gail finished snipping and gave her mother a hand mirror. "*Ist gut, ja?*"

Peg turned her head to one side. "Fine, dear. That saves me a few bucks at the beauty parlor."

Gail took the sheet outdoors and shook it. Aaron volunteered to sweep the hair up while Peg tended to the casserole. As he finished sweeping, Gail came back in and idly reached for the mirror.

"Another zit," she muttered, holding the mirror out.

"Would you set the table?" Peg asked, setting down the casserole with potholders.

"I hate this nose," said Gail. "Which side of the family's to blame for this nose?"

"Quit fishing for compliments. Just set the table, please."

As Gail started placing the silverware, Doug entered with Slim at his heels.

"Well, hallelujah!" Peg exclaimed. "Aaron delivers again!"

"This dog still stinks," Doug announced.

Feeling good, Aaron watched the three of them and focused on Gail, who sneaked a finger into the rice pudding. It was his mother who had shown him that trick with the tea.

Dori arrived a minute later, big beneath her dress and looking pale.

Dinner was lively. The girls went on about graduation and how bad the class singing sounded at rehearsal, griping about how winter storm cancellations had forced the date back by a week. Hunched above his plate, Doug ate steadily and said little.

"Forgot to say," Peg spoke. "I got a call from Jerry Jr. He got himself a bad ankle-sprain in the woods but he'll be down here for the great occasion."

"Oh, good!" said Dori. "He's so funny."

"I'd sure be peeved if he couldn't make it," Gail said.

Aaron listened with interest. The idea of meeting the fifth Ferguson appealed to him.

101

Peg shook her head. "Gawd, I remember the night of *his* graduation — the state he came home in! And at 3 A.M.!"

"Was two-thirty for me," said Doug.

"Well, then," Gail spoke, "it's up to me to break the family record."

"Oh, no it isn't," Peg intoned.

Gail set her fork down. "No, of course not. And how come? Cuz I'm sugar and spice, and everything nice — and save the advice!"

Peg leveled a stare. "Save the wise remarks. Whose house are you in?"

Slouching, Gail crumpled her napkin in her fist.

"Besides," Peg added, "the boys could tell you about the grief they got for that."

"Grief?" Gail countered. "You mean the old 'let's not see that happen again' sermon? Talk about grief! What would *I* get, Mom?"

"Gail, don't get so worked up."

Dori smiled at her half-eaten dinner and Doug rolled his eyes.

"It wasn't so bad!" Aaron protested.

Doug chuckled. "Nope, except I got indigestion and a headache."

Birds lamented sundown as Doug and he toted their guitars along the road, headed for Neil's. Aaron was finding the subject hard to drop. "Jeez, if it was my home I wouldn't . . . I mean, why can't? . . ."

Doug sighed. "Look, I know you mean well. But it's like I've got this allergy, understand? I can't help it."

After practice Aaron had to get his laundry at the house, and there he and Doug found Jerry eating a late snack. "Well if it isn't Future Teen Idols of America!" he said, swallowing.

They said hello and Doug kept on through the kitchen. Synthesizer rock filtered in from the TV. Aaron put his case down and patted Slim. "So this guy's not too popular with skunks, eh Jer?"

"Hm." Communication still wasn't a top concern for Jerry. "What was business like tonight?"

"Too little to crow about, too much for hanging myself."

Aaron looked at him chewing on cold chicken and felt a pinch of irritation. He bent for his basket of clothes but Doug called. "Aaron, come see this!"

He went into the living room, where Gail lay on her stomach before the TV while Doug stood behind her. A video from a new English group was on. To the song's skipping, generic beat, the pompadoured band members were being chased by ghouls and monsters through a haunted mansion.

"Stupid or what?" Doug said.

"Shut up," said Gail.

"How can you like them?"

"They're cute. Shut up."

Doug left the room but Aaron stayed. Gail yawned, her face outlined in the screen's light, and snuggled her chin into her forearms. She asked how practice had gone and Aaron started to tell her, just as the video ended and the opening credits of another came on: "Danny Webb and the Red Sky Band — 'Racing the Fire' — *Thunderhead*."

Like a ghost his father appeared, dressed in white and playing in a vacant lot with Red Sky. The video was a jumble of band shots, with snippets of a bedraggled Spider wandering through one setting after another — a jungle, a desert, a circus, a factory — apparently in search of something. The face flashed. The voice hammered.

"Could you turn that down?" It was Peg's voice.

103

Aaron jerked around and saw her there in her nightgown. "Sorry to startle you," she said.

"I'm just leaving," he blurted. "Thanks again for dinner. I'll bring your basket back tomorrow."

"Oh, no hurry on that."

He said quick goodnights and left with his case and clothes.

Lugging his double burden down the sidewalk, he thought again of the need to be realistic. Realistic and resigned. Facts were facts, and these things would happen, and he would have to relax about it. Staying realistic — that was the key.

Outside the store, the basket slipped from under his arm and capsized. He nearly kicked it but settled for cursing at the top of his lungs.

6

▼

The next evening, he and Doug had fun jamming together at Neil's, with Neil hunched solemnly at the sound board. Shortly before the other two showed up, Aaron paused to look at Doug, who was seated on a sawhorse and picking at low volume. This was how it should be, he thought. Too bad that the Spider wasn't here to check it out, as a refresher course.

On second thought it was great that he wasn't here, but

was off playing some gigantic hall in the Midwest, or jetting there in a private plane, or rolling there in a de luxe tour bus with roadies and an equipment truck behind.

Practice was fun and left them charged up, wishing the Milo's gig were tomorrow and not a week away. Aaron had never felt sure of his voice, and on harmonies he worked at singing from his chest instead of his throat. Still he was pleased with his firming hold on the material, and though he still heard limitations, the band as a whole was improving. Before dispersing they scheduled another session for Sunday at noon.

Starting his shift on Friday, Aaron found that Jerry had stopped whistling and started talking again. This was a relief, despite a few barbed jokes about the band.

"I think you guys'll be needing a new name before too long," Jerry said. "How 'bout the Dirt-Poor Bums?" He handed Aaron his salary. "Now hold on to this, pal. It'll buy you and Doug a lot of good cheap wine."

Aaron forced a chuckle and withheld comment, wondering what had cracked Jerry's reserve. Then, just before he left, Jerry muttered pensively about a Fox Hill plumber who had just scored big on an instant-winner lottery ticket.

"Wally Burnham," he said. "He bought the ticket here. I've known that guy for years and he's a lazy crook. So twenty grand drops in his lap, just like that." He stared blankly across the street. "Jeez, doesn't that pull your plug?"

Aaron patted his shoulder. "Jer, if it was me I'd give you half."

A deep chortle pumped up from Jerry's chest. " 'Preciate it, Aaron. So long."

Aaron pressed his hands to both sides of the doorway and

watched Jerry head toward the sidewalk. "You think I'm kidding?" he thought.

The next night, Aaron was dispatching a line of customers when a guy called his name from the back. It was Mike, one arm around Laurie and the other waving a fistful of junk food. When they got up to the counter Aaron spent a moment of hopeful talk with them about Milo's. Laurie looked even cuter than before. As they left, Aaron's heart contracted with fondness and envy; it was a familiar combination by now.

7
▼

He was out in the morning air, listening to the clang of church bells up Main Street, when the red Sentra pulled to the far curb. Neil stuck his head out. "Whatcha up to?"

"Killing time," Aaron said.

"Same here." Neil looked at his watch. "An hour and a half till practice. Wanna catch breakfast at the Evergreen?"

Aaron crossed and got in, and they headed for the diner.

"My mom's still in the sack, whining about her head," said Neil. "She better shake it by the time we get there."

"Your mom seems like a nice person," Aaron said.

"Sure, if you like dingbats." Aaron glanced at him and he

shrugged. "I don't know — maybe I shouldn't say those things."

It hit Aaron how much Neil reminded him of two or three guys he had known at Chase. Guys who made you feel like a bit player in a movie starring them. They may not have been as prickly, intense, or intelligent, but they had struck the same poses and come out with similar grand statements. "Playing live," he had said lately, " — it's like war without the blood. Know what I mean? That's what I like about it."

"He thinks he's King Shit," was a recent comment of Doug's, after some friction in the garage.

Though he shared with Neil a chafing musical perfectionism, Aaron would have disliked him except for a certain look he would get sometimes — a fleeting, fragile, almost hurt expression that crossed his face whenever he felt challenged. It usually preceded sarcasm.

He had this same look, for some reason, as they sat in the homey, fast-filling diner.

"I guess I shouldn't badmouth my mom," he said. "She's got her problems, but she tries. We just wear on each other."

Surprised at this confiding turn, Aaron sipped his coffee. "I'm an expert on cabin fever myself."

"Yeah. I guess that's what it is." Neil stared at his own coffee. "It was scary the last time my dad dropped in. I hadn't seen him in months, and he just walks in while my mother's at work. And he asks me about my job, what I'm up to, what the plan is. So I tell him and he shakes his head and says, 'Shirt-sleeves to shirt-sleeves in three generations.' Like I've fucked up on everything."

"Did a number on you, huh?"

"It was really weird. It was sort of what Doug gets from his dad, only he didn't act mad. He just sat there shaking his head and going, 'shirt-sleeves to shirt-sleeves.' I don't know, man. I rag about my mom, but it's my dad who seems like the helpless one. The day he moved out he couldn't get all of his things into the van, so he smashed some of them to pieces and left them there in the driveway. But this last time . . . Jeez, he looked like he couldn't hurt a fly. Like he'd fall over if I poked him."

"My folks are split up too," Aaron said, remembering to keep it general. "Believe me, they've had their share of flip-outs." If only he could say more, he thought. And he wondered whether to tell Neil about Chase, where kids with divorced parents seemed to hold a slight majority. Then it occurred to him that such a report might be interesting but not exactly helpful.

Neil sat back with a frayed sigh. "Yup. It sucks, but what can you do? I oughta go somewhere. I was thinking about music school in Boston, but I'd probably hate it. I might end up going down south. I have cousins in Fort Lauderdale. Hey, where's our food?"

The diner was nearly full now, loud with clinking and chatter as dressy older couples arrived from church. Turning around, Aaron saw their waitress wading toward them with a plate in each hand. She was a rotund, energetic grandmother named Nora, an old friend and customer of the Fergusons.

"Which one had scrambled?" she asked.

They took their plates and Aaron thanked her. "Hang in there, Nora."

"Always do. Enjoy."

Chewing his bacon, Aaron renewed the talk. "About Boston or Lauderdale — that wouldn't be real soon, would it?"

"Naw," said Neil. "For now there's the band. I wish we

didn't have to be so mainstream, but it keeps me from getting too bored."

Aaron fingered his toast. "We can have a blast with it," he said cautiously, "so long as things stay cool between all of us."

"Like with Doug and me?" Neil poured ketchup on his hash browns. "Doug's a buddy and all, but he's sort of naive. I've hooked him into some good stuff, but sometimes it's pretty sad what he goes for."

"Well, you gotta allow for taste, right?"

Neil took a bite and looked thoughtful. "I guess it's what he comes from," he said at length. "His background. I mean, he was *born* in this hole."

Resting his silverware, Aaron stared into his lap. He fumbled for choice words, then decided to let it go this time. He was hungry.

Just then a blonde girl came down the aisle by their booth. "Neil baby!" she chirped, and kept on past.

Aaron, admiring her legs, watched her go to the cigarette machine and pop quarters in. In high sandals, she wore a short green skirt, hoop earrings, and a beige, African-patterned shirt. A tassled purse dangled from her shoulder.

Neil gave Aaron a leer. "Always after me Lucky Charms," he said, attempting an Irish lilt.

Thumping a cigarette pack into her palm, the girl clicked her sandals back up the aisle. Neil turned to her. "Looks like you got some sun."

"Been out at my parents' place on the lake," she said. "Mind if I scoot in?"

Neil moved and she sat beside him, sliding the ashtray over. She had light-blue eyes, and her hair was gathered on one side like a gossamer shoot.

"Elaine," Neil said. "This is Aaron, our new lead guitar."

"Oh, I didn't know you had a new guy!"

"Hi," said Aaron. "So you're one of our billion fans?"

"Absolutely," Elaine said. She pulled a lighter from her purse and lit a cigarette. "Actually, I don't know the other guys. I'm more of a Neil fan." Smiling sideways, she let her free hand play through Neil's hair. "Where's your earring?"

Neil smirked at his plate. "I left it at home. Come on, I'm eating."

Her hand slid away and she pouted. "That's no way to be — 'specially since you skipped my last party."

"I was busy. Does that mean you're going to boycott us at Milo's?"

"I'll see." She exhaled. "I got carded there last time. But I've got some older friends coming over from Bridgton. Maybe I can sneak in with them."

Neil looked at his watch. "Twenty of noon. I have to hit the head and then we'll take off."

Elaine let him out, sat again, and smiled at Aaron. "So, what was the name?"

"Aaron."

"Where are you from?"

"Connecticut."

"Just moved here, huh?"

"Moved? . . . Yeah, a month ago."

Nora came by with a coffee pot but Aaron declined a refill and got the check. As the big woman turned away he heard her call out: "Gail! Sweetheart, where've you been hiding?"

Aaron turned and saw Gail leaning halfway in the diner's door, smiling in a pastel outfit. He could hear her above the

110

chatter, talking to Nora. "Was out on my bike and I thought I'd pop in and say hi."

Nora put the pot aside and hugged her. "Wish it wasn't so busy," Nora said. "I ran into your mom at the bank Friday. So graduation's in a week?"

Aaron was about to get Gail's attention when he heard Elaine snicker. He turned back around.

"What?" he said.

"Her," said Elaine, tapping her cigarette. "She's in my class. I call her Queen of the Mutants — hangs out with some real dips." She snickered again. "It's her hobby, collecting losers."

Aware of the heat all through his face, Aaron still managed to keep his tone casual. "Then why hasn't she collected you?"

Elaine blinked, her smile twitching and then gone. "Pardon me?"

He downed the dregs of his coffee while his stare remained level. "I said — why isn't she hanging out with *you?*"

For a moment Elaine didn't know what to do with her eyes. Then she snuffed her cigarette and got up.

"Don't bump your nose on the ceiling," he said.

From over his shoulder he watched her stiff, clicking exit. Gail was gone and Nora back to giving refills. Slouching low, he watched a wisp of smoke curl from the ashtray. His cheeks still burned.

Neil returned and paused before his empty seat. "Where'd Elaine go?"

"She was late for her manicure."

"Huh?"

Aaron dropped two dollars on the table and picked up the check. "Let's head out."

111

8

▼

Peg was not her usual self the next afternoon, when he relieved her at the store. In something of her daughter's fluttery manner, she told him about the armed holdup of a store in South Windham the night before. She had heard of it on the radio. "It's never happened to us. God forbid, but if it ever does, just shell out. Don't get brave; just empty the register and don't say a word."

"I know, Peg. That's the smartest thing."

"It's getting worse," she lamented. "The milk's finally going sour."

She bemoaned a brawl outside Milo's on Saturday night, which had brought out the cops and the rescue unit. She spoke of a recent case of child abuse involving a Fox Hill family, and of her worries about drunk driving on graduation night.

Aaron looked outside at the greenery and wanted to tell her about New York and even Stamford. "One holdup doesn't make a crime wave," was all he said.

Soon after Peg left, he discovered a library book on the window sill — *Seeds Within: A Guide to Cultivating Personal Strength,* by some minister/psychologist.

Just then Gail appeared, proud over cutting a study period at school. "Didn't get detention, though. I wanted it just once before I graduated, but they didn't even notice. Damn."

She had just come from the print shop, she said, and was scheduled for part time this week, full time the next.

"Coming to see us at Milo's?" he asked.

112

"I'd like to, but the bouncer's the brother of a classmate and he knows my age. I'd be back on the street in a second."

"Oh."

She seemed to detect his letdown. "Well, I'll get to see you guys. Sometime soon."

"Okay. Next time."

She bought a bag of cashews.

"Your mom forgot this," he said, handing her Peg's book.

Gail looked at it, made a face, and told him to have a good night.

She had been gone five minutes when Aaron realized that he was standing with the broom but not sweeping, the store silent except for the radio. Lately he had been leaving the sound low and letting his mind roam more. It often roamed to Gail.

But as he thought of her now, his pledge to be realistic tightened and squeezed the daydreams out. He worked for Gail's father, played in a band with her brother, and felt a particular bond with her mother. Furthermore, she was apparently taken. Case closed.

He began sweeping but soon stopped.

What could he offer her, anyway? What, with all the things he didn't want to tell her?

The admission stung as he swept, but not for long. Toy Soldiers took center stage in his reveries. Three nights to go. . . . Gripping the broom handle, he held the bristle end to his hip and played it till the sound of Andy's pickup spurred him back to the register.

Andy entered with merriment in his eyes. "Gosh, aren't we frisky today!"

113

9

▼

Wednesday was a day of anticipation. Aaron walked to all of his favorite spots but found himself hurrying for no reason. He tried to read his Vietnam book beneath a tree but didn't get far. Then he decided to get a haircut.

Mr. Jarvis, the barber, was an erect, thin-haired man with the face of a jovial otter, barely wrinkled despite his age. He had been cutting hair in this shop since 1959, he said. Pictures of his wife, children, and grandchildren adorned one shelf.

"Nice pictures," Aaron said.

"Yep, they're doin' all right. Want some more off the sides?"

"No, that's fine."

Jarvis took his clippers to the back of Aaron's neck. Aaron wiped hair from his cheek and watched the pudgy young guy who was seated by the door. Dressed in an undershirt and painter's pants, the guy was looking through a news magazine. "That's one thing I could never figure out," he said above the electric hum.

"What's that?" said Jarvis.

"Why we sell wheat to the Russians."

The barber laughed. "It's bullshit to me, Wayne. Sometimes I think Uncle Sam might as well hang a target on his butt and bend over."

Wayne shook his head. "If I was president I'd just tell 'em if you want the wheat, you gotta take our niggers too."

Jarvis laughed.

As the clippers buzzed in his ear, Aaron looked at Wayne, then out the open door. He was thinking of the few black people who had passed through his life. There was Byron Ladd, Red Sky's revered lead guitarist. Whenever he had visited the house in L.A., Byron hoisted Aaron onto his shoulder for a better view of the canyon. There were Byron's twin daughters, a year older than Aaron — he couldn't recall their names but did recall his playing and squabbling with them among the shrubs. And there was genial, bookish Mr. Le-Blanc, who taught biology at Chase. And Carl, the kid with whom Aaron had gotten in trouble for laughing in study hall. There were others, a handful.

"Want those sideburns trimmed?" Jarvis asked.

"Yes, please."

When Jarvis swung him around to the mirror, Aaron found his hair shorter than he liked. He pulled the sheet off and paid six dollars.

Practice — the last one before his Fox Hill debut tomorrow night — was two hours away, but his excitement had ebbed. And though he was certain that his guitar would bring it back, he felt troubled. The sensation drew him out to the woods and train tracks. Stopping after the bend, he gazed up the long thrust of rail to the overcast horizon.

"You want the wheat, you gotta take our niggers too." Had he heard it in any other town or city, it would have been just another poisonous little state-of-the-union address from another brain-dead slob. Brain-dead slobs were hard to avoid, and it would have caused him no more than a sneer. But he had heard it here, and he wanted to go back to the barbershop, kick Wayne out of his chair, and step on his face.

He stood there unaware of time or much else besides his disquiet, until a train's whistle impaled the silence. He jumped up an embankment and into the trees and listened to the swelling rumble. In a moment the black engine surged into view and the train took the bend in a clanking slither. The roar peaked and he watched the grimy boxcars rush by with sparks winking underneath.

Then it was past him, the caboose quickly shrinking with a glum-faced brakeman at the rear. On it ran to that distant point where rail met sky, and the rumble died away. In the quiet a few leaves fell in graceful corkscrews. Aaron's fingers quivered.

10

▼

Thursday. Outside Milo's, Aaron stopped his pacing to look at a chalkboard sign propped by the curb: "Tonite: Toy Soldiers — $2 cover after 9 P.M." The scrawled words brought both a thrill and a tremor, which made no sense. With the Gimmix he had played before bigger and more discriminating crowds than the one that would see him tonight. Yet he had never been this nervous before a gig.

Mike's father's pickup was parked a few feet away. Hauling the equipment here had been no easy task, especially with Neil fretting the whole way about bumps and vibrations. But they had gotten it all inside, where the other guys were now. The establishment had a stained log front with long windows and a carved sign above the door. From the juke box inside,

116

a female singer declared that if you wanted to jump on her, you had to come out and say so loudly. All Aaron wanted, however, was to play two smooth sets before friendly people who weren't afraid to dance.

The door opened and Doug stuck his head out. "Y'okay?"

"Sure. Just getting some air."

Aaron stepped back into the dimly lit place. A few Fox Hill Lumber workers were drinking beer at the tables, and one stood locked over a pinball machine. On the juke the song faded and another came on, too loud. At the bar a brunette waitress cleaned ashtrays and prattled with the hefty, bearded bouncer. Jack Milo, a short, spring-loaded man of middle age, sat on a stool and scribbled in a notepad. A longer extension of the place opened to the right, with a low stage at the end, and there the equipment lay jumbled as Neil, Mike, and Ben tinkered around.

"There you are!" Neil called. "We were thinking you'd skipped town!"

Aaron ignored him and followed Doug to the stage, noting the postage-stamp dance floor — the kind that made dancers into human bumper cars. While Neil finished connecting cords with pliers, Aaron set up a microphone and helped Mike arrange his drum kit.

Then Milo came strutting over. "Hey, dudes."

Neil was Scotch taping the song list to his organ. "Well, Jack, your juke-box selection still stinks."

"Awful sorry, chief. I forgot to consult your expertise. Now I just wanted to tell you guys something." Raising his palms, he waited till he had their full attention. "You guys were good about it last time, but let me remind you — I never asked your ages and I don't want to know. But if you're under, I'm taking a chance just by having you here. You can have all the soft drinks you want but . . ."

117

"We'll keep it clean," Doug said.

"Fine." He dropped his hands. "Just covering myself. Anyhow, have a good time and leave 'em hollering."

"We'll pack 'em in," Neil said, as Milo strutted away.

" 'Taking a chance,' " Neil grumbled. "We play for peanuts — that's the only reason he books us."

"How much do we get?" Aaron asked.

"Just the door," said Doug. "Whatever we bring in."

"Oh . . . Where's the sound man?"

Neil laughed. "In a hick-town saloon? No, we do our own sound." He regarded the p.a. system and then the ceiling. "And if I recall, getting it right was a bitch last time."

"Yeah, all through the first set," said Ben.

"What was it like last time?" Aaron asked. "The whole night, I mean."

Mike chuckled. "They didn't tar and feather us."

"Did people dance?"

"Once they got hammered," said Doug. "They drink enough, it's cool."

After a while Neil called for Milo to turn the juke box down so they could start sound checks. Punctuating their jigsaw noises, the pinball machine rattled and rang.

At a quarter to nine Aaron stood at the end of the bar and gazed at faces along the mirror — some lively, a few worn and morose. Already he had been to the bathroom four times. The place was loud and nearly filled to capacity. Milo poured drinks and handled money with a juggler's agility. The waitress, her tray aloft, grabbed laughs and tips among the customers. On a stool by the door sat the big bouncer, with an ink pad, handstamper, and cashbox on a stand beside him. Neil was at a table with a neatly casual foursome who seemed attentive, listening to one of his orations.

Aaron took a gulp of his iced cola and looked at the clock as Doug came up beside him. "We got people here from other towns," Doug said. "That's good."

Aaron's stomach gurgled. "Shouldn't we be getting ready?"

"Soon, soon," Doug finished his ginger ale. "Come over and sit with us."

They went to the corner where Ben and Mike were seated. Mike was speaking with two guys at the next table — one whiskered and small, the other fat and wearing a Hale Construction cap. Aaron faintly remembered them as customers at the store.

The fat one waved his beer bottle at Doug. "When you gonna get your asses up there?"

"Be patient," Doug replied.

The two, apparently older products of Fox Hill Regional, joked with Doug and Mike about school days. Detached from the talk, Ben appeared ill at ease and Aaron nudged him. "Forgot to tell you — you've been sounding really good."

"Thanks," said Ben. "I wonder sometimes."

"Well, I think we're all getting better."

Ben removed his glasses and cleaned them with a napkin. Aaron sipped his drink, scanning for new arrivals and pretty waistlines. It was almost time. Then he saw Neil rise from his company and wave to him.

"Hey, finally!" said the fat guy.

The whiskered one clapped lazily.

Gathering a breath, Aaron headed with the others for the waiting stage. He all but pounced on his guitar and then started tuning. Amid the bar's racket the others joined in with their random, stuttered notes, and it wasn't until the juke box fell silent that Aaron looked at the milling, sitting, gabbing mass of people. Here and there he caught a dull stare in the dimness. Then he felt a weight magically lift. There

119

was no call to be fantastic — not now, not tonight. They would do their best, and that was all. Turning, he gave Doug a nod and Ben a smile.

Neil adjusted the mike with a crunch. "Good even — " A ring pierced the stuffy air. Neil muttered, then tried again. "Good evening! We're Toy Soldiers."

To scattered whoops and clapping, Neil began the organ intro for Dire Straits' "Walk of Life." Mike started light on the drums. Aaron stood poised, then broke fast with the lead line as they all jumped in. Two couples were on the dance floor even before Neil started singing, with Aaron and Doug on refrains.

> He got the action, he got the motion
> Yeah, the boy can play.
> Dedication, devotion
> Turnin' all the nighttime into the day.

Neil's organ swooped and sailed as Doug meshed with Aaron's lead, and Mike and Ben supplied a solid bottom. Aaron felt it down to his feet. Harmonizing, he watched dancers twist and clown. The song ended to yells and clapping, and the couples quit the floor. Neil grinned over his shoulder.

After that, each song rolled out like a wave and crested to a ragged ovation. The rough sorcery was there, along with the flaws. Mike, flailing happily, went overboard in places. And Neil's problem had shifted, his delivery sounding forced on numbers that didn't require his organ, more natural on those that did. But riding the waves and coupled with his Telecaster, Aaron didn't care.

The others had taken Aaron's advice on space between songs, leaving just enough to catch their breaths. Neil's foursome got up for a couple of numbers, but dancing was sparse until halfway through the set, when a U2 song netted a full floor and Aaron's solo carried them to a feverish level of playing. Bearing down with the sound buzzing on his face, he caught glimpses of people in motion. He felt his blood pump and his sweat run.

And for an instant he saw himself with the Gimmix last summer, at the Club Zero in Stamford, facing a crowd for the first time. At the first swipe of his strings, he had understood — fully, at last — what all the work was for. It was just a morsel of what his father tasted in halls and amphitheaters, but it was enough.

The hour swept by, and the sound system behaved until the song that closed the set, when a loud hum caused some who were dancing to plug their ears. With the set over, Neil grimaced into the mike. "We'll be back in a little while."

"Nice earring!" someone yelled.

Stepping off the stage, Neil stopped to glare into the corner where Doug's two older buddies were.

It was the fat one with the cap, slouched with his beer. "Want us to buy you some beads too?" he called.

Titters came from the near tables as Neil stood there glowering.

Setting his guitar down, Aaron looked at Doug, who smirked and yelled to his friend. "And we got a girdle for you, Fred! Looks to me like you need one!"

Cackles burst from all around, including the fat guy's bearded partner. The marksman-turned-target pulled his cap down over his eyes and wailed, "Too-shay! Down in flames! Too-shay!"

Aaron laughed, but sobered as he saw Neil wriggle off through the crowd.

Ben hopped from the stage and smiled. "So far so good."

"Yup," said Aaron. "Order me a Coke, will ya?"

Aaron pushed carefully past the packed bar toward the bathroom, where he found Neil fuming over the sink.

"Townie morons!" Neil said with a spit. "Doug's always gotta have his shit-kicker buddies around!"

"Forget it. Doug got him back for you."

"That fat moron!"

"Come on, Neil! We just did a good set! You were great!"

Neil scowled at his hands as he dried them with a paper towel. "Those people I was with before — they want to meet you."

Aaron followed him back out and Neil introduced him to the two couples, who were friendly and polite. They were students at Colby College in Waterville, and had caught the band here a few months ago on their way back from a ski trip. One of the women lavished praise on Aaron's talent and the others chimed in. He talked music with them, then excused himself when Neil started grousing about the acoustics.

Over in the corner, Ben chuckled as Doug gave Neil's sniper more grief. "Honest to God, Fred. My old man always said you should get free room and board at the zoo."

"It's all my mother's fault," Fred said. "Blame her. . . . Hey, don't I know this character from somewhere?" He pointed a stubby finger at Aaron.

"Yeah, up to the store," his companion said.

Doug introduced Fred and the other guy, whose name was Bud, and presented Aaron as the Supreme All-Knowing Universal Wizard of Guitar. Aaron shook their hands.

Then Ben leaned up to his shoulder. "I ordered sodas but the waitress is taking her time. Is Neil still pissed?"

"He'll live. Where's Mike?"

"Over by the door. Laurie told him she'd try to get in."

To Aaron's left, Bud drew on his cigarette and doodled with a pen on a napkin, apparently tuning out the talk. Aaron looked at the napkin and saw a bunch of saw-toothed gargoyles with bulbous noses.

"Those supposed to be us?" Aaron said

Bud chortled. "They scare the hell out of my wife." Putting the pen away, he crumpled the napkin and raised his beer bottle.

"So where do you work?" Aaron asked.

"What's work?" He dribbled foam on his flannel sleeve. "Naw, I was at the mill in Rumford when the strike happened. After they busted the union I couldn't get back in."

"Jeez, that's too bad."

"Yeah, well, I'm still looking. Fred here's been trying to get me on at Hale."

Bud began a winding narrative about Fred and him raising hell back in high school. Aaron watched the dreamy, bristled face as he listened. He was still listening when Mike returned.

"Laurie get in?" Doug asked.

Mike shook his head in resignation. "Bouncer says she was here a half hour ago. He told her no and she got a little upset." He sat, dangling a thick arm over the back of the chair. "It was a dumb idea anyway. She looks her age too much."

The waitress arrived with a full tray. Up close she was quite attractive — slender, with dark-brown plaited hair. "Here we are," she said.

Bud turned to gaze at her, then placed a hand on her hip. "Hunnnyy!" he purred.

Fred boomed a laugh.

Holding the tray high, she dipped a reproachful eye. "The name's Tracy, and that's my hip."

Bud withdrew the hand and held it up. "I'll never wash this again — never!"

She set the soft drinks down and handed a beer to Fred, who frowned. "Twenty lashes, sweetheart. I ordered a Miller."

"Oops," she said, and took it back. "Sorry, I'm new here."

"Hey, I'll take it," said Mike.

Smiling at him, she put a hand on his shoulder. "If you guys were legal, you'd be the first to get one."

"Aw, thanks," Mike said, smiling up.

She left with the promise of a Miller for Fred.

"I swear," said Bud, fumbling for a cigarette. "That girl could make a dead minister horny."

Aaron watched the people. The juke box blared, then stopped, and Neil got up from his friends.

"Liftoff," Doug said.

On the way to the stage, Neil gave Aaron a glance. "No Elaine. Guess she couldn't get in."

Aaron stifled a laugh.

They began with John Mellancamp's "Rain on the Scarecrow." To Mike's one-stick Aaron coaxed menace from the opening notes, mounting to the song's hard, lumbering hook as the whole band fell in. Neil dispensed with his jerky mannerisms and gave his most intense performance so far. On the refrains Aaron sounded better to himself.

The rest of the night went well. Aaron watched people dance as he played — here a supple couple having fun, there some guy with a puttering gait and a sloshed, swaying woman for a partner. For Doug's "Scene of the Crime" half of the dancers looked confused and sat down. Doug didn't seem to mind and kept the rhythm going, joining Neil on the chorus.

Land of the free, home of the x-ray eye.
Everyone knows the code of the secret lie.
Land of the free, that's where I'm doin' time.
Life in a small town, death at the scene of the crime.

They followed this with an original of Neil's, which lured a few dancers back, and the next number filled the floor again. They wound up with their Psychedelic Furs cover and headed for a table, but Fred and Bud got to their feet — Bud tipping his chair over — and let out wolf howls that quickly had everyone clapping and shouting for one more. Flushed and sweaty, the five of them trooped back up for a furious "All Day and All of the Night." People pressed bumping within inches of the stage and as Aaron played the final riffs, a chubby blonde woman stumbled sideways and wrapped her arms around his waist. Her wide-bellied partner looked annoyed as he pulled her off. Aaron thanked them for coming.

"*Adios!*" Neil called. "Careful driving home."

As Aaron put his guitar down to claps and whistles, he spotted a couple necking by the pinball machine. He paused. It reminded him of those times after club dates with the Gimmix, when older girls would glide up, make conversation, and eventually come on to him. They were hyper, faintly desperate girls whose eyes remained secretive as they talked and talked. But ending up in their beds felt like a natural sequel to the night. The first one was a politically minded Lisa, another a Tarot and astrology dabbler named Debbie, the last one a Jane or a Janet who was trying to swear off coke and who cried about how her mother hated her. With Lisa he made the mistake of telling her about the Spider, then endured a barrage of excited questions. After that he withheld the information from girls he met, no matter how close the conversation got. Each time, listening to them in the dark, he held them to his side and stroked their hair. As they slept, he cherished the lightness of his body and the clarity of his senses. Then his thoughts would turn surreal. The walls whispered to him and the posters came alive; the chain of plastic-wrapped condoms could have been a ceremonial necklace and the room itself a hushed castle chamber. In those fleeting moments life appeared purified, transfigured like a bomb site, with only a magical essence left behind.

Yet he had made no effort to see those girls again, preferring just to wonder what they were really like. Memories of their faces and warm, urgent skin mixed with the taste of ashes, and he wished that Gail had been here tonight. Then again, maybe it was best that she hadn't.

With the equipment all loaded, Ben and Mike spread the tarp.

"Let's just get the money and go," Neil grumbled. "I'm gonna call in sick tomorrow. They can fire me if they want."

They went back inside. All the lights were out except the one above the bar, where Milo and the bouncer sat drinking whiskeys. Mike was at a table with Tracy, the waitress, gabbing and chuckling as she tallied her tips.

"Ah!" Milo said, and placed the open cash box on the bar. "Good time tonight, boys. We'll see about having you back again."

"We might consider it," said Neil, who took a large wad of ones and started counting.

"Tell ya, though," said Milo. "I'd sure like you guys to have a couple of birthdays."

"We just *look* young," Aaron said. "I'm forty-two, myself."

The bouncer chuckled. "Clean livin' — that's your secret, right?"

126

The take came to $44 for each of them. "Aruba here I come," Doug mumbled, taking out his wallet.

Careful not to step on the equipment, Aaron climbed into the back of the truck with Doug and Ben and sat on the edge, holding tight. Another job of unloading awaited them at Neil's, but they enjoyed the ride down slumbering Main. Hugging themselves against the night air, Doug and Ben lauded Aaron's and each other's playing — a lot better than last time, they agreed. Ben spoke of getting his diploma this weekend, and Doug moaned about the "family stuff" that his sister's graduation would entail. Aaron braced for the rail crossing, smiling as he heard Neil swear at the bump, and watched the public buildings pass. Happily drained, he felt content with the roll of bills in his pocket.

"Uh-oh," Ben said, just as a cruiser shot from the lot of Talbot's Hardware, with lights flashing.

Doug leaned over and thumped the rear window as the cruiser gained. Mike pulled to the side.

"I hope it's Porter," said Ben.

"It's Conehead," Doug growled. "Didn't you see how he cowboyed out of there?"

The cruiser braked behind them and a figure got out with the lights still blinking. The cop's hat was on but the pear silhouette was unmistakable. He approached at a quick stride and holding a flashlight, and in its glow Aaron glimpsed the scowl. Without looking up at them he went to Mike's window and shone the light in. "License and registration," he said.

Mike handed them over.

"Okay," McDonald said. "You're getting a ticket for that right taillight. It's out." Mike's response was low and courteous but the cop cut him off. "You also have a guy riding

127

on the side back there. Y'realize I could also nail you for driving to endanger? You listening?"

Aaron lifted himself off the edge, hunkering next to Ben as McDonald yammered on like a terrier.

In the blue-light throb from the cruiser, Doug yawned into his knees and whispered, "Before I get out of Fox Hill I wanna do something to that guy. . . . Something bad."

11

▼

Showing up for work, Aaron found Jerry making small talk with Bud.

"There he is!" Bud said. "You guys were good last night!"

"Well, thanks for the support."

"Hey, I had a blast. Even if I can't remember all of it."

Jerry looked retiringly at Aaron, then stuck his hands in his pockets and walked outside. Bud reached for his bag of groceries and Aaron wished him luck on the job hunt.

With Bud gone, Jerry came back in and cleared his throat. "I was going to tell . . . um, ask you something. Gail's ceremony is Sunday and I'd like it if you could . . ."

"Do a double shift? No problem."

"No, I'll open the place. Just come in around eleven. I meant to ask you sooner."

"Fine by me. I hope the weather's nice for it."

"Thanks." He cleared his throat again. "Well, have a good one."

Aaron waited on customers more cheerfully throughout the evening. Welcoming the chance to do his boss a favor, he was also glad for the check that it might put on Jerry's attitude. The scales between them had righted a little.

Business was slow on Sunday. Alone in the store, with sunlight pouring in the window, Aaron was reading *Newsweek* when the Fergusons' jeep pulled up outside. He watched them get out.

The sight of Jerry in his charcoal suit and red tie nearly made him laugh. Peg, despite a few extra pounds, looked almost glamorous in her heels and plum-colored dress. Wearing a tie and sports coat, Doug got out of the back and Gail out of the other side, clasping her cap and diploma. Her white gown fluttered in the breeze and she looked like a mischievous angel.

"Working hard?" Peg asked, smiling as she entered.

"I'm expecting another busload any minute," Aaron said.

Jerry chuckled. "You can handle it. Give me a bag, if you'd be so kind."

Aaron handed him a bag and he started loading up on beer, soft drinks, and munchies.

Doug and Gail leaned side by side against a cooler. Gail let out a breath. "Over. Over and done. Yipee."

Doug loosened his tie. "Man, that gym was hot! They should've had it outdoors."

"Naw, too windy," Gail said.

"Well, at least the wind might've drowned those speeches out. Same crap as when I graduated."

Peg shot him a look. "I thought some of them were all right!"

Doug raised his eyes rapturously. "We must strive to strive! And in our striving, we must strive for that for which we have striven!"

"Please, no instant replays," said Gail.

Peg expressed appreciation for Aaron's twelve-hour day, but he waved her words aside and congratulated Gail.

"Thank you," she said. "Hey, look what Mom and Dad gave me!" She skipped to the counter and opened her fist, revealing a tiny velvet box, which she unsnapped. There were earrings inside. Smiling brightly, she held them up to her lobes. "Real pearl! Aren't they nice?"

"Sure are." For a second he thought of his own graduation present, whose wreck now rusted off the Connecticut coast. Then he noticed a tear stain on Gail's cheek.

She put her earrings back. "Those are so neat, Mom."

"Glad you like them, dear. I'm sorry they couldn't be diamonds." Peg looked out at the lot. "Jerry Jr. said he'd be over in a minute. I don't know how he can drive with that poor foot of his."

"He's probably still chewing the fat with somebody," said Doug.

"Well, he'll have to hurry if he wants to meet Aaron."

Aaron had forgotten about the fifth Ferguson. "He wants to meet me?"

"Sure," said Gail. "We told him all about you. He likes meeting people."

Jerry put the bagful of items on the counter and asked for another bag. Taking it, he turned and touched Gail lightly on the arm before striding down the canned-goods aisle.

Peg, walking stiffly on her heels, had gone back out to the jeep and returned with an Instamatic. "Aaron, come around here. I want to get one with you."

Aaron hesitated. "Aw, Peg — I don't . . ."

"Come on! Do an old lady a favor."

He came around and Peg directed him and her children outdoors, where he and Doug stood on either side of Gail. Gail put her cap on and the tassel dangled in her face. Peg held the camera up and stepped back. "Smile, Aaron. This isn't a mug shot."

Aaron worked up a smile as she snapped it.

"Fine," she said. "That'll be nice."

"I hope that one of Dori and me comes out," said Gail. "It'll look like a sobbing contest."

Just then a blue Impala swung into the lot and parked.

"Finally," Peg said.

The door opened, crutches slid out, and a tall, bearded young man hobbled onto the blacktop. "Taking pictures without me?" he called.

"We weren't going to wait all day," Peg replied. "Come and meet Aaron."

Aaron met him halfway with his hand out. Jerry Jr.'s firm shake and ruddy, genial face put him at ease.

"So you're Dad's latest victim?" said the younger Jerry.

"Beats unemployment," Aaron said.

Jerry Jr. laughed. "I put my time in here, so I know how it is."

His hair was messy, the dress shirt unbuttoned below his sunburned neck. In spite of the ankle held carefully off the ground, the laugh and face and broad chest denied pain. The crutches could easily have been for a joke.

"I hear you're quite a musician," he said.

"Working at it."

"I always wished I played something, but you can see I'm not all that coordinated."

"So you're a ranger?"

"Yup — dealin' with critters and tourists. Hard to tell 'em apart sometimes."

The elder Jerry came out with his loaded bags and Doug took one.

Peg sighed. "Gosh, Aaron — I wish you could come over."

"Naw, I feel grubby standing next to you guys anyway."

Gail started to the jeep but turned around. "Oh! Aaron, a friend of mine's having a party up on Ash Road tonight. You should come."

He scuffed the blacktop with his heel. "But it's probably just for your class."

"Hell, no," said Doug. "Every derelict in town's invited. The other guys and me'll be there."

"Okay."

"Mike's picking me up after work. You oughta be done by then, so we'll swing by."

To Aaron's query, Jerry Jr. said that he would be sticking around only until this evening. Aaron held the car door open for him, returning Peg's wave as the jeep drove out. Jerry Jr. lay the crutches on the back seat.

"Thanks," he said, and they shook again. "Catch ya next time, okay?"

"Good. Take care of that ankle."

Walking back inside, Aaron wondered what it took to have a face like that — a face that left the impression of a permanent wink.

When they got to the party that night, Mike parked along the road and they each took a beer from a bag that Neil had brought. Cars lined one side of the long driveway, which led to a ranch-style house with brightly lit windows. In the dark of the yard, laughing groups of kids stood around while heavy metal played from a speaker on the porch.

Doug introduced Aaron to one loud, friendly group of people who were well into their beer and flasks. Aaron recognized half of them from the store. Doug spoke with a recently married couple about last year's graduation party, and Aaron listened to tales of outrageous acts and hangovers. Then Fred appeared, still in his company hat, and clapped Doug on the shoulder.

"How's it goin'?" he asked. "I hear Conehead nailed you guys!"

As Doug spun a vivid account of the incident, Aaron spotted Tommy at the edge of the group, sharing a pint of something with two other guys. No sign of Gail. Over by a bush Mike was talking with Tracy, the waitress from Milo's. Some of the more upscale kids had congregated near a birdbath, and there Neil was speaking with Elaine. Aaron thought he saw Elaine notice him and then look quickly away.

Holding a plastic cup, Ben emerged from the house to the lighted porch and paused to survey things. Aaron walked over and congratulated him, and they moved behind the buzzing speaker.

"So what's up for work this summer?" Aaron asked him.

"I didn't look too hard, but Doug says they're adding another dishwasher at the Patch and he can get me in."

"And after that?"

Ben looked troubled and slurped his drink. "I didn't get to tell you guys — I got accepted at Bates. I want to take art."

"Yeah? Great."

"The school's just in Lewiston so I could still play." He contemplated his cup. "Maybe . . . I hope I can."

Aaron forced a shrug. "It's like Doug said to me — we

133

could hang it up tomorrow, but we'll have fun while it lasts."

Ben seemed to relax. "Right, yeah. Milo's was great, and we've still got the Battle of the Bands ahead of us. I'll be psyched."

The music cranked along and high-pitched laughter tumbled across the yard. Aaron looked through the open door to the kitchen, where a middle-aged couple were talking with a group of girls. Arms folded, the man looked somber and the woman wore a flustered smile. Unopened soft-drink bottles and a near-full punch bowl sat on a table, between towers of plastic cups.

Just then Gail, in jeans and a T-shirt, detached herself from the group and waved to him. Then she bounded out to the porch and threw an arm around Ben. "Benjamin! We made it!"

"Don't speak too soon," he said, hugging back.

She coughed and giggled. "This is bad. Two beers and I'm looped." She thumped Aaron on the arm. "How are you doing?"

He smiled. "Not as good as you."

"Well, work on it!"

A wide-hipped girl with feathered hair trotted up to the steps and thrust a sixteen-ouncer into Gail's hand. "Finish this," she said. "I'm hiding from my parents."

Gail held the can above her head. "Sti ni ya'sou! That's the Greek toast to your health."

"Whatever," the girl said, and stumbled to another part of the yard.

"That's Vicki," Gail said. "The hostess with the mostest. We both start full time at the print shop tomorrow. Work — ugh!"

"So Dori couldn't come?" Ben asked her.

"She decided not to."

"Too bad," said Aaron. "I guess she has to take it easier."

"Was good to see my big brother, anyway."

"Yeah, he's cool." He looked at her T-shirt, which bore a print of the United Nations plaza. "When did you visit New York?"

"Never," she said, and burped. " 'Scuze me. . . . No, we had a Venezuelan exchange student and he gave me this. You ever been there? New York?"

"Plenty. I lived near it."

She cocked her head and put a hand to her hip. "What was it like?"

"It was . . ." Stung by caution, he rolled the beer between his palms. Gail looked at him and waited. "It's intense, like everyone says. Another world almost."

"Ever go to Broadway?"

"A couple of times."

"I did with my parents," said Ben. "We saw *A Chorus Line*."

"I've always wanted to see that!" Gail gushed. She raised the can to her lips.

Glad that Ben had taken her attention, Aaron finished his beer and placed the empty on the step.

"I have to get down there," she said. "Sometime in the next few —" She broke into a spasm of coughing and Ben patted her on the back. "Stupid!" she sputtered. "I took a major hit off some Hawaiian stuff. It always does this."

"What a waste case," Ben chided. "Industrial strength, huh?"

She took a careful breath. "Rumor has it some idiots went up to Lewiston and scored some coke for tonight. Lovely, right?"

Aaron watched a guy roll on the grass while a girl doused

him with beer. Thinking of New York, he tried to picture Gail or any Fox Hill kid running the gauntlet of street dealers there: "Check it out. Check it out, man. It's real Jesus bread tonight." At Chase, too, Gail would have been lost for words. Within those ivied walls and practically under teachers' noses, piles of contraband had gathered like Halloween candy. Coke and hash were standards, but the spectrum ran to ludes, acid, ecstasy, MDA, and for one horrific week in '85, angel dust. Aaron's own weed dealer, a corporate lawyer's son, had taken a number of dust hits one day and gone on a screaming rampage during math class. In the mind of the student body, the incident managed to link dust use with stupidity and killed the demand for it.

Aaron shuddered, thankful that he had been bright enough to avoid the chancier junk. Or had it just been luck? Idiot's luck?

Ben went to the kitchen for a refill.

Viewing the activity on the lawn, Gail leaned against the banister. The sixteen-ouncer looked comically big in her hand. "Poor Mr. and Mrs. Ballard. I don't think this turned out like they planned."

"They do look kind of dazed," said Aaron.

She set her can down. " 'Scuze me. I gotta see if the bathroom's clear."

She went back in and he hopped off the porch to walk around. His mood had soured and he avoided talking to people. He felt exposed, stranded outside the fun, and knew it would soon be time to leave. A cheerful, shirtless guy stuck a beer in his hand as he passed, and wished him a merry Christmas. From the speaker, Ozzy Osbourne screeched like a castrated cat.

"Come on, turn it down!" a girl yelled.

"If it's too loud, you're too old!" a boy yelled back.

Aaron spent a drifting half hour around the party's fringe. At the dark rear corner of the house he saw two people in a make-out clinch by a tree; a second glance revealed them as Mike and Tracy. Reversing his direction, Aaron thought of the Prince song about life being just a party. It was true, in more ways than one.

The music was off as he returned to the front yard, and Vicki's father stood on the porch, looking grim. "Excuse me!" he called out. "Everybody? I need your attention!"

The chatter and clowning subsided.

"Listen, we don't want anyone driving home drunk. If you want to leave but you're even just a little shaky, we have tea and coffee inside and you can wait awhile. Or we could even put some of you up on the floor tonight if . . . " The man twitched as shouting burst from near the driveway. Then two guys spun like a small cyclone through the crowd, punching and kicking each other. They fell writhing, but several boys dragged them apart as the man rushed up to them. "What the hell's the matter with you guys? You wanna settle something, take it somewhere else!"

Restrained by their friends, the pair eyed each other sullenly through the harangue. One was a clean-cut guy in a varsity jacket, the other T-shirted and skinny with a sweatband and a bloody nose.

The man went on yelling, stabbing the air with his finger. "You come here, you act civil! Understand?"

Aaron spied Doug, Neil, and Ben conferring on the other side of the yard. In the doorway Vicki's mother looked on fretfully. Then he noticed Gail standing on the right side of the porch, staring not at the confrontation but down over the banister. He walked to the porch and stood below her

137

on the ground. Her face was emptily tired. Then he saw what she was looking at.

Against the house, Tommy lay curled up with vomit down his chin. A friend bent over him and prodded his knee, then turned and called: "Rick, you gonna have room in your car?"

"Yeah," came the weary reply. "But wait till you're sure he's through."

Putting his can down, Aaron looked up at Gail and spoke softly. "Want me to walk you home? I'm going."

It was a moment before she nodded, turned, and came down the steps.

They crossed the yard, slipping past the fidgety crowd and down the driveway. The noises faded behind them.

"Last party we went to, the same thing happened," she muttered. "Was all I could do to get him home in one piece. I should've begged off after that, but no . . ."

"He won't be the only one tonight," Aaron mumbled.

Aaron figured he had been at the party for just over an hour. It would seem funny tomorrow but for now his heavy mood refused to lift, even with Gail walking beside him.

Their pace kept even as they turned down the dark road. Passing the elementary school, he saw her look toward the playground with its swings and jungle gym.

"Thinking back?" he asked.

She coughed. "Looks a lot different since they built the new wing."

A mottled slice of moon hung above them as they walked. The night was crickety-quiet, warm and breezy, and from up ahead came the stream's low babble. When they reached the log bridge Gail abruptly stopped and sat on the railing, facing the road. Aaron sat beside her. They stared for a long moment into the deep, black mass of the trees.

"Your head on overload?" he spoke.

"Sure it is," she said. In his side vision he saw her look at him. "Yours is too, a lot of the time, isn't it?"

He folded his arms and shrugged.

She turned her eyes away. "Always this huge incredible mystery."

He heard a little irritation in her voice, and knew that he couldn't leave it at this. "That bugs you? That there's no big fat file on me?"

She flipped her hair back. "You seem to know a lot, but you're really careful. When you're not saying anything it's like I can feel your wheels turning."

"Relax, Gail. I'm not an escaped convict."

"Then we'll narrow it down some more. Let's see . . . What does your father do?"

Aaron raised a foot onto the railing and let the other dangle. "He's in sales." It was no lie.

"And your mom? Tell me about her."

"She's in a mental hospital."

Gail tucked her chin into her chest and didn't respond right away. "I'm sorry. I get stupid when I'm buzzed,"

"It's okay," he said. "Sometimes I think I belong at the Ricochet Motel too. Except they'd probably kick me out for being too weird."

She laughed, and her laugh mingled with the water and crickets.

Aaron glanced down at the stream and put his hand to her back. "Don't fall. It wasn't that funny." Touching her sent a tingle down his spine. He withdrew his hand.

She hacked a cough and wiped her eyes. "Aw, yeah, me too. Me and my whole family. We're all sort of off the wall in our own ways."

"You're all okay as far as I'm concerned."

She rocked gently. "I know I'm fortunate. Even with some of Mom and Dad's attitudes."

"Well, I haven't seen any whips around your house."

"No, no whips. But to them I'm still their little humming-bird — that's what Dad used to call me. Maybe I always will be, but even hummingbirds need to cut loose when the time comes."

"Yup."

She stopped rocking. "I'm grateful and I hope they know that. They never got any free rides. And Mom . . . she didn't have it easy with us. Or with Dad, for that matter." Her voice trailed off. "I suppose I'd like some muffinheads of my own, one of these days. But it won't be here." Stretching, she yawned to the stars. "Nope. Not here." She gazed up, not dreamily but bound up inside herself. "I have something to confess, and it might as well be to you."

"Go ahead."

"It's about Dori. It hit me that I was sort of relieved she wasn't there tonight."

"How come?"

"Oh . . . there are just these times when I'd rather not see her. I love her and it's awful to say, but I look at her and I get scared. I can see her living in a trailer with the baby crying. When she first told me, I tried to talk her into an abortion, told her I'd get hold of some money for her and keep my mouth shut, but she just shook her head. She was into the idea."

"Money was no object where I went to school," Aaron said. "Wasn't a big school, but in my junior year there were about ten pregnant girls and ten abortions."

"Wow," she murmured.

His small flash of candor made him tingle again. But he

skipped telling her about the eight failed suicide attempts and the two successful ones. For some reason he had kept track of such things.

"It's awful to say," she repeated. "Especially since . . . You know what Dori told me today? Today out in front of the school, everybody was laughing and crying and taking pictures, and she took me aside. And she told me if it's a girl, the middle name's going to be Gail. Virginia Gail Carpenter . . . or Sanford, if Prince Frank comes back to sweep her away, like she thinks he's going to. Ha!"

"Yeah, but that's nice," he said.

"Virginia Gail," she whispered. She chewed her thumbnail and looked at her knees.

Aaron wanted to put his arm around her but held on to the rail. "Come on, you're a free girl now. Now you can strive for things to strive for."

To his disappointment she didn't even smile. "I'm just thinking about Tommy. I should've seen ahead. We always got along, so when he started asking me out in March I said sure, fine. I figured we could keep it light, but after a while it was like he had other plans. I would explain it to him and he seemed to understand, but then he'd be pissed off cuz I wouldn't want to see him every night." She wiggled her head. "The week before the prom I tried to get through to him once and for all, and he didn't want to hear it. The prom went okay, but the way he carried on . . . He was into this Tommy-and-his-woman thing. Maybe I should've waited till summer was over but I could see things just building up. I tried again tonight but he just walked away." Her voice dropped back to a hush, the sort of bruised tone that couldn't be faked. "Mom took our picture today. I'm going to hate to look at it."

141

"Don't feel too bad," Aaron said. "Sounds like it was . . . you know, like it couldn't have turned out much different either way."

She coughed and flicked her hand. "To myself I look like a hypocrite. Dad would make his little remarks and Mom would start to get on the subject, and I'd yell at them. Now it's like I bought their whole line on Tommy, like I bought it all along. He graduated by the skin of his teeth, just like Dori. Basically I think he's gonna pump a lot of gas and drink a lot of beer."

"You never know." It was all Aaron could think of to say.

She frowned. "No, you can never tell. I'd love to be wrong about him, and about Dori. But I don't think they're ever going to get out."

"Well, somebody has to stay."

"That's true, and it's their business. But they still scare me. Life sort of just happens to them."

"Uh-huh. Them and a lot of others."

They fell quiet as a pair of headlights appeared from the direction of town. The vehicle was almost at the bridge and slowing when they saw that it was a police car. With some relief Aaron discerned not McDonald's face but that of Porter, an easygoing cop who had been at the store a few times. Porter stopped in the road and rolled his window down.

"Howdy," Gail said.

" 'Lo, there," said Porter. "Enjoying your freedom?"

"More or less," she replied.

"Been busy tonight?" Aaron asked him.

"Not really. Some kids rear-ended somebody at the Seven-Eleven but nobody got hurt."

"That's good."

Porter shifted gear. "Well, take care."

"You, too," they chimed, and the cop drove off.

They remained silent as the taillights vanished. The breeze had died but the air felt cooler. Gail hopped down and strolled across to the other railing while Aaron sat still, watching her. He didn't want to go home.

Stretching her arms wide, Gail heaved a sigh. "Ohhh, Toto. I have a feeling we're not in Kansas anymore."

"Still looks like Kansas to me," he said.

"Well, maybe so, but pretty soon it won't be." She stood with her back to him, slender and slight against the gloom. "It's not like I'm not nervous. I think about what's ahead and how I want to be."

"How do you want to be?"

"Besides outrageously happy?"

"Yeah. And able to cuss people in Korean."

"Besides that?" She twirled a lock of hair around one finger. "I don't really know. Charismatic, I guess. Charismatic and poised. And helpful in some way."

Aaron could only watch her.

She chuckled. "But, as they say in Moscow, *nikto mozhet videt* . . . No, what is it? *Niktu videt mozh* . . ." A fit of coughing seized her. Aaron got off the rail and went to her, but she had recovered. "Damn that joint!" Straightening up, she hugged herself. "I've got goosebumps. Let's go."

They continued toward the dull light of Main. As the watersound fell away, tree shadows slid over them like those of big, noiseless nightbirds. Aaron looked down at the pocked pavement. He listened to Gail's light breathing and felt her moving alongside him, and his arms ached. Then, as if obeying an outside force, his steps slowed. Gail slowed with him and then they stopped walking. She appeared worried or

143

uncertain as he turned to her, but in the next instant she didn't. Unblinking, her eyes looked like two wet pennies. He put a hand to her shoulder. Almost imperceptibly she nodded, then put a hand to his neck, and their faces came together. She squeezed back as he held her.

They were still kissing when they heard a car coming.

"Let's not get run over," she whispered.

She took his hand as they stepped into the trees. From deeper dark, they watched the car whip by from the party's direction. He looked at her and his heart was pumping fast. She put her cheek to his chest and he stroked her hair.

"This is tricky," she said.

"Maybe too tricky?"

"Maybe . . . Shoot!" She thumped him gently on the back. "I wish I'd met you somewhere else! I wish you were just some guy from another town!"

"So do I."

"Some guy from Portland or Bridgton, instead of whatever!"

His hand went still on her hair.

Holding on to his arms, she stepped back and muttered something too low to hear. And though he could barely see her face, he sensed words teetering and felt her hands tremble.

"It's dangerous out here," she spoke. "In the woods."

"What? Bears?"

"Yeah, and lions and tigers." She snickered. "Actually I meant something else."

"Oh . . . Right."

As they stepped back onto the road, she let go of his hand. Their stride was more hurried, and neither spoke till they were almost at the corner.

"This is so quick!" she blurted. "I don't know what's going on!"

144

"Tell me about it," he said.

"I wish you didn't work nights. It'd be easier to see you."

"I know. But we'll talk about it, all right?"

She cupped a hand to her mouth and wheezed. "Jeez! I'm tired, I'm dizzy, I'm all . . . I'm not going to broadcast this to anybody. Not yet. Not to Mom and especially not to Dad."

"Right. Neither will I."

At the corner of Main, they saw a blue light flashing down by Milo's and lingered a moment. The car they had seen earlier was parked ahead of the cruiser. With painful care, a T-shirted figure walked a straight line while McDonald's shape held a flashlight.

"The Pear," said Gail.

"Conehead," Aaron corrected.

They kept on up the sidewalk, passing from one pool of street lighting to the next, and reached the corner of Lark. In a downstairs window of the Ferguson home, a light shone.

"Mom's probably waiting up," Gail said. "My eyes aren't too red, are they?"

He took her hand and checked her eyes. "They'll pass."

She yawned at his feet.

"Sorry to make waves," he said.

"Well, you oughta be."

"I'm really not, but it sounded good."

Smiling, she kissed him on the lips and let go. "Good night."

"Night."

She headed toward the house, and he walked on.

"Thanks for walking me!" she called.

He halted and looked back. "Any time!"

He thought he heard her groan.

For the short remaining distance to the store and then up

in his room, Aaron floated on euphoria. All worries were scattered and he didn't want to think. And tired though he was, sleep came hard that night.

12

▼

He didn't see Gail the day after. Oddly, he wasn't sure whether he wanted to just yet. To talk and fumble, decide or not decide — whatever happened when they next met, it was bound to rattle his warm, tight memory of the bridge and the road. Yet he knew that postponements would soon rattle it anyway, along with their nerves. And their schedules, as she had observed, would not make it any easier.

An hour before work, Aaron encountered Dori outside a craft shop and congratulated her. She detached her Walkman and said that graduating was a relief, but sad too. He asked whether she was feeling better. Smiling through her freckles, she patted her round belly and nodded.

But her smile had a serious edge. And when the small talk ran out, she scratched her chin nervously, then looked him in the eyes. "One thing I have to tell you," she said.

"Yeah?"

"Take care with Gail. Please be careful with her."

She let her handbag swing like a slow pendulum at her knees. The Walkman's music crackled faintly.

"You don't have to worry," he said.

"You seem like a good guy to me," said Dori. "But I just had to say that."

He nodded at a fire hydrant. "I hear you."

"Well, see you at the store maybe."

She put her earpieces back in and left him.

Though time was short, Aaron kept wandering. From the rail crossing he hiked up the tracks and paused before the power line. There, at right angles, a corridor of grass and bare ground opened on both sides, running with such definition to the horizon that it looked like the work of a single titanic axe-blow, or as if the trees had leaped apart in fright. Above tree height and at wide intervals along the swath, towers stood like metal sentinels set for orders. Black cables stretched high between the towers and over the tracks, their hum like a million compressed hornets. Passing under the hum, Aaron had the sense of breaching a force field whose purpose he couldn't tell.

He hiked another quarter mile and took his shirt off. Catching his breath, he felt the sun on his shoulders and viewed the shade-flecked woods and shrubbery, all pregnant with afternoon light. A goldfinch flitted like a yellow spark from bush to bush. He knew he would be late for work, but at least Peg was there today and not Jerry.

He gazed down the tracks to that far point where the sky began and felt the lost regions yawn wide. Fox Hill was back there, the world out there with its heart laid open — teeming with other stories, other faces. It brought an odd feeling of comfort, to see a way out — there for anyone to take or refuse.

Peg threw her hands up when he rushed in, ten minutes late.

"I'm sorry!" he blurted. "I walked too far."

"No, that's okay," she said. "I'm just glad to see you! Doug said you disappeared at the party."

"Oh . . . " He wiped his forehead. "Guess I should've said something. The party kind of wore thin on me."

"Well, I wish it had worn thin on Doug. I called home at noon and he sounded like he'd just rolled out of bed." She came out from behind the counter. "At least Gail wasn't out all night, in spite of her threats."

Aaron felt an annoying skitter of guilt. Peg had the radio on the Iran-contra hearings; a solemn male voice asked a long question and another began a long answer. "Uh . . . They finding out anything?" Aaron asked.

"It's clear as mud to me," Peg said. She put two fingers to her temple. "What was I supposed to tell you? . . . Oh, Doug says Neil called, and he got you guys a date at Randy's Roadhouse."

"Really? When?"

"Middle of next month, I think he said." She shook her head. "You guys! I hear that place is a snake pit."

"So what's one night in a snake pit?"

"A lot can happen in one night, honey." She patted his shoulder. "Glad you're safe and sound. Bye-bye."

It was a basic slow Monday. Aaron gathered his patience for idle talk with customers — about the heat, about the hearings. But once they were gone, Gail would fill his mind again. Several times he glanced at the open door, half hoping and half worried that she would walk in. But around eight-thirty, it was Tommy who showed up.

Aaron straightened. "Hi, Tom."

Tommy mumbled hello, went to the back, and took a six-pack from the beer cooler. Aaron bit the inside of his cheek. Placing the beer on the counter, Tommy avoided his eyes.

148

Aaron didn't move. "Sorry. I'd get fired."

Tommy gave him a tense, simmering look, but when he spoke it was more plea than challenge. "Come on, nobody's here. I'll give you two . . . I'll give you three bucks."

Aaron looked at him — the frayed sweatband, frizzy hair, and drawn face — and shook his head. "I can't risk it. If a cop catches you leaving here with that, we get all kinds of hell."

Tommy turned and gangled quietly out.

Aaron sighed through his teeth and returned the six-pack to the cooler. Then he stared into the dark outside and remembered Tommy's crumpled form last night: the puke on his chin had seemed a fateful mark of some kind, or an ugly incurable sore. Aaron saw himself leaving with Gail, leaving Tommy crumpled there with his friends, and felt no guilt. It was more a numb acknowledgement — that life was a rigged contest, and that the unfairness of it had served him well this time.

On the radio, lightweight funk played like a fitful merry-go-round. Returning to the counter, he took a copy of *Rolling Stone* from the magazine rack. He flipped absently to the "Random Notes" section, then winced as he blinked at the photo. Like a puppet's face, his own stared flat from the page. The people in the background seemed to be having a good time; he recalled hating those cheerful expressions, just before the photographer's lens came up like a gunsight.

"Webb of Mystery," it said underneath, and a paragraph followed.

Danny "Spider" Webb and his revitalized Red Sky Band — together for the first time since its 1981 breakup — capped a rousing April 27 tour opener at the

Garden with a bash at Webb's Manhattan digs. Webb's current lady love, model Kris Allyn, played hostess for the party, which featured several industry luminaries. But then who should show up but the star's own son, 18-year-old Aaron? Aaron, a budding guitarist and song-writer, has reportedly inherited more than his father's physical appearance. (Pass the torch, please.) Within days of the festive event, however, the young man dropped mysteriously from sight. The Spider, now in the midst of touring, is said to be deeply concerned about his son and hopes that he will soon resurface.

After Jerry had arrived and done his counting, he eyed Aaron appraisingly. "Better get some sleep tonight, pal. You look worse than Doug did today."

Upstairs at his table, Aaron got a pencil and paper and started scribbling. Raw melody and lyrics had been cycling in his head lately. After a minute, he threw the pencil down and stared at his window. The raspberry curtains looked ridiculous.

PART FOUR

▾ ▾ ▾

A Little More to Life

1

▼

It was a rush to be driving a car again, especially with the road nearly all to himself. But then he grew mindful of police, and slowed down as tides of leaf and meadow green rewarded his eyes. Flowers and goldenrod spiced the country for as far as he could see.

Neil had been generous to lend him the car, and on short notice. ("Just don't put a dent in it, or I will feast upon your living heart.") The guy had his good points.

It was also cheering to think of the fifties and sixties compilation albums in the back seat with his guitar. Finding that "used and reissue" bin at the record store in Portland had been like striking oil, albeit under his father's unsettling poster gaze.

As Fox Hill came in sight, Aaron remembered that there was something else to take care of. A moment later he parked in front of Arrow Printing and got out, hoping he could act casual enough.

Vicki looked up from a copier and smiled. "Hi! Here to see the kid?"

"Yeah. Is she around?"

Vicki turned to call but Gail had already appeared, in an ink-smeared T-shirt. Nearing the counter, she raised her blackened hands. "Mah-vel-ous to see you!" she warbled, and reached for his face.

153

He cringed. Vicki laughed and went back to work.

Aaron was grateful to see Gail so apparently at ease. "I take it you're working hard," he said.

"I take it you're easily fooled. I wish our boss was."

He leaned closer. "I have a request."

"Yup?"

"Could you meet me at the square Friday night, 'round eleven?"

She smiled gamely but lowered her eyes. "Sure."

Aaron noticed a furtive glance from Vicki in back.

"It'd be sooner," he said. "But I have practice tonight and tomorrow."

"I know — the life of a celeb. Okay, I'll be there." Letting her inky hands dangle, she sighed and looked up again. It was a deep steady look, and he wanted to forget the ink splatters and reach for her. "Well, I better get back to the offset," she said. "Mr. Peterson's due back any minute."

"Yeah, I have to go pick Neil up."

"Lucky you. Well, see ya."

"Take it easy."

He moved toward the door and looked at her again. She glanced over at Vicki, who was busy sorting copies. Then she raised two fingers and blew him a kiss, printing her lips black in the process. He laughed as she looked first confused and then embarrassed, and left him with a backward wave. At that instant he could have rolled in ink with her and not minded.

Neil emerged from the Briar Patch damp with sweat and full of five o'clock disgust. Sliding into the car, he rolled his window down. "Another senior citizens' tour bus for lunch. I've seen bigger tips at my mom's bird feeder."

154

"You want to drive?" Aaron asked.

"Naw, go ahead."

They picked up Doug at the Fergusons' and started for Neil's. In the back seat Doug discovered the three albums and took them from the bag, reading their titles aloud.

Neil smirked. "What? No waltz music?"

"I just thought we might have fun with a few of those," said Aaron.

Squinting into the sun, Neil frowned. Aaron saw that this would be no less tricky than expected.

Later, while Neil showered, Aaron went to the hi-fi and put on "Good Lovin' " by the Rascals.

Doug leaned forward in his chair. "Isn't there some soda commercial with this in it?"

Aaron hid a grimace. "I don't know. But can't you see us cranking up a crowd with this?"

Jiggling his foot, Doug nodded. "Yeah, I can see it."

The song partied its way through the organ crescendo, then reeled to its end as Ben and Mike walked in, earlier than usual. Aaron took the record off and put on the fifties compilation. "Listen to this, you guys. If there's a definition of rock 'n' roll, this is it."

He dropped the needle on "Lucille." To honking horns, Little Richard banged the piano and shrieked like a mad warlock: "Looseeaalll!" Mike and Ben grinned.

Neil, shirtless and drying his hair, came downstairs and stood listening. Lowering the volume, Aaron gave him an exuberant look. "Outrageous, yes?"

The phone rang and Neil went to get it. Aaron sighed, then turned to Ben and Mike. "I was just talking about maybe getting some classics into our set." They nodded thoughtfully.

155

On the phone Neil made a series of low, hurried responses and hung up. "No Mom this evening. She's making another big sale over lobster. What a gal."

"So anyway . . ." Aaron resumed.

"So anyway," Neil said, and tossed his towel on the sofa. "What's this thing you've got about old stuff?"

Aaron twitched a shoulder. "I like it, that's all. And with the revival it's had in the past few years . . ."

"Yeah, yeah!" Neil moaned, waving his hands. "I know — oldie stations, movie soundtracks, car commercials. So what?"

Aaron reined in his frustration and went to turn the record off.

"Aaron has a point," Doug piped up. "A lot of bands do three or four of 'em a night, cuz your average bar crowd likes it."

Mike opened his mouth but Neil cut in. "Look, it's not like I'm disagreeing with that. But I'm not gonna be part of a moldy oldies band like those clowns who played at my cousin's wedding! I mean, I was willing to mess around with that Kinks song just for the hell of it but . . ."

"Just a few of 'em," Aaron said. "That's all I'm talking about doing. And it'd be fun. Haven't you ever . . ." He stopped, observing Neil's sullen lip. The last thing he wanted to do was make Neil feel cornered. "Well, listen. I'm not going to scream if you're not into it. But if you gave it a chance I bet you'd take to it, y'know? Sure they're hyping the hell out of it, but it was still a great era."

"You're sounding like a Deadhead!" Neil whined.

Again Aaron contained his annoyance. "Isn't there some old group you ever wanted to cover? Can't you think of just one?"

Wavering, Neil mulled it over as they all watched him. Aaron tapped his fingertips on the hi-fi.

"The Doors," Neil spoke.

"Yeah!" said Mike.

For Aaron it was like a hard-pressed obstacle giving way too quickly and making him fall. He rubbed a heel into the carpet. Jim Morrison and the Doors — of all the icons to survive Neil's acid bath.

"They were good," Aaron said. "But . . . Y'know, nowadays the metalheads own Morrison. It's mainly just the metalheads who listen to . . ."

Neil's killer grin stopped him. "What was that you sermonized me about the other day? It doesn't matter who else listens to it, it's whether you *like* it or not!"

Doug gave Aaron an admonishing eye. "He's right, guy. It's only fair."

Hot-faced, Aaron looked down and held his hands up. "Okay. Sure. The Doors were great. But they're not on any of these records and . . ."

"No problem," said Neil, with the air of a winning cardsharp. He went to his cabinet and removed a worn-at-the-corners album. "Got this from my mother, if you can believe that. She was into the Doors when she was young."

Neil put the record on and when Morrison's snarling incantation rose, Aaron again saw the guys in the dented maroon sedan. He could almost feel their kicks and punches. Still he had to agree that the Doors had a spooky gift.

"This one," Neil said. "This one I wouldn't mind doing."

It was a snapping, jazz-inflected number called "Peace Frog."

"I like it," said Mike, "but it might be hard for people to dance to."

"We could do it a little slower," Aaron offered. "Slower and with more of a back beat. We could bring it off."

Neil went to the hi-fi, lifted the needle, and gave the slightest of nods. "All right. I'll give it a shot."

It was a night of clumsy, happy discovery. With frequent trips from the garage to the stereo, they threw together rough versions of "Peace Frog," "Good Lovin'," and Johnny Kidd's "Shakin' All Over." All five of them seemed bitten by a bug, and near the end of it any onlooker would have thought it had been Neil's idea. The Randy's date was two weeks from tomorrow, the statewide Battle of the Bands one month away. But as he poured out his guitar fills, Aaron didn't dwell upon the calendar.

2

▼

Before practice the next day, Aaron and Doug spent two hours taking turns on Doug's old amp. Doug said he had gotten standing permission from Peg for Aaron to come over in the daytime and use the amp, even if no one was home, " 'cept of course if my dad's around."

At Neil's garage they found him seated on a bench and reading *Rolling Stone* — the current issue, with the photo.

"Listen to this," Neil said, and started reading aloud.

Not moving, gripping his case handle, Aaron tried to listen.

It was an item about a Florida minister who had organized the public burning of several thousand records and tapes. Teenage members of the clergyman's church had sung hymns while torching the work of various performers, ranging from Mötley Crüe to Lionel Richie.

"All right!" Doug laughed. "Begone, Satan!"

Neil read on in a monotone. " 'Young people here have come to see that this noise is in fact one of Satan's most potent drugs,' the Reverend Mr. Goodwin said. 'In destroying this filth, and the satanic messages therein, we have struck a blow against sin itself!' "

Doug picked at his strings and sang in a country twang. "Satan he's my buddy — Satan he's my pal — He buys me drinks at Milo's — When we go chasin' gals . . ."

"To hell with practice," said Neil. "Let's just do a human sacrifice. Any volunteers?" He turned a page. Aaron chilled inside.

"Can I see it after you?" Aaron asked.

"Sure. In a minute."

Finding an article on pop music in the Soviet Union, Neil read in silence as Doug tuned his instrument. Aaron put his case down and stood there. Then Neil lay the magazine in his lap, stretched, and handed it to Aaron.

Making a nonchalant exit to the kitchen, Aaron flipped to the "Random Notes" section. He avoided looking at the photo as he detached the section, hoping that Neil wouldn't notice it gone. Then he rolled the pages into a ball and stuffed them deep in the garbage bin under the sink. As he did so, the line came back to him: "The Spider is said to be deeply concerned . . ."

" 'Deeply concerned,' " Aaron thought. It would be great if they could print the buried truth, the truth that mattered.

159

"The Spider is described as too busy making money to think about his life or much else, but plans to sometime in the near future, barring schedule conflicts."

At one point in the evening, Aaron asked Mike to let up on the drums a little. Mike nodded agreeably.

"Don't worry," Neil said. "You can still go hard with Tracy."

Mike smirked down at the drumheads but the moment turned uncomfortable, with dumb smiles all around.

3

▾

Friday night, having closed the store, Aaron waited for Jerry. Doubtless he would feel no more at ease with him than he had all week; but once Jerry was gone, it was off to meet Gail and put an end to their quandary — or to draw it out. Who knew?

He disliked this sense of covertness — the feeling that had made him somewhat hyper today, while talking to Jerry. He would have to act cooler; a guy like Jerry could detect un-usuals and not let on. Joining the band had been one strike against him, and this thing with Jerry's brown-eyed daughter, for all he knew, could be strikes two and three. He considered whether he worried too much, but the thought of discord caused a quiver in his stomach and a thin whine between his ears.

Gail, though — she was worth the trouble.

Then Jerry was at the door and Aaron let him in.

"Hi, boss."

"How was it?"

"Mostly straight out till nine."

"Sounds promising."

Jerry hummed drowsily as he loomed about the cash and pecked at his calculator. Aaron eyed the clock and started pacing. Moving to the coins, Jerry looked up at him. "Why so caged up, tiger?"

Aaron stopped pacing and snapped into a casual pose. "Just revved up from all the business."

"Ah, that's what I like to hear." Jerry went on counting.

After Jerry finished and left, Aaron lingered on the back steps for ten fidgety minutes, time enough for Jerry to make the bank drop and go home. Then he headed for the square. He halted once to inhale the night air and then continued at a slower stride. Excitement suddenly overtook worry.

The dimly lit square came into view and he strained his eyes for Gail, but saw no one. He crossed the street and slouched on a park bench, legs outstretched. For the next several minutes he didn't move.

Where was she? Instinctively he braced for anger, for injury.

At that moment he caught the sound of running feet and turned to see Gail hurry from the shadows. "Hi!" he called.

Catching air, she patted her chest. "Stayed too long at Dori's. . . . Let me sit."

They sat, and he stared over at the town hall steps. Then he put his arm around her shoulders and she lay her head back. "I'll unwind if you will," she breathed.

"No sweat," he said.

"Easy for you to say."

"No, it isn't."

She started chewing a nail. With ceremonious care he pulled the finger from her mouth.

"So what's on your mind?" she asked, folding her arms.

"Guess."

"I mean, in particular."

He sighed. "I'd like to think we could pull it off — you know, hang out together without causing any heart attacks."

"That's a nice thought." She reached for his hand, and her touch was reassuring.

"It's funny," he said. "That first night I showed up at the house, I looked at you and I felt like the Glob from Outer Space."

"You weren't the Glob. You sure were a mess, though."

"Anyhow, after a while I started looking forward to seeing you."

"Me too. I liked talking to you. I wanted to know about you."

He looked at her and then across the street, wondering how he could get around this. How little could he get away with telling her?

A car raced up the street, and a young male passenger looked at them as he passed.

"Publicity," Aaron muttered.

"What the hell?" said Gail. "Vicki's already full of questions about you." She rested her chin on his shoulder. "Small town, Aaron."

"Yup. Small town." Stroking her hair, he smiled up at the street light.

"Well, here it is," she said. "For once I'm trying to be

hardheaded." Still holding his hand, she sat up and looked into his face. "In the first place, it's like I said. I have a day job, you have a night job. My weekends are free, yours aren't. And we don't have wheels either."

He wasn't smiling now. "Can't argue there."

Her direct attitude fell away and she dropped her head back on his shoulder. "I wish I'd met you at college or something!"

"Life's a bitch — ask your dad."

"That's no help. . . . But see, college is the other thing. I hope I'll be going in September and moving to Portland. There's a lot of ifs, so it looks like all we have is this summer. And to tell you the truth . . ." She broke off.

"Go on," he said.

"I don't really need anything heavy at this stage."

He nodded.

"It's the way the cards are stacked," she said. "And I guess I'm also feeling bad about Tommy."

"Yeah. I thought of that."

"So I was thinking we could keep it simple, keep it easy."

He squeezed her hand lightly. It felt so smooth, the bones so delicate. "And just make time when we can?" he said.

"Uh-huh."

"That sounds all right. As good as we can hope for, I mean."

She hooked her ankle around his, and they were quiet.

For all his resolve to be hardheaded, Gail had outdone him. This was a relief but also a letdown, deflating not just his fears but his fantasies too. His imagination would be taking a needed rest. Scenes that he dreaded would now fade, along with those he hungered for. No longer could he conjure Gail's mouth, face, and body so eagerly — not if he wanted to sidestep a bigger pain. Still, it was true, this was the best they could do. And now, any news of it that trickled down to her parents' ears wouldn't set off an alarm.

He glanced sideways at her. "I don't know what your problem is. I *like* your nose."

She laughed. "You're definitely a weird guy."

Before they kissed good night on the corner of Lark, he asked her to meet him for breakfast at the Evergreen tomorrow morning, and she agreed.

4

▼

Gail's laughter danced through the Evergreen, sputtered out, then sprung anew as she slopped coffee on the table. Nora was quickly there to wipe it up.

"Still about as tidy as when I used to baby-sit you," the waitress observed. They had arrived before the rush and Nora was doting on them.

"Listen to this," Gail told her.

Holding a copy of the *Sun*, Aaron read the headline: "Love-Crazed Swamp Creature Gets Girl Pregnant."

Nora huffed, waving the stained towel like a flag of surrender. "Elsie Jarvis must've left that there. I think that's where she gets half of her stories." She left them for some new arrivals.

164

"Keep going!" Gail urged. She cackled as he read on.

"Exclusive: How Elvis Cured My Arthritis . . . Justice Department Cites Extraterrestrial Drug Ring . . . Victoria Principal Joins Satanic Cult to Save Career . . . Iranian Psychics Causing Crazy Weather Patterns . . . Miracle Chocolate Helps Weight Loss."

He folded the paper and resumed eating.

Gail wiped her eye. "Well, I guess all that stuff has its purpose, 'specially out here in the sticks." She poked at her eggs with a fork. "Here in the good ol' thrill-a-minute sticks."

Aaron gave a groan and shook his head. "You and Doug! You and Doug and Neil . . . I mean, would you all rather get kidnapped by psychic aliens? Would you rather have a bunch of psychic aliens take you to meet Elvis and stuff you full of satanic chocolate?"

"Sounds like a good time to me," she said. "But seriously, let me tell you something. . . . Once when I was seven I ran away after this big fight with Mom. I was going to Hollywood, which I figured to be towards Bridgton, only farther." She took a bit of toast and wagged her finger. "I'm not pulling your leg — I was going to be the next Jodie Foster. Anyway, I got a mile out of town and this nice old lady pulls over and asks where I'm going, so I tell her. And she did this number on me, told me she was Bette Davis. I didn't know who that was but then she explained, and it seemed like we had a lot to talk about. That's how she got my name out of me and got me to her house. Dad zoomed in like two minutes after she called, and there I was in the middle of wolfing brownies. Jeesh, was I mad!"

Aaron chuckled. "Okay, but you were only seven."

"*C'est vrai, mon cher.*" Gail's tone turned instructive. "But it goes to show how early it starts."

165

"How early what starts?"

"Ambitions and stuff." She dabbed her lips with a napkin. "They may get more down-to-earth later on, but the main idea's still there."

Aaron didn't ponder the statement. Eating more slowly, he was picturing Gail when little, bundled up on a crystalline winter day or playing around the yard in summertime, growing up. It had become his favorite daydream about her. And he would have gazed at her instead of at his food, but he didn't trust what his face might show.

They wound up talking about favorite movies, until Gail had to go meet Vicki and Dori. Vicki had her mother's car, and the three of them were going to the mall in South Portland.

Later Aaron and Doug played basketball at the high school gym, which was open for weekend recreation and still decked with the banners of last week's ceremony. Amid the shouts of other boys and the resonant slap of rubber, Doug took two of three one-on-one games despite Aaron's aggressive guarding.

At the store Aaron found Jerry under a dark cloud. "McDonald." Jerry spoke the name as if it were an evil mantra. The cop had been in for a newspaper and a Megabucks ticket, he said, and had made some remark about litter in the front lot. "Now watch him hit the lottery. That'd be all I need to go nuts!"

Aaron went out to pick up the litter, but found only a few wrappers by the sidewalk.

The week opened strangely. In his prework hours, Aaron felt a change that left his mouth dry and his mind disjointed. His lone walks around town — to the woods, the bridge, even the tracks — had lost much of their serene fascination. His legs grew tired. Thinking about Gail helped some; but watching heat waves throb from the rails, he longed to be in Neil's garage or to do something more active and different.

He carried his discontent with him to work, where the chores, faces, and small talk melted into tedium like a flat stream. The radio did little to quell his restlessness. Once when the Spider's hit single came on, he simply turned it off and continued stocking shelves.

On Tuesday, four high school girls came in and took their time at the magazine rack, chattering over concert shots, movie stills, and star portraits. Aaron watched them vacantly until the shortest one picked up a *Rolling Stone* and started perusing it. Fixing his stare on her braceleted hands, the pages bending and spreading between them, he wanted the girls gone. One with a blonde streak in her hair looked over at him and whispered something to her friends. The shortest one glanced up and gave a low giggle. When they came to the counter, Aaron caught their traded smirking side-looks as he rang up the *Stone* and a *Tiger Beat*. As they went out the door he overheard one of them: "Kind of shy, ain't he?"

He hoped that his face had made less of an impression. That was the fourth copy of the magazine sold since last week.

Late next afternoon he was on the steps behind the store, using his library book as a surface for his pen and paper. He scribbled a line and crossed it out. The melody was in his head, but why were the words so hard in coming? Most of his songs had taken under half an hour to write. But this one nagged and evaded, like the blue jay he had seen dive-bombing a neighborhood cat.

167

From around the corner of the building he could hear Andy lambasting the latest gasoline price, and Jerry telling him to get lost. Aaron raised his eyes from the paper and squinted across the grassy rear lot. Lately he had felt bothered with lodging above his work place — an odd situation, when he considered it. In his off hours, he couldn't sit in his room without sensing Jerry's bulky presence or hearing his muffled voice through the floorboards, among those of customers. It would have been nice to live elsewhere in town, just for the separateness.

"Freeze!"

Startled, he dropped his pen and looked down through a space in the steps. Gail peered up at him.

"Jumpy?" she said.

"Not until now."

She picked his pen from the grass. "Well, you're lucky I didn't find a branch long enough to reach your butt."

He smiled. "You would've had to pay my hospital bills. Come on up to my office."

She climbed the steps and he moved for her to sit. "What's up?" he asked, taking the pen.

Her face had a hint of weariness. "It's been one of those days."

"How come?"

"Mr. Peterson lectured Vicki and me about talking too much on the job."

"That all?"

"No . . . I ran into Tommy on the street. He gave me this look and kept on walking."

He put his hand on hers. "Things like that are going to happen, Gail."

"Yeah, but looking back on it I still feel wicked stupid."

168

"Join the club. If everything you ever did was smart you'd be a tourist attraction."

"Well . . . I'll handle it." She looked at the paper in his lap. "What's that you're working on?"

"This? Words for a song."

"Can I see? Would you mind?"

"No, sure. But it's not finished."

She took the paper and spent what seemed a long time reading it. Aaron felt a sudden, anxious regret at showing it to her.

"Hmmm . . ." she murmured. "Who's it . . . What's it about?"

"I'm not sure."

She handed it back. "Right. Better clam up or I might blackmail you."

He sat still and felt his sense of threat start to give way, toppling before an urge to tell her all. His pulse jumped as revelations mounted on his tongue. Then she took his arm.

"Ignore that last remark," she said.

He pondered his squiggly handwriting. "Deep inside your dark again / I'm trapped again tonight . . ."

"Can't blame you for asking," he said. "It's not exactly *Sesame Street*." He folded the paper and stuck it in his book. "I have to head over to your place. Doug and I — "

"I know. Practice."

He got his guitar from his room and they walked to the house. Gail fretted about the state scholarship — there was still no word on it — but Aaron didn't really listen. He was thinking how close he had come to spilling his whole quirky history.

*

169

Ben showed up without Mike, and they sat waiting in the garage. Neil and Doug bitched about a tyrannical cook at the restaurant. Ben, with no trace of humor, said he thought he was in for a long summer.

By half past seven Neil verged upon a tirade against Mike, who then made his appearance — red-eyed, with a hazy grin — and breezed over to his drums. "Sorry, you guys. Five women in tigerskin aerobic suits jumped me. Wouldn't let me go till they'd had their way."

Doug chuckled. "So why didn't you bring 'em along, you greedy bastard?"

Mike looked sheepish and thumped his pedal.

Neil spoke. "More like *one* woman, eh Mikie? First initial *T*?"

Mike wiped his palms on his knees. Watching him, Aaron recalled his last sight of Mike and Laurie at the store, basking in each other's company.

"It's okay," said Neil. "Every band needs a token stud."

Instantly Mike looked glum and harassed.

"Think you can play stoned?" Neil asked.

"Yeah, I can play," Mike said evenly.

Mike's drumming held up well enough. The edginess passed as they got into the music, and their absorption of sixties material stayed surprisingly swift.

5

▼

Red, white, and blue bunting on the public buildings heralded the Fourth of July, which was tomorrow. Every few minutes a kid's firecracker snapped the quiet. Aaron walked the neighborhood streets until the sun was too hot for him, then went back to get his guitar.

Finding no one at the Fergusons', he recalled his standing permission and went up to Doug's room. He plugged into the amp at high volume and threw himself into his song, which for two weeks had teased and strafed and eluded him. It was a heavy, downward melody, and as he played it he pictured a giant descending a ladder. Immersing himself and mouthing the lyrics, he experimented with the hook until he happened to look up and saw Doug in the doorway.

Doug was in wet swim trunks and had a towel over his shoulder. "Sounds good. What is it?"

"A new thing — still needs work. Been at the lake?"

"Yeah, me and Slim. I finally patched up my bike. Tried to hunt you up to go with me but I couldn't find you. Anyway, sorry to interrupt but I gotta get ready for . . . Hey, shouldn't you be at the store?"

Aaron stiffened. "What time is it?"

"About twenty after three."

"Holy shit!"

He yanked the plug, threw the guitar in its case, and hurried past Doug for the stairs.

171

"Don't worry!" Doug called. "He's not gonna kill you!"

Arriving sweaty and out of breath, he faced Jerry's power-drill stare and started talking. "Hey, I'm sorry. I was . . ."

"Pickin' and grinnin', huh?" Jerry was looking at the guitar case.

"I just lost track of time. I . . ."

"Well, don't have a stroke," Jerry said, and puffed his cigarette. "This is the first time. Just consider investing in a watch."

Aaron was relieved. "Okay. I'll take this up to my room real quick."

"Not so fast, before I forget." From his shirt pocket Jerry produced a wrinkled twenty-dollar bill. "Know where I found this?"

"Where?"

"Under the ticket machine. Peg says it wasn't her who left it there, and I'll be damned if it was me." He waved the bill. "Aaron, this is what we all work hard for."

Aaron squirmed, feeling as if he had been splashed with boiling water. "Well . . . I don't know how it got there!"

Jerry stared harder. "Don't think you might've gotten absent-minded during a busy time?"

"I don't know!"

"Then take your lumps — cuz this is the last thing we want to get careless about. All right?"

Aaron stared into Jerry's plaid chest; its rumpled crossfire of colors somehow stoked his anger. "Okay," he mumbled.

"Fine." Jerry put the twenty in the till, then placed a pen and clipboard on the counter. "Now, tonight I'd like you to do some inventory."

All evening the scalded feeling clung to him, its senseless-ness frustrating him all the more as he moved down the

172

aisles, counting and losing track, jotting hurriedly, and mumbling to himself. He kept talk with customers minimal, gritting his teeth as business picked up. Once there were ten people in the store and he thought of calling Jerry for help, but angrily dropped the idea. In the back of his mind and then in the front of it, he wondered what other time he had felt like this. And in some slack minutes it finally came to him.

It was that time at Disneyland when he was seven — wandering away from his father and getting lost in the vibrant crowd, in the cartoon smiles and the whoosh of rides. His amazement had given way to distress by the time his father found him; and when the big hand fell on his shoulder — "I told you ten times to stick close! See what happens when you don't listen?" — distress gave way to a bewildered shame and resentment. Scalding.

But it wasn't the memory itself that made Aaron stand motionless in the doorway. The Spider's shouting, he now recognized, had been the sound of a shaken man, his grip the grip of a startled father. He thought of the poster in the record store. Could that really have been the same person?

Jerry was pleasant enough when he came in after closing. Aaron didn't look at him directly and kept his responses to yup and nope, nod and head-shake.

In his room he took his shirt off, threw the window up, and lay on his bed. The air still sweltered. This room, he thought, and this store underneath, and all its repetition . . .

After a minute he felt a stray breeze from the window, and the dark walls drew back. He did not want to leave Fox Hill. No place else had Gail, or Peg, or Toy Soldiers. And for that matter, no other place had Jerry. Maybe it would be best to do as Doug had: thank Jerry and explain, then look for another job in town — to make a little distance and lay some of the craziness aside.

6

▼

In the morning he wanted to see Peg — not Gail or Doug, just Peg. The thought of her calm, round face drew him to the house, where he found her out back with a garden hose.

She shielded her eyes as he neared. "Doug's still in the sack, I'm afraid."

"I just came to say hi."

Around her in the spray, a rainbow hovered like a spectral peacock. She pointed the nozzle away. "Isn't this garden a beaut?"

He bent to look, only out of politeness, but found himself gazing at the flowers, at their geometrical blossoms and precise flecks of color. The morning-glories hung like a clutch of porcelain bugles. To one dripping leaf, a ladybug stuck like a tiny painted brooch. A bee burrowed a tulip's throat, while a brass-colored salamander lay on a shaded rock below.

"Glad someone else can appreciate it," Peg said. "Reverend Ryan was by an hour ago but he's scared of bees." She bent down beside him and the light from the flowers tinted her skin. Despite her jaunty tone, something about her seemed removed. "Would you turn the tap off?" she asked.

He did so and she coiled the hose up. "How've you been?" he asked.

Wiping her hands on her shorts, she smiled slightly. "Fine . . . Okay, I guess." She let out a laugh. "I'm not one for straight answers today."

"That's okay. It's too hot to think."

"Stay put and I'll get us something cold."

She went indoors. Waiting, Aaron strolled to a pair of frayed sunchairs and found Peg's "spiritual strength" book in one of them, with a marker in the middle. Peg returned with two icy glasses of fruit juice and Slim wagging behind her. She placed her book under the chair, and for a minute they just sat and watched warblers flit among the crab trees next door. The dog panted and Aaron stroked his ears.

"So the Rev was by?" Aaron spoke. "I see him at the store. Always buys gum. He chews with his mouth open."

"Everybody has his dark vices," Peg said. "He must be a little concerned about mine, cuz he came to ask me back to church. I really should start going again. Maybe they need me at the bake sales."

"My folks were never big on church."

"No?" She scratched a bite on her arm. "Oh, well — some are, some aren't."

"It sounds like it matters to you. Do you want to go back to it?"

Peg mulled. "Our old minister was great. He could make you laugh and think at the same time. Mr. Ryan's a good man too, I suppose."

175

Aaron's curiosity sharpened. "Is it him, or is something else missing?"

She eyed him in mock reproval. "You think I'm out to plant my hang-ups in a young brain? Gimme a break."

"Maybe my young brain's already hung up," he said, returning the look.

"I would hope it wasn't, but what's hoping?" Closing her eyes, she sighed. "Well, I walked past the church last weekend and he had this sermon posted on the board outside: 'Pray to Win: God Wants You to Succeed!' For a second I thought it was a raffle announcement or something. I don't know. It just . . ." Taking a long sip of her drink, she flicked a hand. "Seriously, I better not get going or I'll start sounding like my husband."

Aaron plucked a cube from his drink and dropped it on the grass for the dog to lick. Occasionally his mind had turned on mystical questions; but then he would catch some stilted bit of dogma from a TV preacher, or hear one of his mother's bubbly, borrowed lines of Zen wisdom, or recall those flat-eyed smiles at Times Square, and the proffered pamphlets. "Read this! It's all about getting to heaven!" And like ripe garbage the whole subject would suddenly repel him.

He decided to withhold his own impression of Rev. Ryan, who seemed to him one of the world's dimmer lights. He was just thankful to feel more detached from the questions than Peg did.

Peg scratched her bite. "I suppose I'll go back and pray to be successful. Or just to be tough. That's a tall order when you have teenage kids, though." She took a gulp. "Your own mother could tell you what it's like."

"She never got around to it."

"Then I'll tell you. It's kind of like waiting for a photograph to develop. I'm sure there are better ways to describe it, but that's mine. You do your best to make sure the lighting's right and the lens cap's off — the basic things. But then the picture's been taken and all you can do is hold tight. And pray, maybe."

"I don't think you have to worry about that too much," he said.

"Oh no?" Again she closed her eyes and put her head back. "They're good children — in that department I hit the jackpot. But who's to say they won't marry the wrong people or turn into alcoholics? It's just about out of my hands now, so what can I do but say a prayer for them? And for Jerry, that he'll at least quit smoking. And there's the world, of course — that's a biggie."

Aaron placed his drink on the grass.

"Speaking of Mr. Ferguson," Peg said. "He tells me he gave you a pretty hard time."

"It was my fault," Aaron said. "I mean, it probably was."

"Well, he felt bad about it."

"Did he?"

"Oh gosh, yes. Furthermore I convinced him to close the store this afternoon. You're invited out to the lake with us for the bash."

"What bash?"

"Nobody told you?" She squinted at him. "Every Fourth, old Andy gets a permit for fireworks and badgers the Chamber of Commerce into footing most of the bill. He buys some rockets cheap and sets 'em off on some public land by the lake. Half the town shows up and has a cookout."

"Sounds like fun."

"It is. Doug'll be working but Jerry Jr.'s coming down. It'd be nice if you came along too. Just show up here around six."

He declined her offer to stay for lunch. As he left, he heard her scolding Slim away from the garden. Then he thought of his mother. What made one person strong and another fragile?

The question pricked him as he sat in his hot room, trying to write the letter. "Dear Mom, Sorry I didn't write sooner. I want you to know I'm okay." Through the floor came the deep, indecipherable roll of Jerry's voice, chatting with someone. Aaron crumpled the paper and left for a long walk up the tracks.

When Aaron returned to the Fergusons' their jeep was gone, replaced by Jerry Jr.'s blue Impala. Gladdened, he found its owner in the back yard, in split-kneed jeans and cavorting with the dog.

"Hey there!" Jerry Jr. called. "Dad told Andy he'd help set things up at the lake, so they're already down there."

With Slim in the back seat they drove off. Jerry Jr. asked about Doug and the band. "Gotta hand it to Doug for sticking with it like this," he said. "I'd be a little worried about him, 'cept I think Dad does enough of that for everybody. Doug's no straight arrow but I know how Dad is." He gave Aaron a telling smirk. "I suppose you do too, by now."

Aaron flickered a smile. "It's not so bad."

Jerry Jr. didn't slow for the rail crossing, and as the jolt struck he let out a circus-sized laugh. "I just . . . I had this flash from one winter when I had your job. We were fixing wind damage on the roof and Dad was having a bad day, which means I was too. So we're up there and it starts to sleet, so I monkey down the ladder and duck inside. Then I look outside and there's Dad, getting soaked and pointing at the sky, and it's snow-rain, rain-snow. And he yells up, 'If you're gonna do this to me, at least make up your goddamn mind!!' "

Aaron laughed, picturing it. He reached back and patted the dog. "Jerry . . . I mean, your Dad's a cool guy."

"Yeah, he really is."

Past the outskirts of town, the woods and meadows came up. Then Jerry Jr. swung the car down a dirt road lined with cars and pickups. He found a parking spot and they got out. The air carried the faint smell of smoke and food and the babbling of a throng. As they walked down the road Jerry Jr. stopped to throw a stick for Slim, and it occurred to Aaron that he could have used an older brother, one like this six-foot leprechaun whom he had met only twice.

Where the trees ended a fire engine was clumsily parked, with members of the volunteer department eating hamburgers around it. One of them called a greeting and Jerry Jr. stopped to talk. Aaron took in the pageantry before him. Crowded with kids and adults, a wide expanse of grass rolled gently down to the lake. Smaller children dashed around, trailing sparklers. Near the shoreline stood a flag-topped gazebo with a table piled with food and condiments, and a cordoned-off area just past it. Grills flamed at various points in the crowd, beyond which the lapping lake glittered like medallions. A red-glob sun presided over all.

Jerry Jr. finished talking and they strode toward the food, Slim trotting closely behind and full of canine amazement. Out on the water a speedboat droned along with a skier in tow. Aaron picked out familiar faces but avoided hellos, preferring just to drift through the laughing chatter. And to eat — the warm hollowness inside him wasn't from enjoyment alone. They got hot dogs from the first grill they came to.

"Bodacious or what!" Jerry Jr. exclaimed. Ignoring the plea

179

in Slim's eyes, he gobbled his hot dog and wiped his fingers on his jeans. Then, dreamily, he looked at the lake and rubbed his beard. "I was going to, um . . . I mean, just so you'll understand about Dad — believe it or not he's got a good feel for people, for what goes on in their heads. I guess he thinks that if he lets on that he sympathizes too much, everything'll go slack."

Finishing his own dog, Aaron nodded. "I can believe that."

"Well, it took me years to see it. Doug still doesn't, and that's funny cuz it hits me sometimes — he's a lot more like Dad than I am."

Aaron stared out at the bobbing white speck of a sailboat. "Wow — you think so?"

"It's a fact, my friend."

A family with a spaniel on a leash breezed past them, and Slim barked. Jerry Jr. seized him by the collar and held him in place, then smiled up lazily. "It's wild when you think about it. You grow up and in one ear you're hearing you're supposed to fight for all the marbles, and not take any shit while you're at it."

"Yeah . . . right," said Aaron. "And in the other ear . . ."

Jerry Jr. let go of the dog and gave a sedate chortle, more like his father's. "In the other ear it's 'Take whatever they throw at you and be a good guy.' Gives you plenty of excuses for going off the deep end. Whenever I look at Dad and Doug, that's what I think about. Sometimes Dad's so pissed off he can't hear himself, and I bet that's where Doug's headed."

Just then a chorus of girls' voices called Jerry's name. Gail appeared with Vicki, Dori, and two other girls and flung her arms around her brother. "Ow!" she yelped, and hopped back. "I forgot about my sunburn."

Turning halfway to Aaron she squeezed his arm, then knelt

to feed the last of her burger to the dog. The other girls smiled hello. Jerry Jr. talked with Dori about her infant-to-be, and Gail used the chance to take Aaron aside.

"So I hear Dad chewed you out?"

Aaron rolled his head back. "Shit, Gail! Did it make the evening news?"

"No, but did you think it wouldn't come up at dinner?"

He swatted a mosquito. "Where are your folks?"

"Somewhere over there." She pointed toward the cordoned area.

He spotted them with Andy, who was in a tropical shirt with palms and yellow triangles. Jerry was laughing and he and Peg had an arm around each other. It had been weeks since Aaron had seen them together. Remembering his first night at the house, he marveled that two months ago he hadn't known that the Fergusons existed, nor they he. To him they still seemed absurdly perfect, perfect even in their imperfections. The last time he had looked at the photos in their living room, he had experienced a bizarre resentment that he wasn't in them.

Gail and the others were all talking at once, but Aaron stood apart for a moment. In the lake's reflected sparkle the entire scene took on a trembling, fragile appearance. Even the biggest people looked small and delicate as Aaron stared, and this green place of refuge felt stripped of the safety that he had first imagined. Everything was fun, everything celebration — yet the water rippled a warning, the grass quivered a promise of pain. What would come from the horizon? The sky, once protective, suddenly did not belong to the tiny, untroubled beings who played beneath it. Calamity, sorrow, disintegration — though far off for now, these monsters could come. They could swoop down or invade by night.

Two little girls in smudged dresses ran by, and their squeals made Aaron's eyes sting. Quickly he looked at Gail and her brother, then at Peg and Jerry in the distance. He felt the happy-sad pinch inside, then a flicker of hate for anything that might hurt or scatter them — all the preying, prowling meanness of the world.

He was faintly sorry that Doug couldn't have been here to complete the picture, but Doug probably wasn't minding it much.

Gail, pink-limbed and wearing tan shorts, looked prettier than Aaron had yet seen her. She prodded Jerry Jr. to pass around a snapshot of his Millinocket girl friend, an attractive blonde who he said was a bank teller. Pressed by Vicki about marriage prospects, he joked around the subject. Then Gail unearthed some family folklore at her brother's expense.

"It was right down there by the picnic tables," she said. "Mom tells me we're heading home, go get your brother — and I find him wrapped like a freakin' python around Penny McAllister."

The girls cackled, the dog barked, and Jerry Jr. hid his face tragically. "Come on, she attacked me!"

"Fourteen years old," Gail went on, "and there he was — the bad boy of Fox Hill. So I go back to Mom and she asks where he is. And I go, 'He and Penny are . . . They're, um . . . They're catching grasshoppers.' "

Everyone laughed. They moved to another grill and as hamburgers and soft drinks went down, other tales rolled out — blowout parties and schoolyard fights, eccentric teachers and long-gone pets.

Sunset turned the lake a shimmering rose. Grill flames died but a bonfire crackled to life, throwing orange light across the crowd. Taking Slim with him, Jerry Jr. left to locate his parents. Gail and Dori remained with Aaron as the other girls

182

drifted off. Under the human babble, the lake sloshed like a slurred murmur as Andy circulated, his small, bright-shirted form moving from group to group.

"Mr. Greene!" Gail called. "Do we rate a visit?"

Andy wandered over and looked at Aaron. "Ten bucks of the no-lead, de-ah."

"You'll have to wait on that."

"Great shirt," said Dori.

"Why, thank you. How're you all doin'?"

"Fine and dandy," Gail said.

"Wonderful. My son-in-law's runnin' a final check on the rockets. Fire chief's got the jitters as usual, so you kids know to keep back from the roped area, right?"

"Yessir," said Gail. "I remember your big speech last year."

"So do I," Dori said. "Good thing you made it too. I thought McDonald was going to start shooting people."

Andy gave a dry chuckle. "Fawchunately he's out on patrol this time." Firelight tinged his gray hair and rawboned features, and despite the noise and frolic there was a kind of serenity about him. He glanced at his watch. "Well, gotta get back down they-ah. You kids enjoy yourselves."

"Thank you," they each said.

The tropical shirt moved off through the spectacle. "Everyone respect the ropes!" he called out. "One hundred and fifty feet from point of dischahge! Regulations!"

"When they finally put up his statue they oughta dress it in that shirt," said Dori. "Well, I think I'll go track Vicki down."

"Write if you get lost," Aaron told her.

Dori left and Gail looked at him. "You finish your song?"

"Not yet."

With night fallen, the bonfire's thrown shadows became a

borealis of limber phantoms. On the gazebo roof the Stars and Stripes wafted feebly, illuminated by a beacon beneath it. Then, down near the dark shoreline, people began herding closer together. Aaron felt Gail's hand slip into his.

"Gonna come see us at Randy's?" he asked.

"We were discussing it," she said. "I'm fishing around for a fake I.D."

His heart lightened. "Wanna go catch grasshoppers?"

Gail suppressed a smile. "No comment. Besides, we'd miss the . . ."

The first rocket whistled up in a spray of sparks and burst in a shower of fluorescent red. Its report mixed with a whoop from the multitude, and Fox Hill declared happy war upon the night. Missile after missile wriggled skyward and splashed red, blue, green, and white above the water, bathing upturned faces in fleeting daylight.

"Yee-ha!" Gail shrieked, and gripped Aaron's hand tighter.

Two rockets shot up in quick succession, one chasing the other as they mounted the darkness. Diverging, they ruptured, the first red and the second blue, and their glowballs spread in two perfect blossoms. Their pops resounded, reaping another collective cry as the colors spilled down.

Aaron went numb. Within the strobelike flashes he had glimpsed the gaunt, shadowy, gigantic face of his father.

When it was over, Aaron and Gail joined the migration from the littered grounds, and Jerry Jr. drove them and the dog back to the house. The Mr. and Mrs. were there just ahead of them, and Doug was already home. Everyone except Jerry Sr. sat around the kitchen, listening to Doug's funny description of his frantic night at the Patch. Then Aaron heard the low wail of bagpipes. He got up and went to the living room, where Jerry sat contentedly with a beer, a cigarette, and the record.

"Greetings," Jerry said. "Enjoy the mob scene?"

"Yeah, thanks for the night off."

"Actually you can thank my wife for that, but I figured you deserved it." He thumbed at a can of beer on the side table. "This Bud's for you."

Aaron took it and sat across from him. Listening to the stereo, he recognized the bagpipes' strain as "Amazing Grace."

Jerry spoke. "I ever tell you about the kid I had at the store between Doug and you?"

"Only that you canned him for being stoned."

"He was sixteen, I think. Even before I caught him with his weed I was suspicious about a few missing six-packs. So I'm saying you stack up pretty well, all things considered."

Aaron opened his can. "Well, thanks."

"I know it's not the greatest job on earth for a smart kid like you."

"Didn't expect it to be. I mean, I don't have my Ph.D. yet."

"Right, yeah. That's a good way of looking at it." Jerry tapped his cigarette in the ashtray. Stuck in a mound of ash, the butts in the tray looked like a clump of spent warheads. "Tell ya, Aaron, when they parcel out the headaches, they're not very evenhanded about it." A flat chuckle escaped him. "I wonder about all that when the tourists start arriving. In the summer they come to point at cows, and in the fall they come to point at leaves. They do a lot of smiling."

"Yeah, I've seen a few of 'em."

"I've seen a few thousand. But who cares, long as it's cash in the till."

Jerry Jr.'s laughter sounded from the kitchen, laced with

185

the others'. Sipping his beer, Aaron watched the smoke scroll up from the elder Jerry's hand. The bagpipes troughed and peaked, and he felt peacefully cradled.

"My father," he spoke, "he said once that you have to pretend you're in a comic strip every so often, or else you lose it."

Jerry yawned. "He got that right."

It surprised Aaron that he had pulled out a quote of his father's, though he couldn't recall what had prompted the remark or when the Spider had made it. "Jer, what did your father do? For a living?"

Shifting in his chair, the bearish man looked at him curiously. "My, um . . . He worked for the highway department. And before the war he was a logger. Used to say if he had a nickel for every black fly that bit him, he'd be golfing with Rockefeller."

"Was he in the war?"

"Yep. Came back from Italy with shrapnel in his hip." He snuffed his cigarette. "When I was stationed in Germany I took a trip down to Rome and poked around the graves at Cassino. I'm happy I was born late for that one."

Aaron nodded. "Me too. That one and all the others."

Jerry's expression turned sardonic. "Well, let's hope your luck holds out — in all categories." He put the beer aside and locked his fingers behind his neck. "Your luck and Doug's too — not that he's going to stop pushing it. You I still don't know too well — but Douglas! I swear his head's a lot thicker than the ice he's skating on."

Aaron glanced uneasily toward the kitchen, but heard the talk still going strong. "Doug's no fool," he declared.

"Well . . ." Jerry patted the air. "I know that. Of course I know that. But I'm a man who's tried talking sense to the

186

deaf, so let me spout off some. And look, at least I'm not one to play dirty. If I was enough of a bastard, all I'd have to do is change your work schedule. That'd sure screw up your little project, wouldn't it?"

"I'm glad you're not a bastard."

"As you should be," said Jerry. "I know there's no point in that. No matter what, you guys are set on having your fun."

Jerry's voice had tightened, and Aaron dug for the right response. "Doug has his fun, but he works hard too. If you could see him at practice you'd know it isn't just messing around. Besides, if you say we've got lots to learn, don't you think this is one way of doing it?"

"Not for anything that's going to be of much use to you, so far as I can see. And it's not like I'm telling him to rope the moon or else I'll disown him." Jerry gave a throaty cough. "I raised my share of hell at your age. . . . " Hunching his shoulders, he looked into his lap. Slim came into the room and lay on the rug between them. The Highland hymn dissolved, but Jerry didn't speak again until the record clicked off. "Don't misunderstand me on this. For one thing I can see him not wanting to work for me. Once in a while I don't even blame him for going the opposite way — looking at my situation, I mean."

Aaron was perplexed. "What about your situation?"

"Uh . . . I suppose I'm not alone, but there are these days when I look around and think, 'So that's it?' And it pulls my plug for a minute, makes me wonder if maybe I missed the punch line." The tightness had left his voice and he chuckled sleepily. "Sometimes the Mrs.'ll tell me, 'Just remember you're younger than Paul Newman.' She's a funny one." He stretched, rose, and went to the stereo.

187

Downing his beer, Aaron smiled at him as he put the record in its sleeve.

"Give me credit for being honest," Jerry said. He excused himself and went upstairs.

As Aaron returned to the kitchen, Doug was leaving for bed and said that he would see him in the morning. The other three were still talking at the kitchen table. The coat of arms on the wall caught Aaron's eye, and he examined its shield with the boar's-head emblem and knight's helmet, and the Latin motto above it: Dulcius ex Asperis.

"What does the Latin mean?" he asked.

"That?" said Peg. "Happiness from . . . what is it?"

"Joy from struggle?" Gail offered. "I never took Latin."

"Sweetness from adversity," said Jerry Jr.

Peg insisted that Aaron borrow a spare electric fan and Gail brought it down for him. With his goodnights said and the fan tucked under his arm, he headed back through the still night.

7

▼

Dear Mom,

Well, as Sitting Bull said to Custer — Surprise!

Here is my promised letter telling you I'm fine. I am not living in a cardboard box and eating garbage. I have not gone to Africa as a mercenary. I have robbed no banks. I have no nasty diseases. Everything's fine, except I've joined the Moonies and become a compulsive gambler. Just kidding. Fact is I've found a place I really like, with great people, so you can stop worrying. Getting better should be your highest priority. And I sure hope you're feeling better.

There's a lot on my mind tonight and I'm not sure where to start. It was just over two months ago that we sat under that tree outside the hospital, but it seems more like two years. I wasn't in the best mood then and things went unsaid. I'd like to fill in some of the blanks now. You said you didn't blame me if I was mad at you. I told you I wasn't, and it was almost the truth. I felt pretty numb. It wasn't you I was mad at so much as what you were saying and how you were saying it, especially about dear ol' dad. When you tell me I should start accepting certain things, I want to scream. Why don't you go look in a mirror and repeat those words, several times loudly? Like you say, it's hard for anyone to be consistent in this world, but I wish you'd listen to youself more. Don't your doctors tell you that?

The other thing is how your voice gets when you talk about the Bay Area days — Land of Sixties Rapture, the Summer of Love, Hippies in Toyland, beads and bells and music and gurus and garlands, etc., etc. It's not the subject I mind. I've always been curious, and that's why I let you go on about it. After all, if none of that had ever happened, *I* never would have happened. For me it's still mysterious. The basic idea, as far as I can tell, is that a bunch of people out there decided to trash the old and ring in the new. Result: the biggest, longest party in history. Sometimes I wonder if really I'm jealous of you, of the fact that you were right in the thick of it and have it to remember.

Anyway, it's not the subject that bugs me. It's just that

dreamy tone of yours — I swear it's like hearing someone read off a batch of greeting cards, over and over. All I can think is, "Yeah, Mom. Must have been a great time. By the way, have you noticed where you are?" And here I go, getting sarcastic again. I don't enjoy sounding like this. Shit, I never know how honest to be with you! I'm just frustrated cuz when you talk about your hippie-girl days I know it's just another way of talking about *him*.

Whenever I went to see him you encouraged me, said it had nothing to do with visitation rights, that it was good for me and everything — and I think you meant it. But it's also that I'm a connection with him, right? You want to keep that, even though it stirs up more bad memories than good ones. And at the same time you're scared I'll get changed or damaged or sucked in like you were, by that whole Rock Star Legend power scene of his. Am I right? If you think I'm off base, tell me so. But it seems that after all these years and trouble, you still want to stay hung up on him, and that's why you're still hung up on Back Then (I don't know — maybe it's the other way around). So when you gasp and sigh and do your Scarlett O'Hara — "Trapped! Trapped in the Spider's web!" — you'll understand why I don't laugh. I'm not trapped and neither are you. You'll have to see that, if you're going to start living again.

All of this might explain why I've blown my jets some-times, like when he sent me the car for graduation. I had to yell it out of my system before I wrote the thank-you note. And maybe now you can imagine how it felt when the Gimmix showed me the door and the lead singer — Gary, the biggest weenie of the bunch — said, "You wanna be a star like your father, go do it with some other band!"

190

That's always been weird. To the kids at Chase it seemed to be some sort of interesting joke. Nobody else there had a dad who'd busted out of the smokestacks and made a pile of money on songs and a monster guitar. A guy like him was someone you heard on a record or the radio — you didn't have him for a father. But I know I can't blame it all on that, for the way it was at school. The kids I got along with figured me for a rebel type and the others for a snob, but truth is I was just lazy. I'd think of trying to fit in, of making the effort, and this laziness would come over me. It seemed useless. In biology class I studied flower and insect mutations and thought of myself.

God, now I'm starting to sound like you!

I think I told you, I ended up not going to the Garden concert. I was vague about the rest, but here it is. That night I spent a half hour waiting in line, then threw my ticket and backstage pass down a sewer grate, and went for a long walk around mid-Manhattan. I came back to watch the crowd leave. For a minute I was sorry to have missed it but then I wasn't, because in my ears it would have been just so much feedback and distortion. The older songs in particular — you know what I mean. So I gawked at the glassed-in poster of him and Red Sky, and all these people wearing T-shirts with his face on it. First I felt dizzy, then so mad I nearly choked. I took a subway to his high-rise, feeling ready once and for all to look him in the eye. For years I'd had this fantasy about owning a blowtorch that would burn away all the lies and bullshit, and that night was going to be the Great Spider's turn to burn. I had a mouthful of fire ready to blow at him.

But when I got there I found a post-gig party in full swing. John Dwyer was there with his new Swedish wife. How that guy plays keyboard with all those rings on his fingers I'll never know — he makes Liz Taylor look like a nun. Anyway, he introduced me to Larry Logan, the new bass player — this bloodshot pretty boy who's a lot younger than the rest of them. He slopped his drink on the carpet and kept saying, "Great show, huh?"

Byron Ladd and Bobby Clive were there too, of course. Them I was glad to see, even though Byron referred to me as "Little Spider" (yeeech!). Bobby had one hand soaking in an ice bucket and held a drink in the other. Supposedly he's still a tornado on the drums, but he reminded me of a big old British pirate who's too laid back to rob anybody — the way he leaned back and said, "Ah, decadence!" His hairline's higher and he's gained weight. Byron's heavier too but he still wears that wide-brim hat and looks like a statue made of black iron, with that hiding-the-joke expression of his. I asked them both about their kids — remember I used to play with them in the canyon, out behind the house? Everybody kept offering me drinks but I wanted to stay sharp for my business with Mr. Legend. Byron and I talked guitars until I got antsy and excused myself.

There I was, just wanting to get this over with, but people kept getting in my face. Fulton, Dad's new manager, went into this drunk rap about getting a demo of my songs together and all the industry connections that were waiting for me. And as if that weren't enough, this reporter cornered me: "You have a pretty unique standpoint, and no doubt you've followed your dad's career. With the new album in mind, where do you think he's going?" "Philadelphia," I said. "Check the schedule." And I left the twerp standing there but not before a photographer popped one of me (see the next-to-last *Stone* — it's charming).

So I shoved along through the noise, wondering where

192

the hell he was, when I glanced into the den and saw Logan there with a little glitz-doll, both of them hunched over the desk. He was using a credit card to scrape some coke lines together. Then he noticed me and grinned. "Larry the Rock Star," I thought.

Then I ran into Kris, Dad's latest one. You asked about her and I forget what it was I mumbled, but actually she seemed nice enough. She's in her early 20s — a looker, naturally, but still nothing like you. Anyhow, by that time it was obvious I was in no shape for small talk, and I'm sure Kris was spooked. I felt bad, but the guilt made me angrier. She told me Dad was holed up with a reporter in the next room but to go right in — he'd be so glad to see me. What happened next was like . . . I wasn't scared, but I didn't move or say anything. At that second I realized that it wouldn't live up to how I'd always imagined it. And I also saw there was a better way of making my point, something I hadn't even considered. And I bolted out of there, so quick I knocked a drink from someone's hand. No awards for politeness. When those elevator doors slid together, they were like blades cutting me free.

I'm telling you this because I had to tell somebody, and I hope none of it upsets you. I also wanted to explain my frame of mind on my last visit. Going away was something I needed to do, and it wasn't to punish you. Someday when I feel ready I'll call you. Until then, if you want to write me back, please address it to Cunningham instead of Webb, c/o Ferguson, and please don't tell *anyone* where I am. I've gone to some trouble to make myself scarce and I'd like to keep it that way.

Well, I don't know what time it is but it's late. Keep fighting, Mom. There is only one Sylvia.

Love,
Aaron

Aaron stretched his arms, folded the letter, and stuck it in an envelope. The fan's soft whir had made him drowsy. Neatly he lettered the return address and then his mother's — The Institute of Living, Hartford. He would mail it tomorrow.

He pictured her face as he had last seen it, in leafy shade. Such a face she had — a fine-boned, neat-lipped oval of beauty. Only in the lines around her smoky green eyes could the damage be seen. With a dandelion tucked behind one ear and a leaf's shadow dancing on her smile, she leaned forward to beckon a squirrel. "C'mere, you. C'mere, sweetie." For that moment, all of nature smiled back and she was the princess, crowned with a dandelion and reigning kindly.

Once, one of her doctors had tried to explain it to him — her bumps and starts, and those novas of despair. "Your mother's a good person with good intentions. Clearly the past dominates her but that comes from a deeper problem, some terror she has about uncertainties. I wish I could tell you more. People are complicated, aren't they?"

Yes, doctor, they are.

8

▼

Aaron brought renewed diligence to his job, cleaning and arranging shelves during slow periods, while the radio played. When it got busy he concentrated on being efficient but still joked with customers. Thursday's gig beckoned but he kept his excitement in control.

A few breezy, bronze-skinned tourists dropped in for gas and postcards. "So where's the accent?" asked one middle-aged guy. His sunglasses were fish-tank green, reflecting pretzel images of Aaron's face. "Have a wicked good visit," Aaron said, putting on his best Down East drawl. "And don't forget to buy our lobsters." The man cracked a broad smile and gave him money.

On Tuesday evening McDonald strutted in for his newspaper and a lottery ticket. Handing him the ticket, Aaron grinned. "Hope it's a winner!"

McDonald darted him a look and grunted.

Gail phoned shortly before ten, with an invitation.

After closing, Aaron found himself at Dori's house, propped against the couch with Gail and sharing a wine cooler. Dori lay behind them, buttressed with pillows as they watched a rerun of *Remington Steele*. Her parents were away at a Lion's Club function.

"Gail?" Dori whined. "Let me have a sip."

"I'll go get you a root beer," said Gail.

"No, I want some of that."

Gail reached up and gently patted Dori's stomach. "You're a teetotaler for now, babes. A sip this time, a gulp next time, and then you'll be a chug machine like last summer."

Dori pouted. "It's from our fridge. I gave it to you."

"Yeah, so now it's mine." Gail took another swig. "Think of the ba — "

"I know," Dori moaned. "Gawd, nine months! Not five, not seven — nine stupid months!"

"Won't be too long," said Aaron.

"It's already too long."

Dori's sigh was extinguished by Gail's as Steele rushed onto the screen, knocking a muscle-headed henchman out a window and urging the female murder witness to testify. "Dumkopf!" Gail said with a sneer. "Do what he says!" Handing Aaron the bottle, she thumped him on the knee. "Why aren't you a private detective in a suit?"

"My suit's at the cleaner's. I threw up on it last time I saw this guy."

She crossed her arms severely. "Envy can do that."

Aaron watched the well-tailored star gun his car for a chase scene. Life without envy would be nice, he thought. "I don't know. Take away the looks, brains, and charm and what d'ya got?"

She hugged his arm to her side. "I'm just teasing."

Feeling her body's warmth, he inched closer to her and wished that Dori would fall asleep.

The program ended and the late news came on, starting with footage of testimony in scandal-plagued D.C. Almost immediately Dori nodded off. Aaron moved an arm around Gail, putting his lips to her cheek as she laughed at one jowly, droning senator. Just then a report from Beirut came on and Gail quieted. One quick cut of film showed a young medical worker clutching a bloodied infant and screaming to his comrades. Staring at the screen, Gail turned glum and inert. She stayed that way until she noticed Dori's slumber.

"Guess we should pack it in," she muttered.

She lay a blanket over Dori and they left.

"She was going on about Frank again tonight," Gail said as they walked. "Still thinks he's going to show up at the door with a ring in his hand."

"Any chance that'll happen?"

She shook her head. "Can't see it."

196

They passed into elm shadow near Fox Hill Savings.

"Tell me this," she said. "Is there anything that ever makes you want to cry your eyes out?"

It was one of her more original questions. "Neil on his bad days," Aaron replied.

"Why do I bother asking you things?"

"Okay." He pondered for a moment. The dark helped him think. "At night sometimes I look out the window and I think about what's going on out there. The worst stuff you could ever dream up. . . . I know it's always happening, or going to happen. To kids, old people — everybody. And nothing can stop it. I don't really want to think about it but it's like I make myself." Their pace had slowed. He noted Gail's sidewalk stare. "See, you should've stuck with my first answer."

"Tell me about 'out there,' " she said.

"You think I'm some kind of expert?"

"Come on, humor me. I mean, you've lived in New York, right? And maybe other places?"

"Not New York. It was Stamford, Connecticut."

"Always?"

"No, it was L.A. before that."

"No kidding?"

She stopped walking. He went on a step and turned around, and she faced him attentively. He glanced at his feet.

"Were you ever on a movie set?" she asked.

"My mom and I were extras in a crowd scene once. It was fun."

"So that's where you were born?"

"No, that was San Francisco."

"Jeez, you sure moved around!"

"Not really."

197

In the weak light Gail's face was brightly curious. "What did you say your dad's business was?"

Lies swarmed in his brain — advertising, imports, architecture. . . . "He's a professional musician."

Gail smiled. "Oh! I guess that explains plenty."

Staring past her to the brick wall of the bank, Aaron felt a sudden twirl of excitement. He was eager to talk, eager to tell. "There was this club in San Francisco called the Troubador. It's famous. That's where they met one night." He smirked. "Back when hair was long and acid was cheap."

"Wow. Was your mom a . . . a whatzit? A flower child?"

"Uh . . . Yeah, I suppose she was a flower child. Truth is I don't remember any of that cuz we moved to L.A. when I was a year and a half. That's where she had her first crackup."

Gail turned somber. "Her first? It goes back that far?"

"Yes, but she came back strong from that one. After their divorce she remarried and we moved to Connecticut. . . . " Aaron faltered as his excitement turned to alarm. "My mother's had her happy days. I . . . " He looked at Gail. Though she didn't smile, that nibbling curiosity filled her eyes. He felt shaky. "Could we walk?"

Sagging, she leaned against him and put her hand in his back pocket. "Sure, whatever."

Lark Lane came in sight. A car passed with a soft brush of air.

"It was Trouble in Paradise when I got home last night," said Gail.

"Doug and your father again?"

"No, Mom and Dad."

"Really?"

She chuckled. "You sound shocked."

Her amusement irked him. "I'm not shocked!"

"Well, surprised, anyway. People butt heads, Aaron. Nobody's going for sainthood."

"Okay, okay." He was surprised, though more at his own anxiety. "It wasn't real bad, was it?"

"Oh, no. See, Mom was typing letters, lining people up for some hearing on water quality. And Dad starts in, saying she's bonkers to think that all that stuff does any good in the long run. And that sets Mom off, saying she's sick of hearing those things. They both got pretty sulky."

Aaron frowned. "Glad I missed it."

"Well, they don't fight a whole lot. It was funny, really. . . . Um, here we are."

They halted and he saw they were across from her corner. Putting his hands to her hair, he leaned down and kissed her. Their arms locked around each other, and it was a while before they let go.

"So now I'm supposed to sleep?" she murmured.

Shortly after, as he sat on the steps behind the store, his head swam with set-piece visions of Gail and himself. He didn't resist them. "Why should I?" he suddenly thought. Nothing could be predicted, and this left as much room for dreaming as it did for fears. However dumb or drab or sad life was, happy things flowered as well. He had witnessed it in this town. Then he thought about Toy Soldiers. The band had something unique, and what if they did get a break somehow? Then he would have prospects all his own to share with Gail. Less likely things had happened to people.

He leaned back, closed his eyes, and laughed quietly. Tumbling through worry and hope, he wondered what had happened to their hardheaded selves.

*

199

The next evening they sat on a fallen tree by the tracks. Brushing pollen from her jeans, Gail glanced at the guitar case between them. "Aren't you going to be late for practice?"

"They can wait a little. I told Doug to head there without me."

Her face seemed pleased with the answer. Across the tracks, fireflies glimmered in tall grass, winking their mystery code. Gail took a deep breath. "You know, I don't think I've been out here since I was little."

"Wow. I would've been out here all the time."

"I just stopped coming at some point. I like it, though. It's peaceful."

"Yeah, except when a train comes." He swung the case down to his feet and looked at her. "Your hair's nice."

She ran her fingers through it. It was shorter, with kiss curls and a hint of henna. "Thanks. Vicki did it at lunch time. I was just sick of how it was."

Watching the fireflies, Aaron longed to lose the moodiness that had burdened him for most of the day.

"You nervous about Randy's?" Gail asked.

He shrugged. "Piece of cake."

"Aren't we cocky?"

"I'm not really nervous. A little, maybe." He bent to pluck a toadstool and twirled it between his fingers. Time had dwindled but he didn't want to go. "Wanna come with me? Over to Neil's?"

She looked surprised, then thoughtful.

"That's if you won't be bored," he said. "You could watch a movie on the VCR if you wanted."

"Thanks, I'd rather not."

He flicked the toadstool away. "Yeah, I guess that would be going public."

She shifted closer to him. "It's not that. I don't care so much about that now. But Neil's kind of hard to take, and also I'm steamed at Michael. He's a nice guy, but right now he's being a real jackass."

"You mean about his girl friend? Yeah, that's true."

A mist was rising over the grass, the fireflies like tiny lighthouses calling the lost.

"Jerry said something about you," Gail spoke. "Just before he left he says to me, 'There's a lot going on between those ears of his. I can almost smell the smoke.' "

Aaron half smiled.

Rocking, Gail stuck her legs out straight. "I also think he picked up on us."

"Your brother's a smart guy." It was time to leave. Aaron slipped off the trunk and took her hand.

Her mouth tightened sternly. "When you make your first million, you better remember me!"

"Sure I will. I'll buy you an RX-7."

"A Jag," she corrected. "Red with white side walls."

She hopped down and they enwrapped each other, her arms pressing even tighter this time. Then, with a decisive tilt of her chin, she took her lips away and let go. "See you tomorrow night."

"Hope you get in. I'll be ripped if you can't."

She headed in one direction and he in the other, carrying his case, but a short distance down the tracks he stopped and turned. Gail was a toylike figure, arms out as she balanced along one rail. He wanted her in a way he had never wanted any girl, in a way he had never imagined. He yearned to be closer and help her absorb the jolts that lay ahead. Yet from what he had seen, time could warp good intentions till they were deadlier than bad ones.

Jerry Jr.'s words came back to him: "In the other ear it's

'Take whatever they throw at you and be a good guy.' " What did it take to be a good guy? Maybe foresight had something to do with it.

When Gail clung so tightly, who and what did she believe she was clinging to? And beneath her statements, what was she feeling? He recalled the look in her eyes last night, the keenness in her voice whenever she spoke of life beyond Fox Hill. Letting her in on his main secrets, he sensed, would only make it worse. And keeping the past at bay was hard enough already.

He turned and started walking again. On both sides of him, gauzy shadows crept through the trees, bushes, and brambles. He thought of how people evolved, of what fate or chance did to them. How the shocks of a single encounter rippled outward till they encompassed whole lives. Shock waves, ripples — on and on.

His mother had begun like Gail, with a heart that was ripe and whole. Never a vanity queen, she had regarded her own soft magnetism as a minor, lucky accident, though in the end it proved neither minor nor lucky. Hers was the fuller sort of beauty that boys and then men sought to own, not just touch. Attraction and pursuit — the game was set up that way: an intricate maze with lures and deceptions and stratagems, plus penalties for guessing wrong. There was no escaping this maze, and all you could do was stay alert. But shrewdness had been alien to his mother, and when the blue-eyed Spider came along it was as if she had been waiting for him. For her he must have carried the promise of something more than just the game's end. And she gave herself in anticipation of that fabled thing — some prize that had glimmered long in her sight, out of reach like a firefly.

*

"One derelict down," Doug greeted him. "One to go."

Mike wasn't there yet.

"Sorry," said Aaron. "But these five women in tigerskin aerobic suits . . ."

"Yeah, yeah," Neil said.

Mike made a blasé entrance soon after and seemed inured to Neil's razzing. Practice began right away.

Four hyper hours later, Doug raised his arms in jubilation. "Are we good?!"

Neil lay his palms on the organ and leered up. "We're good. We're good."

They were.

9

▼

Randy O'Brien was blocky of build, with thinning hair, small gray eyes, and a wisp of mustache. In another time or place, he might have been a TV repairman or a small-time loan shark. But he was a club owner, and his purple designer-name windbreaker made sure that no one forgot. One of his pet phrases was "I'll level with ya."

"I'll level with ya," he said. "For our purposes here, I prefer bands with a girl singer up front."

Seated on bar chairs beside him, Aaron and Neil traded

looks. "Okay, Randy," said Neil. "Now that you've told us how much you value our services . . ."

"Now, Neil, don't get defensive. I'm saying I'd be tickled pink to have you guys here more often. Personally speaking, I love your stuff. But it's a fact of business that more people will shell out for a girl singer with curves. Now, I'm a businessman . . ."

"I know. You keep telling me."

Without looking at the bartender, O'Brien took a bottle of Mexican beer and fondled it. "I'm just answering your initial question, and all I'm saying is I don't know what's in the future. You're here tonight and that's fabulous. If life was fair, I could book you on a regular basis and offer a better financial arrangement. But let's face it, your name doesn't exactly light up the night." He took a long guzzle.

Aaron fished a pretzel from his bowl and crunched it. Neil was humming to himself.

O'Brien turned slowly in his seat and surveyed his kingdom. "We're growing and changing here. Next week we'll take the juke box out and put a big video screen over there. People need a place like this out here in the boonies. And word seems to be getting around, cuz we're starting to get a more sophisticated crowd." He ran a finger along his mustache. "Lately I've thought about maybe changing the name to something, um . . . well, something more sleek."

A laugh hovered in Aaron's chest, and for distraction he looked around. Seven o'clock, and there was only a sprinkle of locals. Two guys did stellar combat in the video-game corner, dispatching alien vessels with bleeps, boops, and rumbles.

Located on the Naples line, Randy's Roadhouse had been converted from a cold-storage place and was twice the size of Milo's, its stage higher and wider and the dance floor more spacious. A raised walkway with railings bordered three sides, with tables and chairs arranged on the floor below. The mahogany bar where they sat ran the length of one side of the walkway, left from the main entrance and right from the stage. "Tip Me or Die of Thirst," warned a Scotch-taped sign on the register, although the sallow young bartender looked more gloomy than menacing.

Randy's voice rose and dipped amiably, leveling with them.

"Whatever," Neil muttered. "Sure, Randy."

A short while ago Aaron had put some quarters in the juke box, which held some oldies. Now the Spencer Davis Group came on.

"Good box y'got there," he said.

O'Brien nodded. "Yeah, Adam — brings me way back, those songs. But the box has to go. The screen'll add a lot, I feel." So far, despite having been corrected, O'Brien had called Aaron by three different "A" names. Taking his beer, he eased off his chair. "Well, gotta go make phone calls." He winked at them and raised a fist. "Take no prisoners!"

As O'Brien moved away Aaron squeezed an imaginary trigger at his back. Then he returned with Neil to the stage, where the other guys were. Except for some wiring, everything was set for doing the sound.

"Why do I talk to that guy?" Neil groaned.

"Don't get defensive," Aaron said. "Personally speaking, I think the man's fabulous. I'm tickled pink about him."

"That spiel about girl singers — he pulled the same shit on us last time, just so he could Scrooge us on our money. So we didn't make people faint! They still liked us okay!"

O'Brien had insisted on a $150 ceiling on the door take, to help keep his public need-fulfillment in the black.

205

Doug, Mike, and Ben met them with smiles.

"So what did Randy-O have to say?" Doug asked.

Neil curled his lip. "Since he's got such a swank operation here, he's thinking about giving it a new name."

Doug handed him a pair of pliers. "Unofficially it already has one."

"What?"

"Randy's House of Herpes."

With the sound done and the club nearly full, the five of them got soft drinks and took a table near the stage. They all seemed keyed and ready. Aaron was calmer than he had expected, thinking more of Gail and whether she and her friends could get in.

The crowd was more of a mix this time — flannel-backed Fox Hillers, including some of the Milo's crowd, and a smoother, dressier set who kept more to themselves. Two overworked waitresses circulated. A red-bearded bouncer sat with a stamper and cash box by the door, while an immense bald one hulked along the walkway.

When the juke box went silent the band took the stage. Voices rumbled as they tuned up. The naked feeling descended on Aaron but he shook it off, struck a chord, and glanced at Ben. "No prisoners," he said, and Ben nodded.

There were yells and claps as Neil gripped the microphone. "Good evening! We're Toy Soldiers. We don't have a video yet but we hope you'll like us anyway."

On Neil's four-count "Good Lovin' " soared gloriously, followed by a string of their eighties standards. Aaron's and Doug's harmonies were strong and Mike's drumming more controlled. Neil's excessive posing appeared briefly, but Aaron didn't mind.

Dancing, however, was unremarkable through most of the set. Introducing one of his originals, Neil announced, "I wrote this next one and if you don't want to dance to it, may you find a bug floating in your drink." The remark had little effect. Angered by O'Brien's sleeker clientele, Aaron did the wind-up solo and scanned the crowd for Gail. He wondered if she had failed to get in.

"Shakin' All Over" came next, and with the first cascading riffs it was as if someone had scattered a wad of twenties before the stage. One couple got up, then another, then several at once, and the floor swarmed. Neil's voice snaked out and struck:

> Quivers down my backbone
> I got the shakes in my thighbone
> I got the quivers in the knee bone —
>
> Shakin' all overrrr . . .

The song writhed and sprang, shut down for the instant that it took Neil to hurl the three words, then struck again. The dancing boiled right up to the end, when claps and hollers rushed from the floor.

"That's more like it," Neil spoke, and with that Aaron began the ringing, building, clamorous intro to Tom Petty's "American Girl." Ben's bass joined in, deep and slow, like a calm voice answering a wild one. Doug's guitar licked around the edges and Mike made the skins suffer, and then Neil let go:

> Well she was an American girl
> Raised on promises.
> She couldn't help thinking that there

Was a little more to life
Somewhere else.
After all it was a great big world
With lots of places to run to.
And if she had to die
Trying she
Had one little promise she was gonna keep . . .

Aaron played to the limit as Gail's face flickered in his mind, and he wished that it was himself singing, graced with a voice like Neil's. On the final note he spotted Gail way over to his left, pressed against the rail of the walkway with Vicki and one of the girls he had met at the fireworks. He waved happily and Gail waved back smiling.

"Sit tight," Neil called through the applause. "See ya in a bit."

Two half-drunk older guys in faded denim met them as they left the stage, identifying themselves as musicians and spouting praise. Immediately Neil sat on the steps and started rapping about the Maine music scene. Aaron slipped past him to the table, where he and Doug grabbed extra chairs for the girls. Breaking into a smile, Gail squeezed his hand as she sat.

"Just get here?" he asked.

"About a half hour ago. *You* sound great!"

"Shucks."

"What about me?" Doug demanded

"*Meraviglioso!*" she exclaimed. She gushed several other Italian compliments before Doug cut her off.

"Okay, sis. Okay, thanks."

The harried waitress unloaded a fresh tray of sodas and Aaron shared his with Gail. Vicki and the other girl, whose name was Sharon, were anxious to know where Neil was. Aaron pointed him out, huddled with his two admirers.

"He'll probably give 'em his autograph," Mike said. "Whether they ask for it or not."

Sharon, giddy and petite, cast a long look in Neil's direction. "He is one cute package."

Doug gagged. "Gawd, break out the Maalox!"

Just then, over by the video games, a fight erupted in a whirl of fists and curses. People leaped aside. The bouncers were there in an instant, prying the two men apart and forcing them out the door.

"Another laid-back night at Randy's," Ben muttered.

Under the table Aaron held Gail's hand as the clatter of voices rose again. Customers thronged the bar, O'Brien working one end while the young bartender scrambled at the other, and steam billowed from the automatic glass washer. A big middle-aged woman spilled her drink and laughed hysterically. On the juke box, the Rolling Stones snarled like revenge.

Aaron looked at Gail's face and at those of the others. A smile came to him, and with it a reflection: on some long-ago night, in a joint like this, his father must have felt as he did now.

"You sure you want a Jaguar?" he asked Gail. "How 'bout a T-bird?"

She smirked. "I'll get back to you on that. Ah, look who's here!"

Fred lumbered up to the table with Bud behind him. " 'Scuze us," Fred said, tugging the bill of his cap. "We had to check these ladies close up."

Gripping his bottle, Bud teetered above Gail and clutched at his chest. "Pardon these scummy eyes gazing upon your beauteous self . . . your luscious loveliness . . ."

Gail snapped her fingers. "Darn, I knew I should've brought my shovel."

"Sure," Bud said. "Throw my nice compliments back in my face."

She gestured to Neil's empty chair. "Bud, just sit down and tell me how your wife's doing."

Mike left for the bathroom and Fred took his seat, quickly lighting Vicki's cigarette.

At that moment a rattlesnake riff started on the juke. Then the Spider was singing. "A hundred miles on the ambush trail / Racing the fire, racing the fire / Gonna find the ending to a jester's tale / Racing the demon's fire . . ." Aaron stared among the tables, expecting to see his father barreling toward him. Then he excused himself.

In the bathroom he found Mike sullenly drying his hands and asked what the matter was.

"That girl Vicki," Mike said. "She knows Laurie. I just asked her how Laurie was, and she looks at me and says, 'Why would *you* wanna know?'" He pitched his wad of paper into the bin. "Nobody has to tell me when I'm an asshole. I know." He stalked out the door. When Aaron came back out Mike was over with Neil and the two jabbering fans.

Back at the table Fred was pressing Doug about why the band didn't play any ZZ Top. Aaron asked Gail how Dori was, and she said that Dori had experienced some nausea and taken to bed. Bud was doodling with a pen on his place mat; Gail leaned over to view his toothy gargoyles. "Bud, I swear you're possessed!"

"The word is hammered," he said. "It's gonna be another sleep-on-the-couch night."

A wave from Neil ended the break.

"Sure you feel safe leavin' these honeys with us?" Fred said.

"We don't mind baby-sitting," said Gail.

They opened with the Romantics' "What I Like About You," Aaron's guitar scarring the air as people poured onto the floor. Everything went well until their Stevie Ray Vaughn cover, when Mike hit the drums too soon and Neil fired a look over his shoulder. Mike muttered an apology and they readied again.

In the lull, some guy yelled: "Do Def Leppard!"

"We don't know any of theirs," Neil responded.

"That figures, you faggot!"

Neil twitched, then peered out over the tables as the noise level sank. " 'Scuze me?"

"You heard me, faggot!"

Aaron spotted him at a table in the middle of the place — a stubble-faced blond guy with his head lazily cocked. The three guys he was with leered and snickered over their beers. All but a few couples had left the floor.

Neil stepped back from the mike, took an audible breath, and leaned in. "Okay, this here is what they call 'audience control.' "

Aaron and Doug glanced at each other.

"Now everybody here," Neil said, more loudly, "are you with me?" A smatter of yells answered and Neil raised his arm. "Let me put that another way: are you all in the palm of my hand? Come on, be nice! Is everybody in the palm of this little white hand?"

From all corners came a solid wave of cheers and whistles. Alert and unsmiling near the entrance, the bouncers looked like a mismatched pair of pro wrestlers.

"All right!" Neil shouted. "Then on the count of three, I

211

want you to turn and look at that guy — that fella there —
and yell these words: 'Shut Up, Jerkface!' Can you do that
for me?"

An avalanche of "YEAH" replied.

His expression unchanged, the heckler sat hunched and
silent.

Neil wore a mad grin. "So it's one-two-three and then 'Shut
Up Jerkface!' . . . One!" He held up a finger. "Two!" Another
finger. Amid whistles, he paused to let the moment build.
Then his hand swept down. "Three!"

"SHUT UP JERKFACE!!!"

The crowd's shout resounded, followed by laughter and
claps. With a faint smile the stubbled blond guy shifted in
his seat, looking to his companions and then at the glass in
front of him.

"Thank you!" Neil boomed. "I've always wanted to do
that!"

Aaron and the others passed a smile around, then geared
up once more. They lunged into the song and brought some
people back. At the end of it Aaron caught sight of the heckler,
still staring at his drink but no longer smiling. Two songs
later he and the other three men got up and left, and Neil
yelled goodbye to their backs.

Sloshed mayhem resumed on the floor and fell off only a
bit with Aaron's song. Holding fast to the bucking melody,
he watched people cavort to this song that he had tossed off
a whole year ago. He had written it as a theme for every trim,
safe, new-money neighborhood in southern Connecticut and
elsewhere. But tonight its origin didn't matter, and Neil sang
it with biting abandon:

> My car shines like a space ship
> And the sprinkler sprays champagne.

212

The insects on our lawn get drunk
And the weatherman says no rain.
Suburban Stomp is what I do
When report cards make me proud.
It's a dance for when your money's safe
And the TV's way up loud.

Suburban Stomp's the thing I do
So why don't you?
Suburban Stomp's the thing we do
So why can't you?

Vicki and Sharon danced with two Hale Construction guys
for the last couple of numbers. The clapping-in-unison began
as Aaron and the others returned to their table.

Smiling but bleary, Gail leaned to Aaron's ear. "I guess
we're outa here. Vicki wants to beat the rush. Hey, Neil's
good with the ad-libs, huh?"

"Sure is. Well, I'm glad you made it."

In the noise and guzzling, no one seemed to notice their
quick, nervous embrace. She got up with her handbag, yelled
goodbye to her brother, and laughed as Bud gallantly kissed
her hand. Waving, she left with the other girls, and Aaron
watched her to the exit. Then the band retook the stage for
the encore.

Except for Doug, who sat with the construction bunch, they
gathered at the bar's near end. Soon it was last call and the
great bald bouncer loomed about the tables, calling "Drink
'em up" in an oaken baritone. The bartender wiped the
counter, stopping to slide tips into a brass spitoon. Aaron's
ginger ale sparkled in front of him. He felt cozy and content.

Ben turned to Neil. "Quite the showdown with Jerkface there."

"Can't help it if I'm brilliant," Neil said.

The bartender was listening in and a smile crossed his hang-dog face. "Man, you oughta get a trophy or somethin'. I got a kick outa that."

"Well, I didn't, especially." O'Brien sidled up next to Neil. "You'll notice that we still get a fair number of two-legged germs in here, and it's no fun for me or my staff. So why'd you have to go and risk trouble?"

Gloomy again, the bartender left for the other end.

Neil rolled his gaze to the ceiling. "Randy! . . ."

"Seriously, Neil." O'Brien spread his hands. "Let me level with ya. If you're a performer, that's exactly the sort of harassment you've gotta learn to shrug off. If he'd kept it up, my guys would have taken care of it."

Aaron put a hand to his forehead as O'Brien persisted. "I've been in this business a long time . . ."

"Too long," said Neil. "I know a good nursing home."

O'Brien sighed, as he might have done with a waitress who had undercharged for a drink. "All I'm saying is that I know how these things are handled and that wasn't the way, buddy. Anyhow, I'll be around with your money."

Neil's head sank to his forearms as O'Brien turned away. "Thanks for leveling with me, buddy."

The bartender turned the lights up and holdouts started leaving.

"Sometimes I wish I knew how to make parcel bombs," Neil murmured.

"Never mind," Aaron said. "Randy probably got called Jerkface in grammar school." He turned his attention to Mike, sitting quietly on his right. "You were great tonight."

214

Mike didn't look up. "Thanks."

Doug came over and took a seat. He looked serious. "Fred just told me something."

"What species his father was?" said Neil.

"He said that guy you zapped was Dave Nolan. I didn't recognize him with his hair that long, but that's who it was."

"So who is he?"

"He was two classes ahead of us. Dropped out to join the navy. He's wacked."

Neil wrinkled his forehead.

"They called him Bedbug," Doug said. "I only knew him to say hi to."

Mike stirred. "Yeah . . . I remember him. But back then he didn't seem *dangerous*-type crazy."

Doug nodded. "No, but he's bad news nowadays. Fred says the navy booted him and he came back screwy, 'specially when he's hammered — been in jail more than once. They eighty-sixed him from Milo's."

Suddenly Aaron recalled that stubbled face and wiry frame: Nolan was the guy who had caught him dancing to the store radio several weeks ago. Selling Nolan beer, he had noted the red-rimmed eyes and an air of what seemed like shyness.

"Don't know who his friends were," Doug said. "Not from around here, I don't think."

Neil sat up, sliding his glass from hand to hand. "So what are you telling me?"

"Just to be careful," said Doug.

"How? Leave town? Hire a bodyguard?" His tone was irritated, but no one replied.

Having stacked the chairs, the bouncers sat for drinks with the two waitresses. Their chuckles buffeted the quiet. Neil and Doug undid the wiring, and they were ready to load out

215

when O'Brien brought the open cash box over and placed it on the edge of the stage. "Here you go, and I must say you guys earned it."

"And without a girl singer," said Doug. "Imagine that."

Neil sat cross-legged beside the box, watching O'Brien's pale hands count out $150. "Hey, Randy — now that we're the hottest thing since Three Mile Island, why not drop a little extra? Just to show you're a man with taste."

O'Brien handed him the wad. "Sorry, Neil, a deal's a deal. Hey, that rhymed." He took the box and headed for his office.

Neil counted the bills and muttered, "Are you for real, you slimy heel?"

"Let's blow this dump," Doug said with a yawn.

Out in the rear lot, they had just loaded the organ and Ben and Mike had gone back inside for the Leslie amp when a pair of headlights swung around the corner. The mag-wheeled car braked with a screech. Aaron was standing in the back of the pickup with Neil. On the steps, Doug looked up from securing the doorstop. "Oh, shit," he whispered, as four figures emerged purposefully from the car. One of them walked with a stoop but was still the tallest, his blond head glinting in the security light. The four approached at a leisurely gait. Neil stepped between his organ and the endangered side of the truck.

Lugging the amp, Mike and Ben pushed past Doug down the steps and were almost to the truck when they paused to stare. Quickly they loaded the amp and faced the intruders, who halted several yards away. Cocking his head, Nolan put his hands to his hips.

Doug spoke. "What's the deal, Dave?"

"Nothin' with you," Nolan rasped. His face was hard to see, but he stood and sounded like a man facing a dull task that couldn't be postponed.

Neil hopped down beside the others, and Aaron followed suit.

"It'll just mean jail again," Doug said.

"My business," Nolan muttered, and spat. Wobbling a bit, he took a step forward.

Hurriedly Aaron tried to figure the odds. Two of Nolan's companions were of average size; the third was small but husky. Five to four — five sober guys who preferred music to fighting versus four older, not-so-sober guys for whom fighting rounded out the night. Pretty even, he thought, but it would still be nice if the bouncers checked in.

"Nothin' with you, Ferguson," Nolan repeated. He made a lazy gesture to his henchmen. "They're here to watch. It'll just be me and Junior there. I don't take that kinda shit."

"You don't like it, don't dish it out!" Neil blurted.

Nolan's chuckle floated through the lot. "Shut up, fag." His buddies moved up alongside him. One of the bigger guys swung his arms back and forth, boxer style. His arms were thick.

Doug stayed calm. "Come on, Dave. You know what'll happen."

"What'll happen is a queer getting his ass kicked, 'cept if the rest of you wanna get it too."

Ben spoke up. "O'Brien'll just call the cops. You're gonna end up . . ."

Nolan swore, and his voice contorted. "That was your chance!"

At that instant the arm-swinger rushed Aaron. Using the man's momentum, Aaron twisted upon impact and locked an arm around the big neck, forcing him down and head first against the truck. With a guttural cry the assailant rolled on the pavement, and Aaron spun to see the fist-flurry under way. Neil was on his back and Doug grappled with Nolan.

217

Mike had the short husky one down but Ben was having trouble with the remaining guy. Blocking a kick, Ben tripped sideways as Aaron rushed the flailing shape and drove a punch to the stomach. The guy buckled, but then he lurched back and swung. Aaron took a rocking blow to the face. He felt his arms go limp as the man wound up for a second punch. Just in time, Ben grabbed the guy from behind and held on as the bouncers appeared. The red-bearded one went to Ben's aid and the great bald one to Doug's, pinning Nolan to the truck as he cursed and wriggled.

"Chill out!" boomed Nolan's subduer. "Settle down or I'll break your fucking neck!"

Nolan writhed a half minute longer before he slumped gasping under the fat man's weight. Redbeard shoved Ben's and Mike's opponents to the car, while Aaron's victim lay holding his head and moaning.

With a drink in his hand O'Brien stood in the doorway and pointed down at Nolan. "The cops'll be here any second. You and your apes better move out fast, and don't look back."

Redbeard helped the head-bashed guy into the car's back seat. The bald one cautiously released Nolan, who spat and stumbled his way to the vehicle. Getting into the passenger seat, Nolan paused. "Later," he spoke. "*Later,* you assholes." He slammed the door and the car started, scraping a log fence as it backed up. Then it turned and peeled away.

The bouncers lumbered back inside. "Need this like a fuckin' hernia," grumbled the bald one.

Then it was just Aaron and the other four, with O'Brien's blocky form above them. Blood streamed from Aaron's nose and down his shirt. The lot swayed beneath his feet, and a noise like a TV test pattern filled his head.

Cradling his drink, O'Brien sighed and looked over at Aaron. "Y'okay there, Arnold?"

"Fine, Ralph."

O'Brien scratched his mustache. "Well, Neil, this is exactly what I meant. I didn't call the cops, so you can finish getting your stuff."

He went inside and no one spoke for a minute. Doug stood holding his chin. Ben picked up his glasses and examined a broken hinge. Still catching his breath, Mike sat beside Neil on the tailgate. Neil checked a scrape on his arm, then turned to look at Aaron. "Jeez!"

"I'm all right," Aaron said. "I don't think it's busted."

Neil slid from the tailgate, kicked the bottom step, and stormed inside. Doug and Ben followed. From the truck, Mike got Aaron a rag for his nose and he held it till the flow stopped.

Under the bouncers' sullen looks and the skittish eyes of the waitresses, they moved the rest of their gear. They were tying the canvas cover when O'Brien reappeared at the door.

"Neil," he spoke. "No calls in the near future. This was all quite unnecessary."

Pulling a knot, Neil didn't look at him. "Fine with me. There's a lot better places than Randy's House of Herpes."

O'Brien jammed the door shut and Aaron laughed.

On the chance that the mag-wheeled car might be waiting for them along the main route, Mike chose a back road. Halfway home, Aaron hunkered down out of the wind and looked across at Doug. "How's your chin?" he asked.

"It'll be a little swollen," Doug said.

With the bloody rag Aaron touched his nose and cheek gingerly, then scratched dried blood from his lip.

Doug shook his head. "Neil's so weird. He asks me for the tenth time if I'm okay and I say sure. Then he says, 'Man, you know some real morons!' I mean, as if he doesn't know his share! There's more than one type of moron, and he knows a few."

"He just feels bad about it," Aaron said.

The forest smells rushed over them and he felt dizzy again. Beside him, Ben scrutinized his glasses and carefully put them on.

Doug shifted in his cramped space and tilted his head back. "It's true what Mike said — Dave didn't used to be . . . like he is now. I think my brother even went hunting with him a couple of times in high school. It's wild."

Aaron made no comment, since talking hurt his head.

10

▼

He awoke with a landslide headache that didn't entirely dissipate by work time. Jerry grimaced at the bruise on his cheek. "Gawd, Aaron! Ever think of learning karate?"

Throughout the evening customers gave him looks and some asked what had happened, and he condensed his answer to "a fight at Randy's." Men chuckled and women didn't, but all of them shook their heads. Aaron tried to limit the talk. Keeping the radio on Jerry's station, he was grateful for the soothing Celtic airs.

Gail arrived with a pained expression and stayed for a few minutes, condemning Nolan and his friends as human garbage. Aaron almost flinched as she planted a kiss beside the bruise. After Gail, Fred came in and ogled the bluish spot.

"I knew it," he said.

Aaron granted him a fuller description of what had happened.

Fred laughed. "Well then, you'll be glad to hear who's back in the slammer!" In the wee hours, he said, Officer Porter had sighted Nolan stumbling alone on the roadside, and handcuffed him after the guy screamed some drunken abuse. Apparently Nolan had become too much even for his drinking buddies and they had ditched him.

The surge of Friday-night business hit after dinner time. Unable to rev up as before, Aaron made a decision and a quick phone call to Jerry, who arrived in a minute and opened the other register. Side by side they worked smoothly for an hour, and against Aaron's expectation he felt no loss of pride at needing the help. Jerry's large, competent presence was a comfort. They easily handled the rush, which ended in another hour.

"I think it'll be okay now," Jerry said.

"Thanks a lot," said Aaron.

"No problem, pal. I'll be back at the usual time."

Shortly after Jerry left, Peg swept in to examine Aaron's cheek. She touched his face lightly and leaned close.

"Déjà vu — eh, Peg?"

"Yeah, really."

"In case Doug didn't tell you, we won't be playing Randy's again."

"That snake pit!"

"Don't be upset about it."

Just then a touristy-looking couple came in and asked for directions to a hotel. Peg obliged them, and they thanked her and left. She stood there looking outdoors. "Nice people," she said, and rubbed her forehead. Aaron was staring at her.

221

Then she looked at him and smiled crookedly. "I wasn't going to bring this up, but I might as well." She wandered to the dairy cooler and leaned there. "I ran into Nora St. Pierre yesterday. She said she served Gail at the Evergreen not long ago and 'that nice boy who's working for you.' "

Aaron's stare fell into a corner.

"Gail was talking about you at dinner," Peg continued. "About hearing you last night, and about your battle scar there. I watched her and there were certain things I could tell from her face, from her tone. So I talked to her privately — not to anyone else, just to her."

Aaron raised his eyes. "Peg, we're not up to our necks in it, if that's what you're worried about. We talked it over. Gail's got school in the fall and everything. She said it herself, that it shouldn't get heavy."

Peg gave him a sadder, fonder smile. "You're no garden variety eighteen-year-old, but you have lots to find out — especially about females your age. If you're too literal-minded with them you're going to wind up awfully confused."

Aaron opened his mouth but couldn't think of anything to say. So much for the official version of Gail and himself, he thought. If only Peg knew how familiar he was with that gap in people — the gap between word and feeling, action and desire.

"Honey, I'm not playing the watchdog Mom here," said Peg. "Well, maybe I am. . . . Now that I think of it, I could've predicted this. But you're both young, and that's just for starters. You and I talk pretty well and you know I think a lot of you. But I still don't know beans about what you're from. Neither does Gail. And what people come from has a lot to do with how they handle things."

Pressing his fingertips on the counter, he watched a fly cross its dappled surface.

222

"Don't be hurt by this," she said gently. "I'm thinking of you too. We all want you around, but you won't be here forever. So what are you going to do? How long do you think all of this'll last for you?"

The headache was staging a counterattack. "I don't really know yet," he said.

"Well, it's not the fairest question, but you see what I'm driving at. And just keep it in mind about Gail, for both your sakes. We're talking about a girl who still has a big stuffed giraffe in her bedroom."

Stiffly he nodded. "So how do you think Jerry'll see this?"

She shrugged. "Aw, he knows you're no teenage werewolf, so don't fret." Chuckling, she shook her head. "Seems I'm always telling you not to worry. I should take my own advice."

With that, Peg's calm nursing style returned. She asked whether he had taken aspirin and he told her yes. She suggested that he come for dinner again soon and told him to sleep well. Then she touched his hand and was gone.

Later, when the last beer buyer had left, Aaron paced around and tried to stop thinking. Dread tangled with curiosity as he went to the magazines and reached for the latest copy of *Spin*. In the "Flash" section he found a single paragraph with no photo.

On June 26 Michigan favorite son Danny Webb and his Red Sky Band hit Cobo Hall in Detroit, scene of the Spider's mid-sixties scuffling days. Proceeds went to a civic jobs program to discourage street-gang activity. During the sold-out performance it became clear that Webb has survived his solo years with temper intact, when calls for his 1969 hit "Eyes in the Storm" prompted him to snap, "I don't do that one anymore!" Tour-related tensions may have been to blame, but afterward the Spider refused comment. Meanwhile his and Red Sky's *Thunderhead* album spent its twelfth week in the top ten and the reunion tour continues to draw its expected legions. Webb's life took one unwelcome twist in May, however, with the strange disappearance of his teenage son, Aaron, whose whereabouts remain unknown.

Jerry got there promptly at ten and did his counting. If he knew anything yet about Aaron and Gail, he wasn't letting on. Moving a stack of quarters, he brushed a dollar off the counter and Aaron retrieved it. Jerry took the bill and looked concerned.

"Sure you're all right?"

"Why?"

"Your hand. You've got the shakes."

Aaron stuck his hands in his pockets. "I wish I'd demolished that guy last night."

"Relax. Be glad he didn't demolish *you*." He resumed arranging the coins. "Keep shakin' like that, your bright future as a minstrel's going to look questionable."

With Jerry gone Aaron walked up the roadside in the other direction, beyond the lights and houses. A few cars drove past him in the moonglow. He stopped after about a mile, with trees on his side and tall grass on the other. A full moon shone through the tree tops, its seas like a ragged birthmark. Farther down on the field side, he could see the plank fence of Andy's junkyard. Then he noticed a small, dark mound near the midline and stepped over to it. It was a porcupine mashed through the middle; with bristles scattered, it awaited the flies of daylight.

224

Peg's voice echoed in the silence: "What are you going to do?"

There was Gail, his job, the band, the statewide contest — this was his life now. But what would come later? And what had he been expecting? It would have struck him as funny, if not for the sick, unanswerable worry that wrung him and wouldn't let go. He touched his cheek and it hurt.

The empty road ran flat from where he stood, tree shadows lancing across the pavement till it faded in dark nothingness.

PART FIVE

▾ ▾ ▾

Shadow Song

1

▼

Walking slowly down the road, they were almost at the corner where Gail had said she would turn back. The sun cast a blinding haze through the woods. Aaron had thought they might discuss their separate sessions with Peg this past weekend, but somehow neither of them had mentioned the subject. His guitar case felt heavier.

Gail picked the petals of a daisy as she walked, then dropped the naked stem. "Why couldn't you blow off practice just this once?"

Her sullen tone took him off guard. "The contest's a week from today. We need all the playing time we can get." She gave no response and he looked at her. Her pearl graduation earrings looked out of place with her jeans and T-shirt. "Next Thursday for sure," he said.

Looking straight ahead, she nodded. A Bogart classic was playing tonight in the basement of the Unitarian Church. She wanted to see it with him and if not that, to do something else together, even if it was just another walk along the railroad tracks.

"Okay," she said. "All right, but it's just such a shitty spot we're in. And it's the middle of July already."

He frowned. The bruise on his cheek hurt. "Look, it's like we both said. I wish it was different, but right now it's not. After the contest maybe . . ."

"Uh-huh. Fine."

Aaron stopped in his tracks and put his case down. Gail halted with her back to him, then turned lazily on her heel. They were just short of the corner. Crossing his arms, he felt queasy. "They're depending on me," he spoke.

"Yeah, of course they are."

"So what about what you said? About keeping it simple?"

Gail's hands fidgeted at her waist but her eyes were direct. "I remember what I said about it, but doing it's a lot harder. Sometimes when I'm with you I wonder if you'd rather be off doing your own stuff."

His arms dropped to his sides. "When I'm with you it's cuz I *want* to be! I want it to be more often!"

"Well, I've seen Doug in this love affair with his guitar, and I've also heard him talk. Guys join bands and they get obsessed. If they're not messing around with their instruments they're thinking about girls falling all over them."

"Didn't you hear what I just said? Is this a 'pick me or pick that' type of deal?"

"No! I'm not like that!"

"Then what is it?"

Her lip quivered, but then she seemed to compose herself. A car sped past and honked but they didn't look. Reaching for her hands, Aaron hoped that she wouldn't pull away. She didn't.

"If you feel bad, so do I," he said. "But next week it'll be better."

"I know. But I just realized what's really bugging me." She sighed. "It's nothing new. There are these moments when it feels like we're close, but then I think, how can that be? You seem far away. You hold yourself back all the time and it's like we're stuck."

230

"You'd rather I was the type to spill my guts?"

Wearily she shook her head. "No, that's not what I'd rather. I just want you to relax and trust me."

He didn't look at her face but at one earring; it gleamed like a congealed white tear.

"I get sad about it," she said. "It's wicked frustrating."

He squinted at the sun. "Yeah, I can see that."

"I better let you go. I'm making you late again."

"Doesn't matter. See ya."

She hugged but didn't kiss him. Holding her stiffly, he pressed his lips to her cheek.

They parted and he didn't look back. A shaky desperation took hold as he remembered Gail's New York reveries, her dazzled ideas of L.A., and all her daydreams. With these she awaited the facts on Aaron Webb, ready to swallow and transform them into some spangled novelty, something that wasn't him but that she might well prefer.

On his arrival at Neil's he found all but Mike flopped around the living room, with a movie on the VCR. "Congratulations," Neil spoke. "You beat out Mikie again." He reached for the remote control and clicked the movie off. "That was stupid anyway. Let's go on out."

Even with the door up, the garage was hot as they waited for Mike. Neil talked about wanting to buy a laser disc player. Ben looked downcast and when Aaron asked why, Ben said he had overslept the morning after Randy's and come to work late. The tyrannical cook had yet to let up on him for this.

Doug said it was high time for deciding which songs to do for the Battle of the Bands. In their fifteen allotted minutes on stage, they could do only four or five.

"We should do two or three originals," said Neil. "The judges might be impressed."

231

"And 'Shakin' All Over,' " Aaron said.

"And 'Rain on the Scarecrow,' if there's time enough," Doug added.

Aaron hesitated before he spoke again, then decided not to miss the chance. "I've been thinking about something we could do instead. Another old one. We still have time to learn it."

"Shoot," said Doug.

"It's by Danny Webb. It's called 'Dead End . . .' " He broke off as Neil rolled his eyes.

"Webb!" Neil spat. "Talk about major-league sellout! You *like* him?"

Aaron opened his mouth but his tongue snagged.

"He's okay," Doug said mildly. "I have one of his records and it's . . ."

"Agh!" Neil cried.

"It's a good song," Aaron muttered, still staring.

"No way," Neil said, with a head-shake. "No geriatric millionaire hippies. As far as I'm concerned, the man sucks." Walking to the garage entrance, he put his hands on his hips. It was nearly dark outside. "And you know who else sucks? Mike! Where the hell . . . ? No, I can guess!"

Aaron looked down at his fretboard and started picking tunelessly. His insides boiled.

Then Mike came striding up the driveway and brushed past Neil without a glance. His face was rocklike, unsmiling as he sat behind his drums and picked up his sticks. "Sorry. I was — "

"That's okay!" said Neil, spreading his arms wide. "Just tell us how ol' Tracy's doing!"

"Shut up!" Mike bellowed, and flung his sticks aside. "I know I'm late but I've had it with all your shit! I've listened

232

to you for a whole fucking year and . . ." He faltered and just sat there bristling, eyes burning at Neil. Then he stared down at his drums and nobody moved or spoke.

Looking hurt and confused, Neil stood there like a wobbly ninepin. "I was just . . . I was just jokin' around."

Mike rubbed his knees. "I know. I know you were. Just don't mention that name to me, okay?"

Neil straightened up and recovered a little. "Wanna beer?"

Mike nodded and Neil left for the kitchen.

Slumping, Mike put an elbow on his snare drum. "Sorry, you guys. I was talking to Laurie."

"How'd it go?" Doug asked.

He shrugged. "Don't know. Mostly it was me admitting I was a dork. She didn't say too much." He gave a sneering chuckle. "Meanwhile I find out that Tracy's got a couple of nicknames — Racy Tracy, Miss Hit-and-Run. That last one sure fits."

"We all mess up," Doug said.

"Not this bad."

"Oh, yeah," said Aaron. "This bad and worse."

Quietly Ben retrieved the drumsticks for Mike, and Neil returned with a six-pack. Taking a bottle, Mike thanked him. Aaron adjusted a string and declined the offer.

Once during the session, Aaron stole a long side-look at Neil and felt his stomach knot up. Later he struck a wrong chord and swore, nearly kicking a mike stand over. Doug gave him a surprised glance. "Too many drugs," Aaron said, forcing a grin.

"Got any left?" Mike asked.

Despite the late start, they quit early and Aaron started home with Doug. "Been meaning to ask you," Doug said. "You and Gail . . . You two have something going?"

Aaron kept his eyes on the pavement. "Sort of. Did she tell you?"

"Naw, she doesn't tell me those things. It's just that when she left Randy's I thought I saw you hug goodbye."

"Oh." Clumsily Aaron switched his case from his right hand to his left. "I'm being a Boy Scout about it."

"Oh, I'm not worried about anything." Doug yawned. "Except maybe your sanity."

"Well, I think she's cool."

"Sure. I know she is. In fact I think it's kind of neat, coming after Tommy. He's a nice guy but he's one hurting unit. Gail's only had a couple of other boyfriends and they weren't too swift either. She's one of these ambulance chasers, y'know? You sort of break the pattern."

Aaron gave a harsh laugh. "Do I?"

"Well, yeah . . ." Doug eyed him curiously. "I mean, so far as I can see."

The scene with Gail at the corner clung to his mind like burdocks, and he wished that Doug had left him on some other note. Still, he knew what he had to do before he slept tonight. At his dimly lit desk, to the whir of the fan, he scribbled on a piece of loose-leaf paper. He cast it aside and started on another. He wished the song was for and about Gail but it wasn't, not by a long shot. The sequence and melody were much clearer now and he wished that he had an amp there with him. But at least and at last, he would get the words down.

Holding his pen, he paused to look out the window and heard his mother: "It's true what they say about the children of famous people — it's not easy living in someone's shadow." Sylvia was bright in the school-book sense.

234

But after all she had been through, she somehow retained the habit of making problems sound like tired nursery rhymes.

Lately he had been waking from dreams that he couldn't remember, except in murky patches. His parents were in them. On this night he had a dream that he recalled distinctly.

The town square was choked with people, and there were jeers, cries, and laughter. It was a festival of some kind. But none of the Fergusons was present and no one acknowledged him. He wanted only to get away. Struggling, bumped around in the mob, he became aware of a voice booming above the noise. It was his father's voice, calling his name with hard insistence. He struggled one way and then another, becoming more and more hemmed in as he strained to see through the crowd, whose noise grew louder and vied with his father's deep, echoing call.

Upright and sweating on his mattress, he rubbed his eyes. It was still dark. He tottered to his feet, pulled the light-bulb string, and went to his desk. The lyrics were there on the sheet, complete, with nothing crossed out. But there was no title yet.

2

▾

Early the next afternoon, up in Doug's room, Aaron worked the music through with a determined ease. Against the outdoor growl of Doug's lawn mower, he upped the volume and crunched out the central riff, imagining the organ and back beat. He sang the words low and played the song several times. Finally he unplugged, put the guitar in its case, and went downstairs.

Doug stood at the kitchen sink, griping as he ran water on a thumb blister. Aaron thanked him and said he would see him later. For now he wanted to be alone with his victory, to let the song thrash around inside him like a netted shark.

He took his instrument back to his room and got a bottle of Gatorade from the fridge. Ambling down Main, he stopped for generous gulps from the bottle and enjoyed the sights: a young mother pushing a stroller, a curbside cluster of kids on bicycles. But all he heard was the jagged melody, stronger than the heat. He shielded his eyes from the window glare and stared at the public buildings, their steps empty in the hard sun. The square itself was brightly bare except for two old men on a bench. In his dream it had been larger and the street wider, beneath a gravel-gray sky.

As the song shriveled in Aaron's brain, he realized that his satisfaction over it was not the happy kind. It was the clenched, acid-tasting kind, like what he might have felt after winning a hellish argument.

*

He was there to greet Gail when she stepped from the print shop. Startled, she eyed him and touched her chest. "Are you drunk or something?"

Equally startled, he shook his head. "Not unless they changed the recipe for Gatorade. Why?"

"You look . . ." She fluttered a laugh. "You look a little crazed."

"Oh." He held up the near-empty bottle. "Thirsty?"

"Naw, thanks."

He guzzled the rest and dropped the bottle in a street barrel as they started walking. A few paces on, he sensed trouble in her solemn expression.

"Mrs. Peterson asked me to baby-sit their kids tonight," she said. "I don't really want to, but that's what I'll be doing after dinner."

"Okay," he said. "You have a good day?"

"So-so. How was yours?"

"I finished my song."

"Great." It was a polite, absent comment. "What are you going to call it?"

'Hate Is No Fun,' he thought. "Don't know. That'll probably take me the rest of the year." The talk lapsed again, and the silence rattled him. She slipped her arm around his, but they let go to cross the street.

"I felt really bad about yesterday," she said.

"Betcha I felt worse."

She smiled, more naturally. "Competitive today, are you?"

"No, just crazed."

When they got to the square Gail wanted to sit, and they took a bench. It was the same one they had sat on three weeks ago, for their first big sorting-out. "I don't know what sort of stuff you're going through," she began. "I get the idea it's heavy and I wish I could help. But whatever it is, it's your business."

"I don't know if I could even explain it," he said. "Maybe you're better off."

Her eyes were fond but her mind was in a hurry. "I wish I could know. I care about you . . ."

He shuddered inside. No doubt she had used similar words with Tommy.

"But that's why I'm laying off," she went on. "You're not ready and I'd just be making it more painful. If I kept pushing I'd be a bitch, which is sort of how I felt last night."

"You're no bitch, Gail."

She turned her face away as the bicycle kids rode past them. A younger girl called hello and Gail waved without looking.

"What do you mean, 'laying off'?" he asked carefully.

"I mean . . . for our own good, I don't think we oughta think of this as anything more than friendship."

His hand tightened around her fingers.

"It would just be a lot easier on us," she said, sounding both tired and urgent. "This way, we're stuck. It's not fair to you, and I don't think it's fair to me."

He nodded, looking at the crude arrowed heart carved into the bench — J.H. and M.L. 1980. Whoever they were, they had reached a happier, cornier stage than he and Gail ever would. Raising his eyes, he noticed white spray-paint words on the chest of the Civil War statue — Mötley Crüe Rules. His gaze moved to the cannon and the pyramid of cannon-balls. "Yeah," he said. "I see what you mean."

Gail nibbled on her thumb.

"Let's go," he said. "You'll be late for dinner."

"You wanna come over? Mom would be glad."

"Not tonight. Soon." Soon — he said that a lot. And he

238

knew that he couldn't blame her. Odds were that this was all for the better, but the thought gave him little comfort.

They got up and walked the rest of the way in silence.

"Sure you don't want to come over?"

"Thanks, but I'm not up for the talk."

Her eyes went dull and she left with a touch of his arm. "See you."

"See ya, Gail."

He watched her cross the street. Then he went to his room for his guitar and returned to wait for Doug. The wait was longer than usual. When Doug at last appeared with his instrument Aaron was seated on the curb, still feeling as if he had swallowed broken glass.

"So you waited after all," Doug said.

"So you're eating with your family now," said Aaron, getting up.

"Couldn't pass up spare ribs. You should've come over."

Aaron nearly laughed out loud when they walked in and found Neil fuming, clutching a pink slip of paper as he paced the carpet. Whatever it was about this time, Aaron didn't care. This whole day seemed part of a scheme to crack his mind, and he didn't want to hear anyone complaining about anything. Neil especially. He didn't want Neil's beer and sandwiches, let along his stupid, scathing opinions. Aaron patted his breast pocket with the folded lyric sheet. If Neil tried to shoot him down on this one — God, let him try — he would be ready.

"Conehead!" Neil spat. "The bastard pulls me over, leans in my window, and his breath stinks like a dump. After he takes the license and registration he goes, 'Nice day, huh?' I go yeah, and he yells, 'Wouldn't be so nice if you pancaked somebody in a crosswalk — would it, hot shot?' Forty in a thirty-five zone, and he acts like I'm burning up the road!"

Aaron's trace of amusement had already perished in the muggy air. He felt pressure building in his skull.

"And the street was clear!" Neil ranted. "There must be something we can do! Some way we can get back at that . . . that . . ."

"I know," said Doug. "I have this picture of him in my mind. He's covered with mayonnaise or something and staked out over an anthill."

Puffing his cheeks, Neil dropped the wrinkled ticket onto a lamp stand just as his mother came in the door. Silently she went to the closet and hung her blazer. Neil looked bemused. "Home early tonight."

"Looks that way," she said. "Disappointed?" Shutting the closet, she gave her son a cool, offhand look. Aaron had not noticed till now how striking she was. In slacks and a silk top she had a fine figure, and a straw-colored perm complemented her lightly tanned face. But the hazel eyes, dark-circled and pinched at the corners, could have belonged to someone much older.

Neil regarded her with mild confusion and shrugged. "No, why would I be disappointed?"

She drew her lips in. "Nice answer."

She left the room and they heard her go upstairs. Neil made a face. "Menopause," he mumbled.

Aaron glared at Neil's back.

Ben and Mike arrived and they went to the garage, where Neil had to repeat his tantrum. Seizing a rake, he held it like a rifle and rattled it. "Honest to God, I'd like to get that shithead in a dark alley and . . ."

240

Shut up, Aaron thought. Looking at Mike and Ben, he guessed that they were thinking the same thing. Both of them seemed crestfallen and Ben actually bordered on morose. So did Doug, whose Band-Aid had slipped off his blistered thumb as he tuned up.

Neil raved on. "I'd like to take that little Hitler mustache and . . ."

"Okay," Aaron said. "We get the idea. Let's do this."

Neil glanced at him. He turned away and picked up his guitar.

They had slogged through a somewhat discordant number before Aaron remembered the paper in his shirt. Digging it out, he looked at Neil. "Got a new song. If you guys like it I'd rather we do this one than 'Suburban Stomp' for the contest."

Though bored-looking, Neil showed no sign of resistance, and the others appeared interested. Aaron lay the much-folded paper on the organ, tightened a key, and plucked down the scale. Then he began. Several grinding notes along he heard some utterance from Neil and stopped, glowering. "What!"

Neil wasn't looking at him. With one hand raised and his head turned toward the kitchen door, he was listening hard. Aaron listened and heard it too — a blubbering sound from deep in the house. It was not the television.

In a moment Neil went inside and closed the door behind him.

Like a small, muffled motor the sound pumped along and then ceased. Aaron blinked at the walls, reflecting how other people's sobbing always hit him in the same way. No matter whose it was, the fitful noise infected him with a sense of helplessness. He hated it.

None of them spoke as they waited. Doug pondered his blister.

When Neil returned, his face was somber. "Look, guys, could we just bag this? I've got a problem here."

"Sure," said Aaron. He nearly added "good luck."

They went their separate ways. No words passed between Doug and Aaron until the house was well behind them.

"Too bad about her," Doug said.

Aaron shook his head.

"One whole practice down the tubes," said Doug. "We'll have to make the most of Sunday. But I want to hear that song of yours too."

"You will. Can't say how good or bad it is, though."

"Mike said he can get his dad's truck again for Portland. I sure hope Neil and Ben can get off work without too much hassle."

The road seemed darker tonight, and quieter.

"I'm getting nervous," Doug said. "Are you?"

"Tell you the truth, I haven't been thinking about it a whole lot." Consciously he hadn't been, but he was now. The competition offered a bigger chance than any other they were likely to get. Dimmed by more immediate concerns, the date had glimmered ahead of them from week to week. Now it loomed like a U.F.O. In six days some thirty bands would gather in Portland to square off, and some of them would be good. It was no longer a mark on the calendar. All along, Aaron realized, he and the others had been climbing with guarded hopes toward the contest.

The air had cooled and a raindrop grazed his cheek.

"Well, the night's still a pup," said Doug. "Wanna come over and watch TV? Munch on something?"

Aaron thought of Gail. He wanted to see her. Then he

pictured her coming in from baby-sitting and the two of them making small talk, straining to smooth it all out, as if none of it had happened.

"Sorry," he said. "Guess I'm just antisocial today."

"Are you okay?"

He shrugged. "I'll snap out."

"Sure, we all will. We have to."

Thunder crunched in the distance, and rain started as they reached Main. "Be cool," Doug said. He hurried toward his house.

Aaron stood on the sidewalk as rain fell, wetting his hair and face. Holding his case upright, he propped an arm on it. Lightning lit the woods to the south. On the trees around him, each leaf was a muttering tongue. He liked the rain, cooling away the bossy summer heat; he loved its sound, canceling human noise for just a while. But the rain's relief would be small compared to that of telling Gail everything, of piling all of his personal rubble at her feet and damn the end results. But end results mattered.

He stared across at the Ferguson home, and its lights flickered in the next electric spasm. The wetness turned cold on his skin.

He had tried to face facts, but the delusions never seemed to quit. He had fooled himself about Gail and how they could be together. Peg was right: Gail, however smart or unique, was also vulnerable. Time would take care of that — her Fox Hill days were running out, bearing her along like a small boat toward the ocean. But for now she could do without his turmoil. All too soon her own waves would rise, and it was best to let her glide on.

A sad contempt cut into him, a contempt for fantasies — for his own, and for Gail's sunlit fantasies of "out there."

3

▼

It drizzled for two days straight, and to Aaron the store felt somehow more cramped than his room. He squirmed with thoughts of next Wednesday's contest. On Saturday Dori came in to buy a jar of peanut butter, and her look of muted sympathy depressed him even more.

"Glad to see you up and around," he said. "How much time left?"

"Eight weeks," she said, crossing her fingers.

When Dori left he wondered if Gail would stop by. If she did, he would let her know more fully that it was okay — that he could see all of her reasons, plus some of his own.

Leaning back on his elbows, he was watching the trickly windowpane when Andy's truck pulled up.

"Howya doin'?" he asked the old man.

"Mil-dewin', mostly. Five of the no-lead and a Megabucks ticket, de-ah."

Aaron shuffled to the panel and set it, then moved to the ticket machine. He didn't look at Andy but felt his examining eye.

"So, did your house burn down?" Andy said.

Aaron glanced up dully. In his cap and dirty slicker Andy stood there, bow-legged, with a droplet at the tip of his long nose. He seemed entertained. "Don't have a house," said Aaron.

"Oh. Your wife run off?"

"No wife."

"Your dog get run over?"

"No dog." Fighting a smile, Aaron pulled a ticket from the machine and handed it over.

Andy's gold tooth sparkled at him. "Well, then, I guess your doin' fine."

"Sure. I guess so."

Andy paid him and headed for the door. "Tell Fergie hi."

A knock on Aaron's door awoke him the next morning, and it was Doug. Yawning, Doug said that he was going to Neil's earlier than planned. Aaron dressed sluggishly and got his guitar. Doug reminded him to bring his song lyrics.

Neil's mother was sprinkling crumbs at her bird feeder when they got there. Smiling, she said that Neil was still in bed but she could wake him. Doug said they would wait and she told them to go on in. Doug did so but Aaron stayed a short while with her, and she told him of her problem with squirrels and chipmunks raiding the feeder. Her eyes looked better.

Then the sound of tuning drew Aaron to the garage, where he found Doug seated with his guitar on a workbench and looking thoughtful. It occurred to him that he and Doug had hardly spoken on the way over.

"Why'd you want to come early?" Aaron asked.

"Just wanted more of a chance to talk to him." Doug struck a chord, then lay the guitar across his knees. "You know, I wish I was a natural like you. You're a natural — I'm not."

"Neither was John Lennon."

Doug looked up. "Really?"

"Yeah, I read that somewhere. In fact, they say the Beatles weren't all that great as musicians when they hit America. But you know the rest, right?"

245

Doug frowned. "Wonder if their dads were anything like mine." Settling back against the wall, he scratched his head and sighed. "Aaron, just out of curiosity, is your dad sort of like mine?"

"In some ways, yeah . . . I guess."

"Well, I mean, does he give you a hard time?"

Aaron set his case down. "I've given out my share of hard times. We don't see each other a lot."

Barefoot and groggy, Neil entered in his bathrobe.

"Mornin', sunshine," Doug greeted him. "We came early to fire you up."

Neil ran a hand through his messy hair. "Think it's worth it?"

"Course it is. We need you. You're our front man, remember? The Star! The Voice!"

Neil let his arms dangle and took a big breath.

"Wednesday we can go to Portland and hit 'em like a diesel," Doug said. "Or we can just go through the motions and wind up sounding like flop from a tall cow."

A sleepy smirk came to Neil's face. Then he mumbled something about getting dressed and left them. Doug started picking again.

"That didn't take much," said Aaron.

"Nope." Doug yawned. "Missed an extra hour's sleep for nothing."

Awake with admiration, Aaron watched him as sun spilled in through the windows.

Neil's mom insisted on making them breakfast and hummed a tune as she moved around the kitchen. Mike and Ben arrived as they finished eating, and both appeared more cheerful than last time.

At the start of the session, Doug asked Aaron about his song. Aaron turned uneasily to Neil. "There's going to be a strong organ line in this. But I kind of wanted to do the singing, just this once. I know your voice is better but . . ."

Neil shrugged. "If you're terrible, I'll be the first to tell you."

Aaron concealed his surprise. They stood back as he got out his paper and readied before the microphone. Tuning, he looked at them. "Feels like an audition."

"Don't sweat it," said Mike.

Aaron cracked his knuckles. "Doesn't have a title yet." He started to play, loosening up as the downward cadence gathered force. Then he began singing. To his frustration he rediscovered the difficulty of singing while playing lead — a problem that had deviled him with the Gimmix when they let him do main vocal. Struggling to concentrate, he missed two notes. His voice flagged as he hurried to a flustered ending. "Damn!" he said.

"Hard to get coordinated at first," said Neil.

"Sounds like it could be good, though," Ben commented.

"Yeah, it's potent," Doug said. "Listen, since we're short on time here, why not give me the lead and you could do rhythm? That way you could relax more."

If ever Aaron had felt possessive about a song it was now. But he gave Doug a nod. Gloomily he wondered whether they could conquer this in one session, but at least the others — Neil included — were willing.

He played the melody in segments for Doug, who duplicated it haltingly and then with greater ease. Doug's old Mustang gave the song a different timbre but kept its stinging edge. Tending the sound board, Neil stayed remarkably quiet. While Mike and Ben tried various back beats, Aaron molded a sharp, simple counterpoint to the lead, after which they combined for a couple of dry runs. They were getting it, building it level by level.

A following attempt came off solidly and Neil improvised

on his organ, curling it around Doug's riff as Aaron sang. Couched in a full background, Aaron's voice hit its stride and grew stronger.

"How am I?" he asked hopefully.

"You'll do," said Neil. "But let's try it a little faster."

They played it three more times, and on the third try the transformation hit — a falling in place, a wondrous sense of shift. Aaron sang from deep in his chest and pushed the rhythm, binding it with Doug's staggered, steely chop. Never had they been so tight, so firmly in sync, and at the end of it Aaron looked at the others and saw that they felt it too. Together they had tumbled over an unseen barrier. Leaving behind something fine and warm and flawed, they had broken through to something better. And the chance to prove it was nearly upon them.

4

▼

The Battle of the Bands overrode other thoughts until the next day, when Aaron relieved Peg at the store. In her face and greeting he detected the same affectionate regret that Dori had shown, and it jarred him to thoughts of Gail. It felt strange not to have seen Gail for four days straight. And it struck him that since she had done nearly all of the reaching out, it was up to him this time. It was his turn to go to her, soon. He felt ashamed for being so tangled up in his own riddles.

Tuesday, he and Doug practiced on Doug's amp and played records. In twenty-four hours they would be on stage in Portland, taking their shot.

At the store Peg didn't greet him with her customary smile.

"What's wrong?" he asked.

"Andy died last night."

He stared at her.

"It was a stroke," she said. "He was working on his truck and his son-in-law found him."

An image flickered: the green pickup pulling into the lot, the little junkman climbing out with the gold-tooth grin — "Ten bucks of the no-lead, de-ah." In all these weeks they had never really gotten past the joking stage, but Aaron had looked forward to seeing him.

Peg propped her back against the dairy cooler. "Funny — I hardly ever saw him except in here, but it's still a kicker. I guess I'm not a good loser, period."

"Me neither," Aaron muttered. "He was old, but . . ."

"Yeah. Some people just seem more alive than others."

Aaron had another flash of Andy, standing there just three days ago with a raindrop at the tip of his nose.

"Anyway," Peg said, "the funeral's Thursday and I have to go see if they're having a wake." She drew herself up and attempted a smile. "So, you boys all primed for tomorrow?"

"Tomorrow? . . . Oh, yeah. We're pretty fired up."

"Well, I know you'll be good. But I'll knock on wood for you."

"Thanks. Knock twice."

Aaron played the radio lower than usual. Andy's death was a running theme with the customers, and there was talk of

249

naming the public land by the lake after him: Andrew H. Greene Memorial Park. At least he had lived a long time, people said; at least he had known that he was appreciated. As Aaron worked on leaden feet, his shock became resentment. Death was smart. Death knew all the hiding places and patiently sought them out, and no amount of music, dancing, or fireworks could ever repel it.

As quickly as his mood had fallen, it lifted with Mike and Laurie's arrival. Mike bent for a bag of chips and Laurie went to tickle his ribs. He retaliated and reduced her to squeals and writhing on the aisle floor.

"You kids settle down," said Aaron, "or I'll call Cone-head."

With no other customers there, they were able to talk for a few minutes. Mike glowed with anticipation of the contest. Aaron wished that the pair didn't have to leave, if only so he could look at them and feel revived. Andy was dead and life was pitifully imperfect — but tomorrow lay ahead, and tomorrow would be all right.

Through the rest of the evening he held the thought: It's going to be all right. It hovered warmly as he read a magazine, passing the last few minutes, when someone entered. He didn't look up, and barely noted the shuffle of feet toward the back. Then, laying the magazine aside, he craned his neck to see who it was. He stiffened. There was the blond head and stooped frame, a twelve-pack of beer under one arm. The head turned with red-lidded eyes, then smiled faintly through stubble.

"Hi," Aaron said.

Turning his face to the cooler again, Nolan closed the door and leaned his forehead against the glass. "Ohhh, man. Everywhere I go . . ."

250

"I'm closing up."

"Everywhere I go . . . same fucking story." Nolan chuckled. With his free hand, he reopened the cooler and reached in. "Let's see . . ." He withdrew a six-pack and slowly tipped it, the bottles dropping and spewing foam as they broke.

By the time the last one dropped, Aaron had hurdled the counter and was rushing down the aisle. He skidded in the puddle and nearly into Nolan, then faced him with arms ready, not knowing what to do next. Beneath his anger he realized that it had been dumb to leave the counter, where the phone was.

Nolan cackled.

"Get out!" Aaron hollered.

"Or what? Get out or what?"

Stepping backward, Aaron glanced up the aisle to the clock. It was past ten, and he thought of Jerry. "Or it's the cops," he said.

Looking at Aaron's knees, Nolan heaved a sigh. It was the same weary, duty-bound pose that he had struck in Randy's parking lot. Then, cobra-quick, he crouched and snatched up a broken bottle. He lay the twelve-pack on the floor and rose slowly, holding the bottle by its neck. "Your little faggot buddy's got his turn comin'. But, like, you're here now . . ."

Aaron's stare caught on the bottle's jagged teeth. Where was Jerry?

Nolan leveled the bottle at Aaron's chest. His hand quivered and one finger bled. "You're gonna learn," he growled.

There were about six feet of space between them, and Aaron thought of how quickly Nolan had grabbed the bottle. Staring at the pale blue eyes, he licked his lips and tensed to bolt back up the aisle. He hoped Nolan wouldn't have time to lunge or cut him off at the door. If he couldn't escape,

251

maybe he could at least get to the broom and use it to fend off the bottle.

But in the next instant he heard Jerry's voice: "Take it and go."

Aaron looked and Jerry was standing up front, facing them. Hands to his hips and with his cap jammed on, he could have been a disgusted football coach. The deep eyes glowered. "Go on. Ten seconds and I'm dialing the police."

Nolan's arm retracted some, and the faint smile returned. His glance darted from Aaron to Jerry. Without lowering the bottle, he squatted and carefully lifted the twelve-pack to his side while Aaron remained braced, watching him. Nolan stood up with his cargo and weapon. Backing away he gave Aaron a long sneer, and spittle gleamed on his teeth. Then he started up the far aisle toward the door.

Suddenly there came a racket of falling objects. Aaron almost slipped in the beer puddle as he took the corner after Nolan, who barreled along toward the front, his bottle arm raking a shelf and carrying all before it. Containers tumbled and rolled in his wake. Then, keeping a dogged hold on the beer, Nolan halted and hunched. Aaron stopped a few feet behind, and past Nolan's shoulder he saw Jerry's glaring face. Nolan brandished the bottle. Jerry was way too close.

In the instant of Nolan's thrust, Aaron felt his own left hand grip something firm and fair-sized and switch it to his right. At the same time he caught another glimpse of Jerry's face — no longer glaring but blurred with alarm, and falling. Aaron's mind recorded the image as lasting longer than it really did — that, and the can's tumbling trajectory for Nolan's head. He had never thrown anything so hard. The split second before it hit, Nolan seemed to remember him and jerked his face around. The can struck. Aaron heard the pack

252

of beer drop, and then the bottle. Nolan rocked, one eye shut and the other twitching. His lips contorted but no noise came out. Then, amid strewn cans and cartons, he crumpled to the floor.

Aaron rushed to Jerry's aid but Jerry was already standing.

"Y'all right?" Aaron asked.

Rubbing his back, Jerry eyed Nolan's fetal-tight hulk, then pulled a cigarette and matchbook from his shirt pocket. "Fine, fine. I just slipped." He lit the cigarette. "Crazy bastard."

Aaron noticed the fanged bottle by his foot and kicked it away.

"Better call Fox Hill's finest," Jerry said. "Keep an eye on him, will ya?"

Jerry also called the rescue unit. Aaron didn't look away from Nolan, who stirred slightly, like a dart-gunned animal. Porter and McDonald were there in two minutes.

"Had a feeling I'd be seeing this one again," Porter said.

McDonald gave Aaron a distracted glance, then bent to handcuff Nolan and haul him to his feet. With a pinkish lump by his eye Nolan emitted a low moan.

Aaron put things back on the shelf, placing damaged items in a cardboard box, then swept the glass fragments into a pile. By then the rescue unit had pulled in beside the cruisers, their beacons tinting the street blue and red, blue and red. Hearing Conehead's rapid-fire bark, Aaron paused to look outside. Nolan sat slumped on the gravel and moaned louder as one of the med-techs shone a flashlight on his face. "Maybe just a chipped bone," she said. "Lucky it wasn't his temple."

Aaron disposed of the glass and got the mop and bucket from the washroom. He stopped to give his version of events to Porter, who had already heard Jerry's. Outside, Nolan started cursing and Conehead told him to shut up. The slam of a car door cut the raving short.

Porter scribbled in his pad. "Well, we're taking him to Bridgton to get x-rayed. There's going to be legal stuff, of course, and you'll be contacted through Mr. Ferguson." He put the pen and pad away and patted Aaron on the arm. "Nice throw there, guy."

As the cop walked out, the rescue van backed up to leave. Its beacon was turned off but in the headlights Aaron saw Gail standing by the pumps, staring inside as her parents conversed behind her. After a moment she rushed into the store and stopped at the head of the aisle.

"Dad says your timing was decent," she spoke.

"Well, it was about time I did something right."

Smiling, she looked at the floor. "Smells like a brewery in here."

"Yeah, I'll use a lot of soap."

They fell quiet, and he watched her stare at the bucket. A police radio crackled.

Jerry and Peg came in as the cruisers left, and Peg was babbling about the town's decline in safety.

Jerry sighed. "Aaron, I have to head down to the cop shop so I'll just stuff the cash in the bag and take it home. I'll leave you to lock up."

"Okay, Jer."

Gail was looking at Aaron now, and there was something anxious in her gaze.

Jerry dug bills from the register. His movements were stiff, but he chuckled. "Mr. Bedbug himself — felled by a can of baked beans!"

Peg exhibited no humor. "He always gave me the willies.

A hundred times I had to wait on him, and I could never relax till he was out the door."

The phone rang and Peg got it; it was Doug at home, wanting to know where everyone was.

Stepping to Gail's side, Aaron spoke low. "I want to talk to you after I'm done. I won't be long. Could you meet me out back?"

She nodded.

Jerry zipped the bank bag and tossed the keys to Aaron. "Just drop 'em off at the house before you turn in. Thanks."

Hanging up the phone, Peg gave Aaron a worn-out smile. "Who said Tuesdays were dull?"

Gail gave him a limp wave as she left with her parents, and Aaron went back to mopping. Then he heard Jerry yell: "I can't believe it!" Running outside, he found them standing around the overturned barrel and its scattered trash. Beside it, the tire ruts veered from where McDonald had been parked.

"God, give me a break!" Jerry fumed. "The one time he's here to be useful, and he leaves me this!"

Peg took him by the arm. "Forget it, hon."

"The man's amazing!"

Aaron righted the barrel and started picking up the wrappers and soda cans. "Head on home. It's all under control."

Jerry pulled his cap down. "Check this kid out — must've had a good teacher."

As the Fergusons finally departed, Aaron caught a smirk from Gail.

With the trash disposed of, he finished mopping. It was midnight when he turned out the lights and locked up.

He found Gail waiting on the steps out back. Easing down beside her, he put an arm around her and started talking.

"Cunningham is what I've been going by. That's the name of the man who used to be my stepfather, but my real name is Webb. My dad is Danny Webb. You'll find him in Doug's album collection."

"In his . . .?" Gaping, she sat up. "You mean he's a rock star?"

"Yeah. In fact he's still one of the bigger ones."

She put a hand to her mouth. "God, this is . . . You know, I think I've heard that name somewhere before. Maybe on the radio?"

"Probably. They call him the Spider. Mom always hated that cuz she thought it sounded creepy."

"Wow." Gail shifted on the step. "It seems to me like . . . I mean, that sounds like it would be kind of exciting. Wasn't it exciting?"

"Sometimes," he said. "Mostly when I was really young."

"So you ran away from that?"

He smiled tiredly. "You think there's something wrong with me?"

"No, no! I . . ."

"It's okay. I've wondered that too."

He told her about the poster in the record store, the video on TV, the song on the juke box at Randy's, and the photo in *Rolling Stone*. He told her about his ejection from the Gimmix, about crashing the Spider's party in Manhattan, and of visiting his mother before he hit the road. As he spoke she leaned lightly against his side; though she said nothing, her gaze never left him. But the story was coming out jumbled. Pausing to order his thoughts, he felt her hand on his.

"My father's from Michigan," he said. "Made a name for himself with a band in Detroit and then came out to San Francisco, just to catch all the goings-on. Remember me saying the two of them met at the Troubadour?"

256

"Yeah?"

"He was there with a psychedelic group called Last Train to Valhalla. Mom and a girl friend of hers showed up, all bummed because their ride to the Monterey Pop Festival had fallen through. Anyway, her friend knew Valhalla's drummer and he and Dad sat with them when the set ended. The way she tells it, it was pretty much an instant thing. They moved in together not long after that. Valhalla fizzled but he got a solo contract, and he even wrote a song for Mom that got on the radio. Then I was on the way and they decided to get hitched. What happened after we moved to L.A. . . . Well, nobody could really say what all the reasons were. But I have a couple of guesses. Someone like her in that sort of beehive, and married to him . . ."

"And with a baby," said Gail.

"Yeah, and that. She got back into pills, too. I think she was slowing down inside while everything around her got faster and faster. My dad's career was taking off. I can see her reading the reviews and articles and feeling the world muscle in, taking him away. But it was some time before I got any real details. The main one is that one afternoon there was a brush fire in the canyon and some fire fighters spotted her walking straight toward it, like she was in a trance. When they stopped her she kept saying the fire would purify her, she wanted to be purified. My father put her in San Benito Hospital. I was five then."

Sitting as still as he could, Aaron let the images come floating back: the open glass doors of the sun room where he played; wooden canyon slopes that echoed his mother's absence; his father's voice and guitar on the radio but the man himself gone somewhere, getting swept to some higher, busier plane of importance. "Our housekeeper," Aaron spoke, "she was this nice Mexican lady and I played with her kids a lot.

She called it the 'hus-pee-tal,' so that's how I pronounced it too. Huspeetal was where Mom had to be for a while."

"That must've been awfully hard on you," Gail murmured.

"Well, at that age you take things more in stride. You're not into being a martyr because you don't even know what that is, and later on you learn that plenty of worse things happen to people. But I did have this idea that when she got better, everything else would get better too. Four years it took her to recover, and somewhere toward the end of that they decided to call it quits. Dad drove me into the hills in his new Camaro and broke it to me — he wouldn't be around as much but we'd all do fine."

"Must've been tough on him, too," said Gail.

Confused, Aaron looked at her. "Tough on him?"

"I mean, he wrote that song for her. He must have really loved her, don't you think?"

He looked away and felt his face grow hot. "Maybe . . . Yeah, maybe. But shit, he drags her off on this big star trip of his and it isn't till she tries to kill herself that he notices anything haywire! And of course by then she's a major inconvenience for him!"

"Still, to have that happen . . . You can't know what he felt, can you?"

"He still had his fun! For her it was back to square one, for him it was onward and upward! Business can't wait, you know?" Gail was stroking his fingers. "You know where Mom's really crazy?" he said. "She thinks I want to be like him!"

"Go on," Gail said.

He let out a worn sigh. "After her release things happened fast, before I could get a grip on them. She'd never looked better, all smiley and excited. But there was this other man

258

with her and that was Roy. Roy the Substitute. They'd met while he was visiting his sister at San Benito. Basket case or not, Mom has her charms. Roy found her there, this beautiful lost person, and he decided to put on his shining armor. He was a network TV exec, about as different from my father as you could get. Short hair, thin lips, suit and tie, and he was older."

"And what happened with him?"

"He got promoted and we moved east, but the marriage only lasted three years. It's funny, but I hardly ever think of Roy anymore. I never warmed up to him, but that wasn't all his fault. He thought he could manage anything and anybody like a movie director. Mom and I frustrated the hell out of him."

"Is that when her trouble started again?"

"Oh, no. Not then. We weren't moving back to California — Land of Ghosts, she called it. And she had a good job at a museum in Stamford." Aaron shook his head. "God, there were days when she seemed so solid — cooking in the kitchen, painting in the attic. She had her moods, but I really thought she'd left all the bad stuff behind. Wrong again. Year before last, she started coming undone and stopped working. One night I found her passed out in the bedroom with a half-empty bottle of wine and an empty one of downers. That was a real close call and it landed her at the hospital in Hartford. After a while she was well enough to come home, but a few months ago she crashed again, and her shrink got her read-mitted." Aaron shrugged. "There's not a whole lot I can do about it. At least it spelled some things out for me. Up until two years ago I had some pretty lame ways of living."

Gail lay her cheek on his shoulder. "What brings it on with her?"

259

"Who really knows for sure? Whenever she hears anything about him, I guess it's like hearing all the old bones rattle. Must make her wonder how it might have been if she'd been stronger, what it would be like now."

"Do you still keep in touch with your father?"

Glancing at Gail, he ran a hand through her hair. "This is taking longer than I thought. You'd better head back."

She gave him a gentle slap on the knee. "Keep going."

"I've seen him once or twice a year, but the last few times it was . . . just strange. He'll blow into New York — he's lived on both coasts for some time now — and he'll call up. We'll arrange something, and the funny part is I actually look forward to it. But then I see him and I don't know whether to shake his hand or start wrecking his apartment. So I sort of freeze. Last time, he gave me a key in case I ever dropped by while he was out. I've never used it." He stared at the ground. "Mom once said to me, 'Don't think I haven't wondered what if I'd made it down to Monterey instead of the Troub.' That's a real teaser, all right."

Gail nodded sleepily. "Yup." Without speaking, they sat there a while longer before Gail got to her feet. "I'll absorb all this in the morning," she said, then bent down and kissed him on the cheek. "I'm glad we had this little chat."

He handed her the keys. "So am I. But you'll keep it to yourself?"

"Por supuesto."

"In English, señorita."

" 'Of course,' I said. That is, until you make it big yourself. Then I call the tabloids."

"Well, make sure they pay you enough."

"You bet I will." She started away. "Good luck tomorrow."

"Thanks. Piece of cake."

Her laugh wafted across the dark lot.

Then he was alone on the steps, feeling the stillness and a soft, hollow sensation that verged on peace.

5

▾

In the morning, Aaron found Doug half dressed in the Ferguson kitchen and reading a note from his mother. "Dad wants you to stop by the store before you leave," it read. "P.S. Clobber the competition." Doug frowned over it and then went to get his shirt on.

"Well, Neil and Ben got today off," he called. "And every day from now on."

"They got fired?"

"They quit. Nobody'd switch schedules with 'em and the chef and the manager kept being jerks, so they walked."

"Oh, well."

"And get this — Ben did most of the yelling."

"No kidding?"

"Wild, huh? Neil told me about it on the phone, said he just stood back and gawked." Doug reappeared with his guitar.

They walked to the store, and some instinct told Aaron not to accompany Doug inside. Arms around his case, he leaned against the building and waited until Doug emerged, holding a copy of the *Weekly Advertiser*. He handed it to Aaron. It was just off the press, and the front displayed an overexposed photo of a grinning Andy with his name and dates underneath. "Next-to-last page," Doug said.

Aaron turned to it and found the bordered paragraph atop one columm.

Budding stars are not confined to New York and Los Angeles! Fox Hill's own Toy Soldiers, a home-grown rock band, will be trying its musical luck at the second annual statewide Battle of the Bands, this week in Portland. Favorite sons Neil Cook, Doug Ferguson, Mike Boudreau, Ben Katz and Aaron Cunningham hope to grab the top prize of $500 plus ten hours of studio recording time. And folks who have heard them play say that they just might pull it off. The event, open to musicians 20 years old and under, kicks off at noon on Wednesday July 22, at Portland's Expo on Park Ave. Break a leg, boys! We'll all be rooting for you!

"Neil's mom must've called them," Doug said. "Nice of her."

As they started for Neil's, Doug's quizzical frown returned.

"What is it?" said Aaron.

"He told me 'good luck.' "

"Well, what the hell did you *think* he'd say?"

"Anything but that. Then he showed me the paper and I told him thanks. That was all. His back's bugging him from last night. . . . Hey, what about that? Nolan got pretty scary, huh?"

"Big time. I never thought I'd be glad to see Conehead."

"I can see that next *Advertiser* — 'Local Hero Beans Bed-bug.'"

At Neil's the band played each of their selections once or twice through, and Aaron's song sounded even better. Then they loaded their instruments into the pickup.

Chuckling, Neil gave Ben a slap on the shoulder. "You guys missed it! You should've heard this guy tell 'em where to stick it!"

Ben gave a sour smile and put his bass into the truck.

Doug reread the *Advertiser* notice aloud and they laughed. But the laughter had a shaky ring. No one spoke as they tied the tarp down, and the mood turned strangely heavy.

Aaron crouched in the back with Doug and Ben and they started down the driveway.

"How come Neil never rides in the back?" asked Ben.

Doug smirked. "Did Elvis ride in the back?"

It was sunny and the wind swept over them as they sped up. Relaxing, Aaron looked down at the flapping page of the newspaper in his lap and reread the friendly notice. His eyes lingered on "favorite sons" and on his name. The names of the others fit snugly in the paragraph; yet his own seemed to bulge from the page, more than it had in *Spin* and the *Stone*, even though it gave his false last name. He folded the paper and sat on it. Aaron Webb, favorite son of Fox Hill. At any other time the idea would have made him wistful or maybe proud, but now it was just peculiar.

Ben and Doug were talking about the contest. Aaron didn't want to talk, let alone yell above the wind, so he started thinking about Gail and how steadily she had looked at him last night, how well she had listened.

At the Main Street stop sign a light-blue Skylark crossed in front of them, going toward the center of town. Doug jerked around and stared after it. "Conehead!" he exclaimed, and leaned to knock on Mike's window.

Mike braked in midturn and rolled the window down.

"That was Conehead's car!" Doug cried. "Follow him!"

"Now?" Mike said. "Why? How come?"

"We're gonna be early anyway. Come on, this is our chance!"

There was no protest from Neil. Mike headed after the car and Doug wedged back into his place, his face almost diabolically intent.

Ben looked baffled. "Whatever this is, are you sure it's worth it?"

Doug didn't answer. As they went down Main he leaned forward to check ahead of them. Then he lunged over beside Aaron and yelled for Mike to pull over. They slowed to the curb and stopped.

Neil stuck his head out. "Now what?"

"He's parked outside Talbot's," Doug said.

Aaron checked and saw the car several spaces ahead.

Doug turned to Ben. "Go down and stand by the door. Wave to us when it looks like he's going to leave."

Still looking puzzled, Ben hopped down and headed for the hardware store. Doug climbed out and stood on the esplanade, rubbing his chin until he spotted something and his eyes lit up. He bounded to a telephone pole with a tacked-up poster announcing a supper at some church. Grabbing the poster, he called to Aaron: "Get my duct tape, will ya?"

Aaron got out, pulled Doug's guitar case from under the tarp, and extracted the roll of tape.

Doug rushed back with the poster, took the tape, and opened Neil's door. "Got anything to write with in there?"

"Think there's a Magic Marker in the glove compartment," Mike said.

"Perfect!"

Neil took out the big red marker and Doug snatched it. Laying the poster face down on the hood, he started printing in large block letters. "Keep an eye on Ben for me," he said.

Down by the store entrance, Ben peered in like a rookie detective. There were no passers-by and traffic was slight, but then a phone company van went past and Aaron saw the driver look at them. Drumming his fingers on the hood, he watched Ben.

"What the hell's he up to?" Mike muttered.

Aaron went to look over Doug's shoulder but Doug dropped the Magic Marker, grabbed the tape, and whisked the poster away. Crouching behind McDonald's car, he began tearing strips from the roll. Aaron started toward him but then Ben came dashing back from his guard post, waving an arm.

"He's coming!" Aaron said.

Doug slapped on a final strip and they hopped to the sidewalk, falling in step with Ben as they slowed to an easy gait. "Keep walking and don't look back," Doug whispered.

Passing the truck, Aaron heard Neil snickering but didn't chance a backward glance till a few strides later. Conehead had a bag in one arm and was opening the car door. In a paunch-tight rugby shirt and white pants, he looked as if he had been forced uncomfortably into the outfit. Only a second look at the bulletlike head convinced Aaron that it was the same man.

He heard the door shut as the three of them turned into the driveway of Newton Drug and halted.

"Think he noticed us?" Ben asked.

"Naw," said Doug. "Too busy thinking about his next speeding ticket."

They heard the engine start and spied around the corner,

down past the truck to the light-blue car, which pulled away without signaling and with Doug's red-lettered sign on the bumper: MY NAME'S CONEHEAD. HONK IF YOU THINK I'M AN ASSHOLE.

They were still laughing when they returned to the truck. From farther down Main came the bleat of one horn, then another, and their laughter jumped to hyena pitch. Mike turned the ignition, did a U-turn, and they were off again.

The exposition building was not what Aaron had pictured, and this brought his first real tug of nerves. With its marquee and glass-door front the structure looked neither stately nor welcoming, just blindly functional. Kids crowded the entrance and sidewalk; cars, vans, and pickups lined the curb, and others crammed the lots on both sides.

Mike turned into the bigger lot and drove to the building's rear corner. There he backed up to a flight of metal stairs with a plywood ramp, leading to an open door. Climbing from the truck they listened to the racket of some band inside, against cavernous crowd noise. Then a tall, shaggy-haired man holding a clipboard appeared in the doorway.

"Steve!" Neil greeted him.

It was the guy from the downtown music shop, wearing a T-shirt that advertised the contest. He took a moment to recognize them. "Oh . . . hi." Neil started talking to him but he interrupted. "What do you call yourselves again?"

"Toy Soldiers," Neil said.

Steve squinted at his clipboard.

"From Fox Hill," Doug added. "Number twenty-two."

"Yeah, okay." Steve made a mark with his pen. "We're only up to number nine, so it'll be at least three hours. I'll explain things in detail once you get your stuff inside." He hurried back in.

Neil looked depressed. "I hope the sound's halfway decent here."

Doug sighed. "If it's bad, everybody else'll sound bad too."

Upon entering they found themselves in a large, crowded chamber with cinder-block walls, each band gathered like a tiny tribe around its instruments. Some stood and others sat; some talked and laughed while others listened to the thrashing sounds beyond the front wall, which was flanked by stair-wells.

The music stopped to sparse clapping, and an emcee's voice sounded from a microphone. "From Freeport, that was Ugly Stepchild."

Shuffling noises came down from the right-hand stairs, along with Steve's loud call: "Eleven! Number eleven!"

"And now," the emcee spoke, "all the way from Bangor, let's hear it for Killer Elite!" There was another shallow wash of applause.

Four sweaty guys hauled their gear down the left-hand stairwell. The bassist, a short kid with a Chinese braid, laughed and swore as he descended. At the center of the space a bleary, long-haired kid raised his hand and called to them: "Hey, great! You guys got it, man! We might as well go home!"

The braided guy fired him a look and put on an apelike posture. "Aw no, man, don't go home. They gotta hear some metal!"

The long-haired one lowered his hand as his fellows turned to face the other group, but his shouted retort was drowned as Killer Elite started playing. The braided one leered, and he and his friends lugged their way to the door as Aaron stepped aside for them.

"Interesting," Neil said.

After they had gotten all their gear up the ramp, Mike

managed to find a parking space. Steve soon reappeared and addressed them hurriedly. "Okay, here it is. Shortly before you're due to go on, get yourselves up those stairs." He pointed to the right. "You'll wait in the wing, then when number twenty-one goes off I'll call you and you'll be announced. Set up quick — it's fifteen minutes, no more. Don't start a song if it's gonna run over, cuz they'll cut you off. Exit to the other wing and get your stuff back downstairs. For the drums we have two mobile risers with wheel locks — one goes off, another comes on — so one'll be waiting for you upstairs. Any questions?"

They shook their heads.

Steve took his pen and a printed white card from his clipboard and gave them to Neil. "Sign your names to this. After you're done, go around front and flash the card to whoever and you'll get in for the rest of the show. Shortly after the last act we announce the winner and the runners-up."

Neil signed all their names and gave the pen back. Wishing them luck, Steve rushed back upstairs.

"What do runners-up get?" Aaron asked.

Doug crinkled his mouth. "Gift certificates for any sponsoring record store."

The five of them stood ogling and listening in the sultry chamber. The music came down loud but garbled, its quality impossible to judge except for a couple of bands that were obviously bad. Hearing one of them, Neil cracked a grin. "This might be easier than we thought."

"Don't say that," Doug muttered.

Each time a performance ended, the deep, clipped voice of the emcee introduced the next one while Steve called the number. And another encumbered group stumbled down the left stairwell — their shot taken, their fifteen minutes burned away. Some laughed with relief while others looked glum or thoughtful as they hurried for the door, and across the way another band trundled upstairs to wait at stageside. Amid the crowd's noise, the thump and twang of tuning would begin like the first pebbles of a landslide, and then the music — all this over laughs and chatter, the bustle of new arrivals, flushes from the adjoining lavatory, and Steve moving in and out and back like an anxious shepherd.

The long-haired kid got louder, directing much of his attention to a bleach-blonde girl in fur boots, a red beret, and a black miniskirt. Leaning in a corner, she snickered with her tank-topped male comrades and then led them up the stairs. Meanwhile a Lewiston band called the Bellviews had been introduced. They sounded good.

Neil pressed his lips together. "We're better than them."

"Hard to tell from here," said Aaron.

Aaron moved to the right stairwell and listened. Against the wall behind him stood a rangy, red-headed guy wearing a sweatband; with a cigarette in one hand and a guitar in the other, he looked equally attentive.

"Not bad," Aaron commented.

"They're all right," the guy said. He bent to crush his cigarette on the concrete floor. "Who ya with?"

Aaron told him and asked the same.

"The Off Center," the guy said. "We're from Yarmouth." He folded his freckled arms and Aaron glanced at his watch. An hour and a half to go.

Stronger applause marked the Bellviews' exit. Upstairs, Steve called for number seventeen while the emcee gave another clipped intro. The Bellviews came trooping down the far stairs.

"They'll eat you alive!" the drummer hollered.

"We'll eat *them* alive!" shouted the long-haired metal kid.

The redhead smirked at the ceiling, and Aaron looked at his guitar. "Wow! You got a Rickenbacker."

Smiling, the guy held it up by the neck. "Yup, it's my baby. Didn't come cheap, either." He let Aaron hold the gleaming instrument. "I'd let you play on it if we had the chance."

Handing it back, Aaron thanked him and stepped aside as the long-haired kid barged upstairs, gripping an orange B. C. Rich and followed by his mates. The redhead asked Aaron his number.

"Twenty-two," said Aaron.

"We're twenty-one."

"Really? Warm 'em up good for us."

"Sure, if they don't all leave by then." The guy took up his guitar. "Well, gotta get back to the huddle."

"Eat 'em alive," Aaron said, and the guy laughed as he ducked away.

Putting a hand to the wall, Aaron felt it vibrate as another band pummeled the auditorium. Then Neil came over. "I'm going to take a look up there," he said.

Aaron went up with him and found three bands waiting in the shadows. Looking haggard, Steve ignored the metal boys as they joked and jostled. Four guys with faces painted white had their drums on the riser, ready to roll out. The group with the fur-booted blonde huddled as she yelled to them above the music.

Leaning for a view, Aaron looked over the milling young audience and at the roped-off judges' section in the far stands. There were about fifteen judges — radio jocks as well as club and record shop owners, according to Doug — gabbing or just reclining with their clipboards. The stage was white and well lit. Near the opposite wing and partly hidden by an amp, a scruffy sound man sat at his board. The acoustics were clear and punchy, although the group playing sounded like no threat.

"They're called the Unbelievers," Neil said. "Pretty unbelievable."

The set ended and the emcee came on from the other side — a lanky man wearing a fishnet shirt and tinted glasses, with his longish hair slicked back.

"Eighteen!" Steve barked, and the white-faced guys scrambled.

"All right," the emcee spoke. "Next we have . . ." He looked at a list in his hand. "From Portland, please welcome Blue Joke!"

The new band hustled out as the metal boys chuckled.

On the floor near the front, a patch of kids clapped and cheered wildly.

"Guess they brought their cult followers," Neil mumbled, bending for a broader angle.

Doug came up behind them and tapped Neil on the shoulder. "Lookin' for Fox Hillers? Don't strain your eyes."

Blue Joke began with a hopping, reggae-ish number. In the light their faces looked less ghostly, more as though they had been hit with cream pies. And the set that followed, though smooth, had a sameness about it.

"Should've just called themselves Joke," Neil scoffed.

From behind the curtain a stocky assistant rolled the other riser into the wing and then disappeared. The girl's band got their drums onto the riser while she frantically brushed her hair. Toting its arsenal, another band came bumping up to the waiting wing. With them was the red-haired Rickenbacker kid. Aaron suddenly felt the hour sweeping toward him like a battlefront. "Getting to be that time," he said.

271

Back downstairs, Ben and Mike stood talking while the open doorway framed late-afternoon light across the parking lot, shining off hoods and fenders. They gathered everything. Meanwhile Blue Joke quit the stage — fans whooping within an otherwise weak ovation — and Barbie and the Wires were next. Their reception too revealed loyalists in the crowd. They went into a campy version of "Lipstick on Your Collar" and the girl's voice was energetic but shrill.

By the time Aaron and the others had hefted everything upstairs, the emcee was announcing War Dog, the metal band, which Neil immediately dubbed Warthog. Halfway through the set, Mike remarked that a real warthog would probably sound better.

Neil fiddled with his earring, Doug rocked his case on its body end, and Ben cleaned his glasses on his shirt.

The assistant returned with the riser, and the Off Center mounted their drums. Waiting in the dim light nearest the stage, the red-haired guy looked over at Aaron and twitched his eyebrows. Even now it was not the face of an adversary.

"Good luck," Aaron called to him.

"You too, guy."

War Dog's wall of noise swelled and shook. The loud-talking guitarist went into a solo and seemed to forget what came next. Undeterred he plowed on, whimming his way from screech to growl to screech until the singer came wailing back. Somehow the song ended and they seemed ready for another, but the emcee waved angrily from the side and pointed to his watch. Applause rippled as they sauntered off.

Steve didn't call the Off Center's number, since they had already moved to the curtain's edge. Holding the Rick to his side, the redhead resembled a guerrilla braced for an ambush.

"Thanks a lot, War Dog," said the emcee. "I'm sure you'll

go far. . . . Now, before our next act, I'd like to remind everyone that this event would not have been possible without the support of Maine's growing music industry. I'd like to mention a few . . ." The audience rumbled as he ticked off record and equipment stores, and the Off Center muttered among themselves. Looking slowly over his shoulder, the redhead bugged his eyes and Aaron gave a shrug. Two other groups had arrived from downstairs but Aaron didn't look at them. He gazed at the quintet by the curtain.

"And now," the emcee boomed, "from Yarmouth, the Off Center!"

The five strode on, greeted by strong cheers from a rooting section somewhere in the rear stands. They plugged in quickly and adjusted the mikes, then the drummer did a roll as the band's other guitarist began a propulsive riff. The redhead came in, swooping around the beat, and they were off on a bulldozer rendition of David Bowie's "Panic in Detroit." Playing synthesizer, the vocalist had a driving delivery. The bass was good too, as were the drums and lead guitar. The redhead was better than good.

Steve came upstairs, then stood tapping his foot as the huffing assistant brought back the empty riser. Aaron helped Mike load his drums, then rejoined the others to peer out and listen.

In the forward part of the floor, much of the milling had stopped and some people were dancing. After "Panic" the Off Center did what Aaron guessed were originals, and the first two showed rare imagination. The third was an elaborate, avant-gardish effort that didn't quite succeed, but the Rickenbacker dove and soared like a jet.

"Well," Neil grumbled, "they're better than the last ones."

"Better than anybody so far," Doug said flatly.

The band made a false start on their final song, which nevertheless came off inspired. Catching Aaron's eye Doug made a fist, but the gesture didn't match the look on his face. The music poured in from the stage, wearing down the seconds, and Aaron's palms were sweaty.

The Off Center crunched their last note.

The emcee reemerged as they filed off and the ovation crested — the biggest response yet.

"Okay, guys," Steve said.

With the others Aaron moved to the shadow's rim; beyond it the hall yawned like a swarming pit, higher and longer than he had realized.

The emcee adjusted his glasses. He looked at the list. "And now . . ."

Neil drew a breath. "Demolition time!"

"From Fox Hill, Toy Soldiers!"

Aaron barely heard the feeble applause as they hurried into the light. Despite the heat, the stage looked like a stretch of Arctic waste, blank and bright, and the sound setup like a mysterious altar. He took the far mike as Ben and Doug took the two nearer ones, and they plugged in. Clutching his sticks, Mike moved the riser into place and kicked the wheel locks shut, then hopped up into the seat and did a thump-and-roll. Neil connected the wires for his organ and its mounted mike. Tuning, Aaron threw a glance to the weary judges and then to the dim, anonymous hundreds of the crowd. Someone near the front giggled.

Just play. The thought came from nowhere. And with it came a deep energy, igniting him as Neil's hand swiped the air.

"Shakin' All Over" came down like a clockwork storm. To the drumbeat and Neil's whipping, elliptical voice, Aaron

274

wrung fire fom his guitar, and only once did he look at the audience. The look told him nothing but he didn't care. Yet the cheers at the end of the number shocked him. Across the stage, Doug too looked gratefully stunned.

Then, in the wing beyond Doug, a tall figure moved and vanished. Aaron froze. Then the figure reappeared and it was Steve — just Steve with his clipboard. It had been something in his stride or maybe the angle of his jaw. No, the Spider was far away, probably at the other end of the country. . . . Aaron laughed and Ben gave him a confused glance. This was no time to crack up, he thought, and recovered himself just in time for Neil's song.

Melding with the riff, he glimpsed people dancing in place. Then they swung into Doug's song, and in the middle of it Aaron remembered that the next one was his, and his to sing. Still he felt limber and poised, though his blood raced with the music.

The number ended and the other guys looked at him, their features keen in the light. Turning from the mike, he cleared his throat as Doug began the churning hook. Neil, Mike, and Ben jumped in and Aaron took up the rhythm. Then he sang, and the voice that came out somehow didn't sound like his own. It was huskier, feverish, matching the fever of his hands. Projecting himself toward some distant point in space, he let the song break free.

Deep inside your dark again, I'm trapped again
   tonight —
But the darker it gets, the better I can see.
Beating to your heart sometimes, I'm blinded in your
   light —
But the brighter it gets, the more you hide from me.

275

And it wasn't gonna be this way,
And it never should've been this way,
But the darker it gets, the better I can see.

Want to rip your shadow up sometimes, or blast it from
    the ground —
But the darker it gets, the more I want the sun.
Want to move up close sometimes, to hear your echo
    sound —
But the louder it gets, the more I want to run.

And it wasn't gonna be this way.
And you never said why, you never gave a reason,
And from where I stand, you look too big for me.

The times I tried to lay the blame
I couldn't even speak your name.
The times my tongue went stiff from chill —
Paralyzed
By shadow eyes —
My hands too numb to kill.

And it wasn't supposed to be this way.

Calling for some kind of answer, trampled in our past
And the louder I call, the less there is to say.
And locked inside this night with you, I see our fate at
    last
Cuz the night's come down, it's coming down
To take us both away.
And it didn't have to be this way,
It never had to be this way.

He stepped back as their playing intensified, bottomed out, then ceased. The ovation rushed at them. Aaron stared at the floor's blank white and then over at Doug, who stood there with a broken string dangling from his guitar.

Cheering peaked as the emcee signaled from the side.

Reluctantly they unplugged, then strode past the emcee and sound man to the opposite wing. Aaron felt the multitude of eyes fall away, heard the yells and clapping trickle out, and that was it.

"Toy Soldiers," the emcee intoned. "Next, from Westbrook . . ."

Mike brought up the rear, pushing the riser, and they unloaded it. The dogged assistant rolled the riser away behind the curtain, just as other music blasted in from the stage. Carrying the cymbal stand Aaron was last to head downstairs, where remaining groups shuffled about in degrees of boredom or nerves. Ceiling lights had come on.

Blinking around, Aaron was slow to remember the prize still hanging in the balance. And it failed to stir him. His drained, dizzy sensation — surprising for only fifteen minutes of playing — wasn't much different from after Milo's, or Randy's, or any of his dates with the Gimmix. Hardly different, except for a vague, gnawing anguish underneath it.

Out in the lot, they said little until everything was in the truck and the tarp secured.

"Think we did it?" Mike spoke.

"It's robbery if we didn't!" Neil declared. "We nuked 'em!"

Doug rubbed his chin. "I don't know. But they liked us."

"Hope that includes the judges," Ben muttered.

Aaron watched them leaning against the pickup, hoping in

the cool twilight as jagged melodies emanated from the door-way above. Then Mike took the truck back to its spot and they went around to the lobby. Neil showed the card to a security guard, who waved them inside, and they positioned themselves along the restless back rows. Far down, on the bright stage, some other band from some other garage was cloning a top-forty hit. Two more hours gaped between now and the judges' decision; Aaron stood apart from the others and steeled himself for the wait.

To crippled applause and the emcee's terse announcements, groups came on and played and left, rounding out a spectrum of types and abilities, though none seemed special. Aaron's eardrums hadn't recovered yet and the music flattened to an aural blur. Periodically he turned to see a spent band filter in, looking dazed or impatient or cocky. The majority of contestants had gathered at the rear of the hall, massed there like hungry mice — just part of the audience now. He noticed Ugly Stepchild's braided bass player, seated in the last row, while at his back the loud one from War Dog stood yammering at him. The loud guy cackled as he reached for the braid, cackling again when the other knocked his hand away without turning around.

Close by, Neil and Doug conferred while Ben stood gazing toward the front. Mike returned with a tray of soft drinks from the concession stand and Aaron took a cola. Loving its cold bite, he felt his strange indifference start to crack.

Through the racket he heard a chirping voice to his right, and looked to see Elaine with Neil. Decked in black and yellow and sporting a stylish new coiffure, she was clutching Neil's hand. "I'm surprised you didn't hear me screaming!" she said. "You were wonderful!"

Neil seemed ill at ease. "Thanks, I . . . So where've you been? I haven't seen you anywhere."

"Oh, I've been busy. But I wouldn't have missed you this time. Some friends and I got here around four and . . . Where are they? I wanted them to meet you."

Aaron's eyes strayed from Elaine as another act came on. It wouldn't be long now. Then to his left he spotted the Off Center's red-headed powerhouse, standing alone.

Aaron went over to him. "Where are your buddies?"

"Hangin' out with the home-town crowd," the guy said. "I'm not into that right now."

"You were terrific."

"Thanks. I'm just glad that part's over with." He dug out a lighter and a cigarette. He had removed his sweatband, and without that or his guitar he appeared oddly vulnerable, with none of the guerrilla look. "Didn't get inside in time to hear you," he said.

"It went all right."

The guy blew a smoke cloud and squinted toward the stage. "I'll be glad when this part's over too."

Aaron offered him his drink. "Wanna kill the rest of this?"

"Aw, thanks!" He downed the drink and tossed the cup away.

Aaron checked the guy's watch and it was almost eight-thirty. "This must be the last band."

"Hope so."

They stopped talking and endured the choked bluster of the lead singer. Aaron licked his lips and glanced over at Doug and the others; facing the action, they stood close together. Elaine was nowhere in sight.

The band cattled off the stage but left their drums behind, and the moment had come. The scruffy sound man got up and walked to the riser. Taking up the sticks, he hopped behind the drums and waited while a flurry of scribbling and

279

discussion got under way in the judges' section. Time stretched. The audience simmered, then boiled to life as Steve, the emcee, and the female judge converged at a microphone.

Aaron eyed the redhead's firm-featured profile and realized that he now beheld a rival. And all of a sudden he too craved to win.

The emcee raised a hand and quashed the noise, whereupon he introduced the woman, a station manager, as the one who would announce the runners-up and then the winner. Claps and whistles greeted her as she stepped forward with her clipboard. Aaron focused on her small, white-suited form.

"Before we announce these names," she said, "we want to thank every band who performed here today, and all of you who came to hear them. It goes to show that the music scene here in Maine is not only alive but better than ever, and we're grateful to you for making this . . ."

"Skip the bullshit," the redhead grumbled.

The emcee and Steve stood to either side of the woman as she spoke, the first with a white envelope and the other with a large manila one. Then the sound man began a drum roll, barely audible at first but building gradually.

"Fifth runner-up," the woman said. "From Portland, the Mall Rats!"

The name triggered a burst of clapping from some section of the hall, as did each of the following names.

"Fourth — from Waterville, Criminal Justice!"

Aaron rubbed his fingers together. With measured pauses the woman went on as the drums rolled louder.

"Third — from South Portland, Barbie and the Wires! Second — from Augusta, Smart Bomb!"

Smiling, the woman shifted the clipboard in her hands and

extended the pause. The drum roll swelled like a giant balloon. Aaron caught his breath and felt his lips move.

"First runner-up — from Fox Hill, Toy Soldiers!"

Stronger, longer applause assaulted his ears, and he stared into a far corner of the ceiling. His arms went limp. He felt the redhead's quick glance. And there was only the crowd, the drums, the cymbal crash, and then the woman naming the Off Center as winners.

In the clamor Aaron turned and shook the redhead's hand.

"Hope I'll see ya again," the guy said, grinning. "Take it easy." He slipped into the crowd, while up front his band mates hopped on stage with the officials.

"See you all next year!" the woman called.

Lights came up and the crowd oozed toward the exits. Rubbing his eyes, Aaron saw Ben and Mike beside him.

"We did our best," Mike said, looking baleful.

"First runners-up," Ben muttered. "That's still pretty good, I guess."

Aaron knew that anything he said would sound feeble, but he spoke anyway. "And we got our name around too."

People bumped past them, and contestants were easy to spot for their stoniness or biting laughter. Looking toward the stage, Aaron saw the redhead speaking with Steve. Doug had gone up to get their gift certificates, his T-shirted body pushing slowly against the crowd's tide, while over by the lobby doors Neil stood with his back turned. Aaron didn't want to speak to either of them just yet, or see their faces.

6

▾

At Neil's house they sat watching MTV with the lights off. A row of perfect girls danced in jerking perfection to the music, but it was more than this that held them here, despite the late hour. Still the talk had taken a philosophical turn, and Aaron sensed they might soon be laughing — about Warthog, Joke, the Unbelievables, and Conehead with the sign on his bumper.

Over by the phone Neil's mother finally hung up, and her bathrobed silhouette moved into the TV light. "I'm turning in."

"Want the sound lower?" Neil asked.

"Just a little."

He turned the volume down. "Night, Mom."

"Night." She started to leave, then paused in the hallway. "I'm sorry you didn't win."

Neil didn't respond.

"We'll get over it," Aaron said.

"Can't keep a good band down," said Doug.

"That's the spirit," she said. "And first runners-up — that's nothing to sniff at, really."

They thanked her again for the late snack and she went upstairs.

Aaron had been studying Doug's expression, which was thoughtful one minute and retiring the next. Now Doug yawned. "We just got our hopes too high."

"So close," Neil mumbled, and folded his hands. "Well, maybe we can still get club dates in Portland."

In a chair by the wall Ben crossed his legs and said something too low to hear. They all looked at him and waited. "I was gonna say," he finally spoke. "I'm going to be starting at Bates in September, and my folks are getting after me. They're afraid this'll take too much time away from school. And I'm thinking maybe they're right."

Neil stared at the screen.

On the couch, Mike stirred and sat up. "Yeah, my dad's been on my case too. It's gonna be a busy season at the market, and besides that he wants me to get more serious — you know, about what I'm gonna do with myself."

Doug looked into his lap and sighed.

They were silent for a while. Then Neil lay his head back, sliding lower in his seat. "Well . . . I guess that does it. World-famous in Fox Hill — that's as far as we got."

"I'm sorry," Ben said. "It's just priorities."

"Sure, I know," said Neil. "Come to think of it, I've got some of my own stuff to hash out."

"Same here," Doug mumbled. "Same here, I guess."

Aaron leaned on his elbow and wanted to say something, anything to unburden the moment. "She's right," he said. "Out of all those bands we came in second." Looking at Doug, he tried to smile. "And you stuck it to Conehead."

Doug only nodded and watched the TV.

Toy Soldiers had existed this morning. Now it didn't. Endings were simple, Aaron reflected, yet it was funny how they knocked all of your clever comments away. But daylight would make it easier to shrug off, and he could wait until then. Nearly always, daylight shrank disappointments to a size you could handle.

He paid no attention to the TV, and a haze gathered in his mind. Then his father's voice and guitar cut through it. Blinking, he beheld the video's tall, striding hero. Splices of Red

283

Sky in action alternated with those of the vagabond Spider, who roamed through one incongruous setting after another. Aaron's vision narrowed to the face — that hard, forlorn face with the impatient gaze.

"Oh — *this* clown!" The comment was Neil's.

Twisting in his seat, Aaron glowered. "Lay off, okay?"

Neil went rigid, eyeing him back. "What's this? Now who's getting touchy about his tastes?'

"I'm just sick!" Aaron sputtered. "I'm sick of hearing you . . . your . . ."

Doug looked alarmed. "Okay, okay. We're all disappointed, and it's late."

"Jeesh!" Neil huffed.

Avoiding the screen, Aaron sat back and ran a hand through his hair. He had to leave but his body didn't move. He felt their bewildered stares.

Doug cleared his throat, as if to summon all of his talent for mending. "I, uh . . . Did you hear about his bass player?"

Aaron shot him a glance. "What? What happened?"

"His bassist OD'd. Coke with heroin, they said."

Aaron's mouth went dry. "Where'd you hear this?"

"Was in the paper a few days ago. They played San Francisco and the next morning they found the guy dead, so Webb's had to cancel the rest of his tour."

The video was over and another had come on. Amid the wrestling of his brain, Aaron perceived Mike's muddled gaze from across the room.

"I don't get it!" Neil burst out. "This is mental! Why are you so hung up on this guy?"

"Because he's my father."

"What?"

"He's my father."

284

Without looking at them he grabbed his guitar case off the floor and left quickly — across the carpet, out the door, down the driveway, and onto the road.

The case bumped against his leg as he walked faster, trying to outpace the stabbing visions that pursued him. He started to run. His legs surged down the dark road and the case bumped and swung until he stopped, out of breath. When he got his breath back, it was the only sound in his ears.

Stars pricked and dusted the night, shrouding all that was forever beyond reach. The night was one of the very few things that a person could count on, he thought. Let everything else be uncertain, you could always count on the night to drain the light away and remind you of what couldn't be. Deaf to your complaints, it didn't laugh or condemn — it just told you.

What it told him now was that running made no sense and never had, and that all along he had been running from one emptier night to the next. Hiding, thinking that he could dream himself into other people's lives.

Suddenly the trees on both sides felt too close, like shadowy jaws closing on him. He started walking again. Coming over a rise, he saw a house at the end of a long driveway on his right and halted. Two second-floor windows were lit, making the place look snug and safe within the blackness. At the mouth of the driveway he noticed two skunks — two patches of white with inky black, nosing around the mailbox post. Noticing him, they went still and raised their tails like a pair of mutant sentries. He backed away to the other side of the road and gazed at them, then at the house. A dog's harsh barking sent the skunks waddling into the undergrowth. Then the dog quieted and Aaron sensed the doors of the home locked tight — the last bolt shut, the last key turned. Locked against him. One light went out and then the other.

In the quiet everything felt inevitable. It had to come to this, he thought. Alone out here — an impostor whose deceptions had run out, a dumb tourist who had chosen to linger and dream.

He turned his gaze around to the hillside. Switching the case to his other hand, he hopped the ditch and started up the slope. Some presence awaited him just over the crest — something he dreaded, even as he let it draw him. As the ground grew level he broke into a sprint and stumbled on a rock. Ahead he discerned the white picket fence, the trees, and the steeple's tip.

As he stood still in the breeze and rustle, his labored breath refused to settle. Then he walked to the fence and swung over. Wandering half blind among the headstones, he eventually found the one he remembered. He set his case down, knelt, and touched the listing, faded, lichen-spotted stone: Samuel Augustus Simpson, 1782–1802, age 19 years and 2 months. Back in his own strange era, what had Samuel Simpson wanted? And how would he have won or lost, had he lived to be old?

Looking past the grave, Aaron saw the row of stunted white markers. Children swallowed in time — this was all that was left of them, their only proof. He sat against the nearby tree and stared at the angel's head atop the stone; its eyes were shut and crudely serene. Aaron shivered as he gazed up through the branches. A meteor pierced the moonless sky like a needle and died. He wondered what would remain of him two hundred years from now, besides a stone. What would be left of him or of anyone he knew, besides a small carved monument, if that?

Aching he curled onto the ground and looked at the grave. Samuel Simpson, however long dead, was his companion now. Sleep pressed down like the weight of dead centuries, along with the visions that he had tried so long and blindly to escape. Now he let them come, feeling the watchful presence somewhere straight ahead past a stand of trees.

"I'm not going to be like you!" he shouted. "I'm going to be better than you!"

He rose and took a few steps. Moonlight suddenly flooded the cemetery, bathing a rubble of uprooted trees and broken headstones.

"You hear me?" he called.

The Spider's thin shadow cut across the ruins. Upon the ruins stood the tall man with his guitar, phosphorescence touching his hair and shoulders. He picked a string. The note thudded once, twice, and again, echoing like giant drops of water. Aaron looked over his shoulder and saw his mother a short distance away, staring past him with frightened eyes.

Then a higher, shriller note skewered the quiet. His father's shape crouched with the instrument and sustained the noise to a piercing cry. Fear gurgled up in Aaron's throat.

"Dad!" he yelled.

The cry stretched on, twisting to a siren wail as the moonglow began to fade. Aaron looked up. Many times blacker than the sky and nearly half as big, a shadow towered from the horizon, arcing like the belly of a vast whale across the heavens. Aaron gaped at the shapeless, widening gulf of black, slowly blotting out the stars and all beneath. His father's single note screamed on. Then it grew fainter as sounds began pouring down, first as a kind of static and then as a cacophony that filled the night — smashing noises and garbled music, with an infinity of crying, laughing, babbling voices. Buried in the shadow's din, the Spider's guitar at last went silent and there was no light, only the shadow and its infinite clamor. Aaron couldn't breathe.

Waking, he found his hands at his throat. His wet eyes darted through the dark, and he discovered that he had rolled several feet away from the tree. His head lay between the guitar case and Samuel Simpson's marker. He fumbled back to the tree and curled up again, unable to tell whether it was dew, sweat, or tears on his face.

"Sleeping in the graveyard," he thought, and shook with quiet laughter. For the kids back at the Academy, this would have confirmed a few opinions about him.

He closed his eyes, and his breaths became more even. Sleepiness descended again, slowly, more like a heavy cloak this time; yet he stayed awake long enough to recall the great sky shadow. It had seemed so real. Briefly its static returned to his brain — the sound, he realized, of everyone who had ever lived, struggled, and died.

7

▼

The nattering of birds roused him to the dawn. Wrinkled and stiff, he stood, stretched, and rubbed his eyes. Sunlight had just cracked the eastern woods, fringing the steeple and headstones with a faint red, and the air was clear, and it would be the kind of day when you could see the mountains in New Hampshire. Wiping specks of grass from his arms, he watched the sky turn brighter blue and the steeple and rooftops start to glisten. He wondered whether this was where old Andy would be buried today, deep in the fresh-smelling earth. Bending to pick up his case he spotted a crushed beer carton by the children's markers; he took it with him down the hill and tossed it into the first trash barrel he came to.

Once back in his room, he slept dreamlessly for a couple of hours.

Entering the store he found Jerry in his charcoal suit, with the newspaper spread before him and a ponderous announcer on the radio. Jerry looked up at him, then at the knapsack and guitar case and the jacket tied around Aaron's waist. Nodding, he puckered his mouth and then turned off the radio. "Greetings," he said.

"How's your back?" said Aaron.

"Still has a crick." Jerry folded the paper. "So what's this? Happy trails?"

Aaron set his case down and stood there.

Jerry lit a cigarette. "Well, Peg and I thought this was a possibility. The way I heard it from her, Doug got home pretty late and spilled it all out about you. . . ." Letting out a puff, he chortled. "Don't know anything about your dad, but I gather you've made Doug's year. I guess it's really something — for this town, at any rate." He looked at Aaron's face and turned sober. "Can't say I thought you'd be leaving quite this soon."

"I'm sorry. I know it puts you out, but I have to. It's not something I can wait on."

Jerry waved the smoke away. "No problem. I think I understand." He ogled Aaron. "Sure you don't want to stick around one more day? We could take you down to Portland, get you on a Greyhound . . ."

Aaron looked at Jerry's small cigarette hand. He would miss the sight of those hands — and the face, and the sound of his voice.

Jerry sighed. "Okay." He took out his wallet, removed a wad of bills, and added a twenty from the register. "This is your full week's pay. Hide it in your sneaker or something." He handed Aaron the money. "Want you to know you were a good worker."

Aaron muttered thanks and put the wad in his back pocket. "I was going to tell you . . . I mean, I was going to suggest . . ."

"Speak."

"Maybe you should ask Doug if he wants to try working here again."

Jerry lowered his head but not his stare.

"There's no band now," Aaron said. "He has some things to sort out, but right now he's not too fond of dish washing."

Jerry rubbed his cigarette into the ashtray. "Well . . . Wouldn't hurt to ask, I suppose. But we'll need a long talk."

"You might be surprised. If he says no, Ben Katz needs a job till September. But you can do worse than hiring Doug back, if you're up for trying."

Jerry smiled a little. "Maybe. I'll bounce it off him." He looked at his watch. "Peg'll be by any minute. I'm closing up for a couple of hours so we can go to Andy's service."

From somewhere down Main came the clanging of a bell.

Peg entered a moment later in her plum-colored dress. As her eyes met Aaron's, dismay hovered on her face.

"Afraid we can't hang around," said Jerry. He gripped Aaron's hand and shook it. "Take care, pal. I didn't pull you off the damn highway for nothing."

Aaron could only nod at the wide chest. Peg reached for him and they hugged. "So soon?" she said, and his arms tightened around her shoulders. Holding his hand she stepped back. "Go over to the house and make yourself breakfast. Doug's still sleeping but the door's unlocked. God, I wish you weren't hitchhiking!"

"Thanks for everything," he said.

She gave him her long-lipped smile. "Ever want to shock me, drop us a line."

"I'll write you."

"Oh!" Peg dug into her purse. "Almost forgot, this came for you." She took out an envelope and gave it to him.

It was a letter from his mother.

Looking outside, Jerry clinked his keys.

Aaron picked his case up and followed them out. Pinching the envelope in both hands, he watched the jeep roll away. Jerry honked, Peg waved, and the church bell clanged through the town.

At the house Aaron threw a ham-and-egg breakfast together and fed nibbles to Slim.

He was quiet so as not to wake Doug. Within the limits of Aaron's secrecy, Doug had been as much of a friend as he could have had here; but the last things Aaron wanted now were wide eyes and eager questions. He would pass up this farewell — let Doug sleep off some of his amazement, then share the remainder with Neil, Mike, and Ben. But Gail was another matter. His next stop was the print shop, for his main goodbye.

291

The letter lay unopened by his elbow. He looked down at the looping, graceful handwriting so familiar to him and suddenly worried that if he opened it here, its bleak spirit might escape and spread like radon vapors through the kitchen. At the very least it might spoil his final minutes here. He stuck the envelope in his knapsack.

Washing his dishes, he glanced at a stack of Peg's toxic-waste pamphlets on the counter and felt a sad tug.

He patted Slim's head and took up his load. As he stepped out onto the porch, Gail arrived on her bicycle. Stopping, she stared at his knapsack. Her bright orange blouse failed to offset the numb expression.

"I was just heading over to see you," he said.

"I just checked your place," she muttered. "I'm on lunch break."

"I already ate."

"S'okay. I'm not hungry just now."

"Wanna go for a walk? Like down to the bridge?"

Unsmiling, she hiked up the strap of her handbag. "Old time's sake, huh? All right, just a sec."

She took her bike around the back and they started walking.

"Well, I was still up when Doug came in," she said. "He was running around like a lunatic and waving that old album of your father's — 'It's true! How'd I miss it? He looks just like him! I can't believe it!' "

Cars were parked a long way up and down from the church — nearly all the cars in Fox Hill, it seemed — with the glossy black hearse out front. The two of them passed in silence.

At the bridge Aaron put his case against the railing and flexed his arm. "So what's going to be happening with you? The scholarship come through yet?"

"Yesterday, finally."

"Congratulations."

Gail propped her elbows on the rail and peered down. "It's a relief. At least I know I'm on my way out of here."

He leaned in beside her. "If I were you, I guess I'd be psyched for leaving too. But I'd come back sometimes." He glanced at her smooth, taffy-framed face with the nose she couldn't stand. "You might tell your brother that too."

Staring down at the stream, she didn't seem to be listening. "When I woke up this morning Mom was there holding my hand — said she had a bad dream about me drowning in the lake. Weird, huh?"

Aaron thought for a moment. "No, that's not so weird."

"And Dori had one about her prince coming back. She called me up just to tell me about it. Dreamed that she answered the doorbell and there was Frank in his army uniform. The way she talked you'd have thought it really happened." She sighed, cupping her chin in her hand. "What about you? Ever going to come around these parts again? Ever?"

"Yeah. But I can't say when."

"Well, who could?"

He put his arm around her waist, and they listened to the water. "You'd be my big reason for staying," he said, wishing for a steadier voice. "But I've got some loose ends to fix, y'know?"

"Sure. I know about loose ends."

"You're going to do all right for yourself. Better than all right."

"Hope so. Hope we both do. It's nice to imagine things." Absently she put a finger to her mouth and chewed it.

"Ever going to stop biting your nails?"

"Shut up." She leaned against him. Their reflections danced in the water's rush — an orange spot beside a dark one.

"Oh . . ." Stepping back, she fumbled through her handbag and took out a snapshot. "Souvenir."

He took it, and it was the picture from her graduation day: with the store at her back Gail beamed from behind her tassel, her white gown billowing as if in flight. Doug, with his tie askew, looked roguishly amused. Aaron wore the thinnest smile, and his eyes looked as if they were trying to penetrate something.

Gazing at it, he thanked her.

"I thought you might like it," she said, and shouldered her bag. "I oughta go now. Mr. Peterson's probably back from the funeral."

Few words passed on their way back to Main. Almost there, they stopped and held each other. Gail started to let go but he didn't, and then she held tighter. She sniffed. "This is a crazy summer."

"Wicked," he said.

With a kiss they released each other. He didn't follow her to the corner, but as she reached it she turned around. "Don't be a stranger," she called.

"I won't," he said, not quite loud enough.

She waved and walked away, while cars filed past with their lights on. Watching her as far as the library steps, he let his best hopes race after her.

He nearly bumped into Bud as he stepped out of Fox Hill Savings. With his bristly beard trimmed, Bud was wearing overalls and a construction cap.

"You're working?" Aaron asked.

"Sure am, finally. What's with the luggage?"

"I'm thumbing south."

Bud looked surprised. "I'm delivering some wood over to Raymond. I could take you that far, if you want."

"Good. Thanks."

In Bud's company truck they started down the street. From the opposite direction, a cruiser passed with Conehead's taut, jowly face behind the wheel. "Ha-haaa!" Bud cried, and gave the cop a double honk. Aaron sank against his guitar case and laughed.

He asked Bud about his job, and Bud began an upbeat monologue as they passed Lark Lane and then the store, where Jerry's jeep was parked out front. Aaron felt that tug again, stronger but not completely sad. Maybe he wasn't really a home-town boy, a favorite son, but for the moment he felt like one.

Letting him out at a bend, Bud shook his hand and wished him luck. The truck rattled away and Aaron looked down a green slope to the tree line, and the low hills far off.

He was leaving the way he had come — back through the lost, shimmering country — and it made him smile. Clutching the broken strap of his sack he stood there for some time, barely aware of passing cars or the sun on his head. You could count on the night, his mind repeated, but you could still hope for days like this and actually get them. And had it been possible to hear colors, the sky's limitless blue would have resounded across the land, as loud as any nightmare.

PART SIX

▼ ▼ ▼

In the Dark

1

▼

His last ride was from a thirtyish Oklahoma man, a full-blooded Cherokee who had recently sold his landscaping business in Tulsa. All the way across Connecticut he played Emmylou Harris on his tape deck and told Aaron about his summer travels, and he seemed disappointed when they reached the outskirts of Stamford.

Watching the van ease out and take the on-ramp, Aaron surrendered to his daze. Seven rides spanning three hundred miles, two days from Ferguson's Corner Grocery, and here he was. It was all still here: the parking garages, the high-tech office buildings, and the voracious suction of New York City. The din of traffic seemed to come from the fume-filled air itself — alien thunder, invincible thunder that never let up.

His pockets were still sandy from the New Hampshire beach where he had slept with the sea wash. His back still ached from last night's slumber in the woods near Sturbridge, Massachusetts. His hair was greasy. Wearily he took up his case and started walking.

It was dusk when he awoke, clean from the shower and sprawled on his bed. In the quiet he gazed at the books, tapes, and albums around the room, and he remembered where he was. He sat on the side of the bed.

299

Home — this was the name a person gave to his own small bastion, that one place where he could wake from any dream and not feel lost. Like warming embers the word glowed, round and full. Yet a deadness hung in the air of this house, and the walls had never looked so pale. And suddenly he didn't want to stay here tonight.

Digging in his sock drawer he found the key and pocketed it. He considered making a phone call before leaving but realized that he had forgotten the number.

2

▼

Surfacing from the subway, he found Washington Square's ragged carnival going strong. Rap music played from a blaster as a bunch of black guys laughed and argued; a husky folk guitarist sang in a lame voice about war and famine; gypsyish street people sat by the dormant fountain and NYU students circulated in small groups, while under the stone arch a cadaverous youth laughed wildly. And as he had on countless other occasions, Aaron wondered where they would go and what they would do with themselves. He wondered who had ever loved them and how they would die. Maybe he would always be curious about things he couldn't know.

For all his past wanderings around this area, his skin hurt with the shock of it. The arch was well behind him now, but he heard the kid's mad laughter break to a near shriek and picked up his pace. He was moving through some kind of netherworld — a glaring, blaring, vicious, nonstop festival where nothing mattered.

Soon he reached the high-rise. At the foot of the steps he paused, waiting for something — waiting to slip into the right inner gear for whatever might follow. Sweating, he chuckled out loud. What if the man wasn't even here? And what if he was? He looked up at the heavy door with the intercom panel beside it, and stopped smiling. Somewhere down the block a car honked and from farther off came the long arc of a siren. In his pocket he pressed the key between his fingers. Then he ascended the steps. He paused again at the intercom, eyeing the button for the apartment, but didn't press it. He unlocked the door, stepped into the lighted foyer, and took the elevator up.

When the doors slid open the apartment was dark, and its silence nearly stunned him. He didn't reach for the light switch. As his eyes adjusted he looked around the living room, then walked slowly down the hall to the bedroom and found its door ajar. Clothes lay strewn about the unmade bed. Aaron leaned in the doorway and mused how nothing ever happened as he planned or envisioned it. It was one missed connection after another. He looked at the framed platinum record on the opposite wall. Well, he thought, what were the odds? What were the odds that he could come waltzing in from the wilderness, unannounced, and have the Spider there waiting for him?

He went to the bed and fell back onto it. Stretching his arms, he wondered at the feeling — how in an otherwise empty place his father's presence could still throb like a hidden generator. From every wall and corner it throbbed, filling

301

the spaces. A smell rose from the sheets — a mix of male sweat and cologne, maybe perfume, too — and Aaron inhaled it. The Spider would return. In an hour or possibly a day, he would be back.

Quickly Aaron sat up, saw the phone on the side table, and reached for it. His finger quivered as he poked the buttons, straining to see their numbers. He pressed the receiver hard to his ear as a faraway connection rang once, twice, again. Then someone picked it up.

"Hello?"

Aaron drew a deep breath. "Gail, it's me."

"Aaron?!"

"How are you?"

"Good, good! — Whew!" She laughed, and he laughed with her. "So you made it home okay?"

"Uh-huh."

"What's up, honey? You sound strange."

"I guess, um . . ." Dizzy, he settled back against the headboard. "I guess I needed to know you were still real."

She cackled again. "Well, let me go jab myself with a pin."

"Naw, I'm convinced."

"A lot of good it did giving you that snapshot."

"I looked at it a lot while I was thumbing." He had, between readings of the letter from his mother.

"Well, I'm all alone here," she said. "Dad's at the store and Mom's at some meeting."

"And Doug?"

"Beats me. He's been crawling in after midnight. The only time I saw him today, he was playing your dad's old record."

"Tell him hello. Tell him I'm sorry I didn't say goodbye."

"Sure. He'll be glad . . . God, it's funny to hear you. It's like you're calling from Mars."

302

"I might as well be."

He told her where he was, describing the subway and the sights of the square. She listened without comment. He told her of wanting to visit his mother as soon as he could.

"Good," she said. "And what about after that?"

Thinking, he raised his feet onto the bed. He suddenly felt as he had nearly three long months ago, after sending his car off the cliff: what now? "I'm going to make a demo tape of my songs. I may not even do anything with it, but I'll see."

"Then you'll get another band together, I suppose. Onward to the Grammy Awards." She sighed, sounding gloomy. "But you know, we're both running out of maybes. From here on it's supposed to get more definite."

"So they say." There was a long pause between them. "College is another maybe," he spoke. "I'm going to think hard about that. I . . ." He could see her leaning in the hall, the phone cord hanging loose around her waist. "Your birthday's in October, right?"

"The seventh," she said. "I'm a fun-loving Libra."

"Pick a weekend around then and I'll rent a car and come up there. We can knock around Portland and then drive to Fox Hill. That's if you can put up with me."

"Oh, I think I could." He saw her smiling. "I might even permit a visit for Thanksgiving. And Christmas. And Groundhog Day. Not to pressure you, of course."

"Pressure me."

Just before they hung up, Gail said something foreign that he couldn't translate, though it sounded nice. "Love you too," he told her.

After hanging up he lay there for a few minutes more, letting the ring of Gail's voice recede from his ears. Her gentle tones lingered and then trickled away, northward over the interstate miles to the woody roads of Maine and the house of soft amber light. Up there the house still stood, they all still lived, and he would be with them again. But right now he was alone, awaiting the one who had towered in his dreams.

He got up and wandered back down the hall. Sinking into an upholstered chair, he took the wrinkled envelope from his jacket and turned a table lamp on low. Once more he read the letter.

My dear Aaron,

Two incredible surprises in such a short time span — can our heroine survive such dazzlement? First there was your letter. The second thing I'll get to in a bit.

They gave me a grounds pass, so I'm outdoors, under the same tree where we last spoke. Beautiful day, hot but mercifully free of insects. Maybe this is just the medication talking but today I feel the universe has decided to give me a break. Or maybe it's inviting me to give myself a break?

About your letter . . .

Once when I got "dreamy" about my "hippy-girl days" I said that in my memory it even seemed like the sun was different, a more mystical sort of yellow. Do you recall your wise-ass comeback? "Hey, Mom, maybe it was just the acid." Then, as now, I had to laugh. And then as now I'll say I bet you would've loved it too: the gatherings, the happenings, the free concerts, strangers being buddies, runaways flocking into the Haight district like little lost sparrows. I bet you would've done what I did — gazed at those kids and wondered who they were, what they'd come from, and why they'd come, and how the saga would unfold. And of course we had the big bad war, and the cops. What do you babes have for something to oppose? We never had to go looking.

But Dr. Whatshisname's been on my case, as you have, to start thinking in harder terms. So I'll add that yes, yes, my sweetness-and-light rap did get out of hand and yes, there were parts I chose to leave out for fear of spoiling the story. Except on rare occasions, I find it easy to forget the three or four friends who got cozy with the needle and dropped from sight, like the earth had swallowed them, and how the party kept on like nobody noticed. At times I felt this strong, scary pull in the air and it wasn't just the drugs. I'm not sure what it all was, but once the first dizzy days were over I saw some lovely people turn mean or crazy, or just lose their way. I can tell you that back then was the closest I ever came to fitting in, but I can also say (how's this for honesty?) that somehow I never quite did. Neither did Danny, really, even after he got more confident.

I could go on, all frank and confessional. But if it's true that there's envy behind your wisecracks, please let go of it now. I never meant to make you feel that way. And if you still do, I'll make a deal: you can envy me for that time if I can envy you for your smarts and your strength. You are a sharp one, honey, and I really shouldn't worry about you as much as I do.

But all of this is just a long-winded prelude to telling you about my other surprise, yesterday.

He came here. He came here to see me. He checked with my doctors, who then checked with me, and the consensus was that I was stable enough for it. Not that I wasn't plenty nervous at first. We sat on a bench outside, and for a minute I couldn't listen to him. All I could do was stare — he's rangier, still good-looking, but with creases around the mouth. Black hair salted gray on the sides, and

305

shorter. To state the obvious, it had been such a long time. So long since we sat in Golden Gate Park, him plinking out a new song on his guitar. Or since I watched him sing you to sleep at our apartment on Russian Hill.

First he asked if I'd heard from you and I told him about the letter, giving no specifics. He only nodded and looked at his feet, but I could see the relief. When it comes to you and what you've had to deal with, he's a better guesser than you think, even if his attendance record doesn't show it.

Aside from the matter of you, he's down on himself about Larry Logan. I trust you've heard about Larry's death from a speedball overdose. Danny said he should have known Larry wasn't ready for the scene, or he should have grilled him more about his habits. He called Larry a fool kid, but I could tell it's really burned a hole in him. I felt sorry. And all of a sudden, death didn't seem so appetizing. It's questionable whether Red Sky will ever perform as a group again, but Danny didn't seem to care that much. He said he was gratified to see people your age in the audience, but at the same time he'd get these flash-backs of playing some roadhouse in the early days, when he was young like the crowd. It made him feel awfully strange, I guess. So at present he's mostly holed up in the Village, avoiding reporters and the world in general.

Oh, Aaron, I don't want you to hate him. Especially not for my sake. There are things you got from him that you should be glad for — your spirit, your musical side. I remember when you came home with your first guitar. You were twelve, I think, and I didn't even know you'd been saving up for it. You hurried upstairs and I heard you practicing chords. You are your mama's child, too, of course, but mainly you're an original. Is that what you needed to hear? I hope so.

Just before he left he returned to the subject of you, and how it was after we split up. He said that every time the two of you got together, you were bigger than before, or there was some other change he'd missed seeing happen. It brought him down. By now you were from a different world, he figured, and maybe you'd be better off if he didn't disturb it quite as often. That may not sound like much of an excuse to you, but he also said there were times when it was hard for him to stay away.

What else can I tell you? — except that you get to a certain point and the verdicts start coming in. Things you did, things you left out — it all catches up. And most of all where kids are concerned. You see, back then having kids wasn't what we were about — wasn't central to it, anyway. We were out to make a noise, to splash on the new colors, right the awful wrongs, work it all through, dance the new dance. (Am I getting too dreamy here?) This was true for Danny too — although before I met him, all he really wanted was to get out there like the big boys did and make people jump. He wanted the freedom and the girls, and the money didn't hurt. But when he got to the Bay and we came together, it was clear there was something huge, something wonderfully different going on around us. And even though he spoke little about it, I think he liked feeling that he was part of it. But the whole business of a family really snuck up on him. Once he chuckled about that and said it was like he'd taken the kind of life they handed him back in Michigan and smashed it, but a piece of it flew off and hit him on the head. See, eventually kids tend to happen. And when they do, it's Amateur Night. No matter how good you are at anything else, it's definitely Amateur Night. The talent varies quite a bit, and I wish that one or both of us had been more talented.

307

I think about all the junk they pile on top of you, straight out of the cradle — what you're supposed to go for, how you're supposed to be — the whole cursed list. What it has taken me forty years to see is that one way or another a person has to shove their way through it, or else they'll never see or decide things for themselves. Let's wish each other luck.

God, some of the squirrels here are almost the size of cats! I just had one come up and take a potato chip from my hand. My sketch pad's with me, and I've been working on a pastel drawing of you. I'm doing it from your school portrait, except I've added some semblance of a smile. So you see you've been much on my mind, my lone boychild. Writing this has brought me a certain tranquility. I wonder how long it will stay this time.

Peace, Love, and Woodstock,
Mom

Aaron lay the letter aside. He touched it lightly, as he wished he could touch her hand right now. "Peace, Mom," he whispered.

Noticing a record on the stereo turntable, he got up and pressed "play." It was an old Van Morrison album, the volume set so low that the music could have been coming from a block away; its dipping flute and violins mingled with the faint city noise. He turned the lamp off, went to the sitting room, and stood before its long, wide window. All those lights, he thought. Against the night they were like a million fireflies stuck on overload. Or stars. And for a moment he had the sensation of staring from the heart of a galaxy that was collapsing slowly inward.

Whether you were happy or lonely, he thought, one mystery engulfed you in the end. Compared with the dark of that

308

mystery, your private shadows appeared tiny and your life microscopic. No person could be called a giant, not even the Spider. Yet endings and limits seemed to make everything matter, forcing questions of what next and how to get there. They made coins matter at the Fergusons' store; they made a night on stage count for better or worse.

Just as everybody was born to a certain face, he or she was born to a certain solitary trouble. Friends could help to a point. But in this secret war, only a lone stand could win you a truce. It did no good to wish and search for a different legacy while hiding from your own. Hiding never made you strong.

His foot bumped an empty liquor bottle by the couch, and on the coffee table he noticed two sheets of paper. He picked them up and held them close to the window. In the ashen light he saw that both sheets bore ink-lettered lyrics for a song titled "Phantom Boy" — one tattered, messy with crossed-out words, and dated May 1985, the other undated but new and neatly printed. He read the words.

First there was me
And then there was you,
One from the other,
A sword from a stone.
First we were one
And then we were two
And the blade of your image
It cuts to the bone.

Searching for you
On a rocky lost shore,
Looking for you

Through a cold iron door,
Down the miles of a maze
Toward the light of a blaze
I look for a phantom boy.

Time doesn't smile
On a fugitive's lie —
Tangled in reasons,
He can't run and hide.
And if fingers of flame
Wrote the truth in the sky
It would kill all his laughter
And burn off the pride.

Listening for you
Through a crack in the wall,
Waiting at night
For your faraway call.
Deep in a dream
Or a memory's gleam,
The face of a phantom boy.

Aaron lay the pages on the sill and peered down at the streets, where cars crept like shiny beetles. Time slowed, though not with the strangled alarm he had known before. He looked out and listened. What he heard was not the city or the music rippling in from the stereo, but the ebb and flow of generations. Under a boundless black, they swept together and pulled apart — waves of uncounted castaways, each alone and grasping for anchorage. Deep in the noise of collision, they grew deaf to one another while shining visions floated around them, promising glory or protection — ways to be and things to win. But these vanished with a touch.

And in time every castaway had to gaze up and face the darkness, to hear its echoing prophecy of an end.

But Aaron was not afraid tonight. Tonight the past was too small to matter, and a tide of sad gratitude passed through him. There would be much to say when his father arrived. But for now it was enough to know that he was one of the lucky ones, and this alone was worth a million songs.

He reached into his back pocket and withdrew the photo of Gail, Doug, and himself. Touching it with the tip of his finger, he knew that Fox Hill was inside him now. They were all inside him — there to hold on to instead of the past — and his gladness swept the great, dense patterns of light outside.

Gazing out, he tucked the picture away. The Spider would return. "I'm here, Dad," he spoke. "Come on back."